Tigers Love Bubble Baths
& Obsession Perfume
(who knew!)

by Mary K. Savarese

ISBN 978-1-63393-710-9

This is a work of fiction. With the exception of verified historical events, all incidents, descriptions, dialogue, and opinions expressed are the products of the author's imagination and are not to be construed as real.

Published by

 köehlerbooks™

210 60th Street
Virginia Beach, VA 23451
800-435-4811
www.koehlerbooks.com

MARY K. SAVARESE

Tigers Love Bubble Baths & Obsession Perfume

(who knew!)

VIRGINIA BEACH
CAPE CHARLES

For Vinnie, Katie, Vince & Amanda.

A True Story

The Sisters of Loretto, Santa Fe, prayed a novena. They needed a staircase to reach their choir loft. A stranger on a burro arrived and their prayers were answered.

For nine days the small group repeated, "We pray for Your help, dear God. Our architect was shot dead and though the chapel's magnificent, he left us with no staircase. Please, oh Lord, we pray for a way to reach our choir loft. We lift our voices in glory to You with no visible space to hold these stairs. We pray for Your help, dear God."

The stranger, equipped with a few carpentry tools, requested only privacy while he worked. The nuns wondered where the beautiful wood the stranger used to build the magnificent staircase had come from. The sisters never saw the stranger working, and he always left for the evening while they were in prayer. The winding spiral staircase that the stranger built was a helix with no central support and constructed without nails or glue. It stretched into the choir loft with a total of thirty-three stairs.

The sisters wanted to honor the nameless stranger for his extraordinary work with a special dinner, but he disappeared before they could thank him.

And he left no bill.

Chapter 1

In her eyes, Angie Pantera never looked nor felt more beautiful. Wearing an off-the-shoulder eyelet dress, she admired herself in her mirror. At forty-eight, she still looked good. More than just good—great. Losing twenty pounds enhanced her curves. Another five or ten pounds would be perfect. *Definitely a work in progress*, she thought, gazing at her reflection. With blonde hair and baby-blue eyes, Angie's incredible smile would sweep a person away like a Caribbean wave.

The special day finally arrived—her and Jay's twenty-fifth wedding anniversary, and the couple would be repeating wedding vows. Standing in as maid of honor and best man, Maddie and Kevin never looked prouder. Although grown, Angie still viewed the twins as her babies. They waited patiently in the gathering space, ready to walk Angie down the aisle.

Jay's last-minute business trip and delayed return flight had tightened everyone's nerves. As the altar boy peeked his head out of the sacristy, Angie's heart pounded. With everything perfect, she smiled as her twins walked her down the aisle. Angie and her twins marched arm in arm between the pews in that small Philly chapel. As they nodded to family and friends, she felt her life couldn't have been better.

Standing next to the pastor, a man in a dark-gray suit held tightly to a manila envelope with her name printed across the front in big, bold, black letters. Staring at the mysterious envelope, Angie's heart pounded.

The man's face, stern and pale, reminded her of the funeral director at her father's memorial. It was the same frightening look she endured when her father died. *Something isn't right.* Taking a few more steps, her perfect life detoured her straight into hell.

"Mom! Mom!"

Grabbing the bars on the side of the hospital bed, Maddie cried.

Kevin glared over at his sister. "Stop screaming at her!"

"Your sister is just scared," the nurse said, adjusting their mother's IV.

"I think she's waking up," Maddie said, wiping away a tear. "Mom? Mom? Can you hear me?"

Angie tried to clear her mind. But the room kept spinning. Staring up at her daughter, she whispered, "Where's your father? Where's Jay?"

Kevin frowned. "Now what do you say, Miss Control Freak?"

"Mom?" Maddie lowered her voice. "You fainted at the altar. You hit your head on the way down. We're in the emergency room."

"Where's Jay?" Angie asked again.

"You broke your nose." Maddie stared at her mother's black-and-blue raccoon eyes.

"Where's your father?" Angie's voice quivered.

"Dad's such an ass," Kevin whispered, gently touching his mother's hand.

"Giving Mom those papers today of all days was really stupid," Maddie said. "You're right, he *is* a jerk."

As reality hit, Angie's stomach cringed. *It happened. It really happened.* One moment, she was walking down the aisle with her twins at her side ready to rejoin the love of her life, and the next she was in a hospital bed with a broken face. Jay, her lover from their college years, had been her only. Now, she was alone.

"It would've been easier if the bastard just died," Angie cried into her hands. A new habit for her, crying. Emotionally raw, she stared at the flat-screen on her bedroom wall. A little after eleven in the morning and she was still in bed. Sweats and pink booties adorned her tired and aching body. Rarely did she step outside these days. The local delivery driver was even used to seeing her in her pink booties. Now an expert at frivolous excuses, it didn't take much to keep her indoors. Too cold. Snowing. Whatever. Angie remained not only hidden from the world, but from herself.

The reality show droned in the background. Angie wanted to escape. Then again, it wouldn't make a damn bit of difference. Playing the scenario through her mind like a broken record, she cringed. Rereading her husband's scribbled note didn't help to ease her confusion. Throwing the manila envelope across the room, it fluttered only a few times before coming to rest under the closed bedroom curtains.

That envelope had been delivered by a paid stranger. Standing on the altar, Father Tim had glanced at her as if he were about to read off her death sentence. Maddie and Kevin glared at the neatly dressed stranger. Father Tim's eyes lowered as he took in a deep breath.

"Oh dear," he said before frowning. "Angie, I'm sorry."

Glancing around, Angie's mind whirled. Where was her husband of over twenty years? "Is Jay in the sacristy?" Angie had asked Father Tim.

Father Tim handed the manila envelope to Angie. On the cover, a scribbled note in her husband's handwriting. Just reading the first few words sent waves of dread through her. Written hastily on a paper napkin, Jay's words burned deeply into her soul.

Ang, didn't know how to tell you. Can't do this anymore. I'm with Taylor now. Sign the divorce papers and mail to my attorney.

"Taylor? Jay's with a guy?" Dropping the envelope, the room spun. As her world darkened, so did her life.

Jay met Taylor while on a business trip. Unbeknownst to Angie, they'd been secretly seeing each other for months. Maybe it would've been easier if Jay had been gay. It wasn't supposed to end like this—blindsided by the man she loved.

For good or bad, in sickness and in health . . . blah, blah.

Those words meant nothing. Words that turned a person's world upside down and inside out. That was exactly where she was—guts on the outside and asking, *What in the world happened?*

"Did I deserve this?" she asked the bedroom walls. "Wasn't I a good wife and mother?"

The last several months had sent Angie on a personal trip through the underworld. To make matters worse, she was still there. Her ticket didn't include a return trip back to reality, back to happiness. Jay pushed for a quick divorce. Disappearing into an endless void, it seemed as if he was divorcing the twins, too. Refusing to forgive him for what happened at the chapel, Maddie and Kevin wanted nothing more to do with him.

Jay spent their hard-earned savings on entertaining his young *bimbo*. With just a little over a thousand dollars to her name, Angie constantly kicked herself for not keeping track of their money. Who was this stranger that she had married?

With no lawyer because of no money, Angie received no alimony. She was mostly the breadwinner anyway. They had zero equity in the family home purchased from Jay's aging uncle over fifteen years ago. A recent consolidation loan was more than the house's value, ultimately sealing her fate. It was Jay who declared he was giving it all back to the bank.

Feeling dejected and useless, Angie started arriving later and later for work. After only a few weeks, they fired her. Embarrassed, she lied to her twins.

"It's a companywide layoff," Angie said, maintaining her happy face.

Christmas was hard that first year her husband left. With Kevin working in the Middle East, only Maddie flew home for the holidays. Although Angie remained brave, a tear still managed to eke out from time to time.

After the New Year, Angie hibernated. More depressed than ever, she gained back all the weight she'd lost to impress Jay. To her dismay, she was even a few pounds heavier. Her bedroom was littered with empty ice cream containers, potato chip bags, and Chinese delivery cartons.

Staring at her face in the mirror, no one would ever think that she'd broken her nose. How embarrassing that afternoon turned out to be. Since the reception had already been paid for, their guests congregated at the Italian restaurant. A few paid their respects at the emergency room with leftovers.

Clicking through the channels, Angie stopped on the Travel Network. A showcase of travel destinations within the United States flashed before her eyes.

That's what I need. Travel to someplace nice.

With no money and no job, the idea seemed like folly. Angie dug out one of the twin's discarded plastic US maps.

I'm going to start over. Let serendipity be my guide.

Placing the map into a leftover Christmas box, she rolled up a yellow sticky note. Closing her eyes, she tossed it into the box.

I do hope it's New Orleans. I need warmer weather right now.

Vigorously shaking the red box, Angie recited to herself, *Take my little rhyme. Promise not to change my mind. But do change my life, to make it again divine.*

She ended with a magic word—*please*. Peeking, she searched for the sticky note, frowning when she found it stuck to the lid. "Can't even get this right," Angie moaned in disgust.

Glancing down she noticed something—a tiny white feather was stuck to the map. But where? Was it a sign? Gently lifting the feather, her eyes widened.

"What? This isn't even close to New Orleans. Whoever heard of Birdsong, Maine?" Annoyed at serendipity's choice, she frowned. "Is it even a city?"

Deep inside, Angie's inner self whispered, *You promised!*

"Fine," she yelled out. "I'll give it six months. What's the worst that could happen?"

Her inner self didn't answer.

Angie's to-do list: sell furniture, tell the kids, pack her clothes, check the weather forecast, reserve a hotel room, leave by Monday at five in the morning, and kiss Philly goodbye. Now living with a purpose, the adrenaline rush of putting her life in order set things in motion. No longer depressed but determined, Angie jumped into action.

Sell the furniture ✓

With a black magic marker, the letters spread across the pure white cardboard, sending waves of relief straight into her soul. Stapling her message around town, Angie's heart pounded. Although her home was on the outskirts and anything but an estate, people flocked to her small house. Seeing the words *GREAT DEALS* in big bold letters always lured buyers.

Tell the kids ✓

"Are you kidding!" Maddie's voice blared through the phone. "You're moving where?"

"Birdsong, Maine." Angie giggled. "Just be happy for me. I want to spread my wings a little. No pun intended."

"Never heard of Birdsong, Maine."

"The feather found it," Angie replied.

"What feather?"

"Private joke. I'll explain later."

"I don't know about this. How will I know if you're okay? Why not come to San Francisco, stay with me for a while?"

"You already have two roommates," Angie replied. "I'd just be in the way."

"No, you wouldn't."

"I'll stay in touch. Call me on my cell if you're worried."

Angie stared at her silent phone. Reaching Maddie was somewhat easy. But talking to Kevin would be a challenge. Sitting in front of her computer, she pulled up her email. Typing in his name, a baby Kevin flashed through her mind. Jay was so proud, bouncing a girl in one arm and a boy in the other. These days he acted as if he never had kids. *Hi Kevin . . .* the email began. After filling in the details, she ended with *Love Mom.*

Pack Clothes ✓

Picking up a pizza for dinner, Angie ran her finger through her list. *What am I leaving off? Did I think of everything?* Pulling into her driveway, she stared at the darkened house that nudged at her insecurities. *Am I making the right decision?*

With a full stomach and a glass of wine sitting on the table, she separated her things into different piles. Pulling out outfits that were now too small, Angie cringed. How could she allow herself to gain all that weight back? Then again, what difference did it make? *No need to impress a husband anymore.* Shoving the clothes that fit her into two suitcases, Angie's mind searched for answers that still refused to come. Did she drive Jay away because she didn't care about her appearance? *I'll bet that bimbo's a twig.* Staring at the empty pizza box, a tear threatened to fall.

"I've gotta go on a diet and quit eating this crap."

The screech of the packing tape seared her heart. Sealing a box with old photos of her and the kids just didn't feel right. She included none of Jay. He wasn't hers anymore. Storing these away should help to heal her wounds.

As for Jay's stuff . . . *What to do with it? Burn it?* Nah, that wouldn't work. *Sell it? Yeah, why not make a few bucks?* He'd never miss it anyway.

Weather Forecast ✓

Only light flurries forecasted for the next few days. Looking farther north, the weather didn't change much. The drive to Birdsong should be relatively uneventful. Just the way she liked it.

Reserve a Hotel ✓

Scrolling through the listings, her hopes soared. A Holiday Inn was right inside the town. Tapping on the keyboard, the reservation was confirmed for Monday night. By the time she finished, another piece of apple pie had vanished.

Leave Monday at 5 AM and kiss Philly Goodbye ✓

With almost a thousand dollars in her pocket and the unwanted junk sitting on the porch for a local charity, Angie didn't bother to lock the front door. Flinging the keys into the air a few times, she smiled before tossing them onto the empty living room floor.

Angie glanced at her watch. One minute before five. Right on time. With an eleven-hour drive ahead of her, Angie prayed her ten-year-old Honda would make it. Constantly tossing *Birdsong* around inside her brain, she was starting to like the sound of it.

"Goodbye, Philly!" Angie yelled from her car as the cold wind slapped against her face. "It may not be New Orleans, but it's a fresh start!"

Chapter 2

The *Welcome to Birdsong* sign greeted Angie. She screamed, "*Woohoo!*"

Stopping the car, she stepped into the freezing air. Standing next to the large words, she read out loud, "Welcome to Birdsong. Population, 3,130." *Made it. It's now, population 3,131.*

As she stared at the sign, her mind wandered back to what she'd read on the internet. In 1888, wealthy New York financier Kerr Bird Song established the small town only fifty miles from the Canadian border. Buying 30,000 acres in the middle of northern country from the state of Maine, he placed his estate on the ridge that overlooked the valley. He christened the town by financing a small chapel. He offered free land to those wanting to live in the new Birdsong Township.

Arriving almost an hour later than planned, snow flurries greeted Angie as she coasted down the main street. All was good. With her adrenaline flowing, she was anything but tired. After checking into the hotel, she could start looking for a job.

Glancing around inside her car, she laughed. Soda cans and hamburger wrappers littered the floor. Patting the dashboard, she said, "Good boy. We made it."

BOOM!

The good-boy car blasted smoke as it limped into a parking space. Shaking, Angie turned off the engine. As the smoke cleared, she stared at the small chapel filling her vision. With its brightly lit stained-glass windows, it was almost as if it was waiting for her to arrive.

"At least I made it into Birdsong city limits."

Opening the car door, a blast of Artic air sent shivers through her. Maybe she could find someone inside to help. The hotel couldn't be too much farther down the road. The place looked friendly enough. Surely, no one would mind if she left her car there for just one night.

Bracing against the torrential wind, Angie marched toward the chapel's entrance. The sign, barely visible through the thick veil of snow, greeted her.

WELCOME TO
THE CHAPEL of THE LITTLE FLOWER

Angie shivered. Lately, chapels were not a good omen.

Five elders knelt in novena prayer in front of the wooden statue of Saint Therese. The statue was also known as the Little Flower. Scattered amidst the pews, the men in various stages of balding whispered into their hands. Sitting behind them, a steely-haired woman stared up at the statue.

Together, they whispered, "Little Flower, please send us the help we need."

Sitting back, they waited.

"Let's hope we get an answer soon." The gray-haired woman glanced over her shoulder at the door. "We're running out of time."

"We have one more day," replied the man with black-rimmed glasses. "We're in day eight of our nine-day novena."

"No," she replied. Sitting up straighter, she clasped her hands together. "I'm quite sure this is the ninth day."

"It is," the other three responded.

"You should learn how to count," laughed the man with a saucer-shaped bald spot bordered by salt-and-pepper hair. A large crash echoed through the chapel.

"Jesus, Mary, and Joseph!" a man from another room cried out.

"He's in the house," said the quiet man, partially bald with platinum strands that ran down his neck. His ruddy complexion and bulbous nose gave him the appearance of a Christmas bulb.

Wearing a brace on his right leg from the ankle up past his knee, Father Joe Methuen hobbled out the sacristy door with his crutches. Dressed in black pants and shirt, he wore his ever present priestly white collar. Simply known as Father Joe, his youth followed him even though he just celebrated his seventieth birthday. Still owning a full head of light-brown hair with only a slight touch of gray, he wore frameless glasses that accentuated his long thin nose.

Over the last thirty years, his chapel experienced both good and bad times. Currently, they were bad. Reconstructive knee surgery due to a black ice fall added more weight to his otherwise heavy cross. His once robust flock of parishioners had dwindled to meager numbers over the last decade with no relief in sight. The parish properties had been folded into the auspices of the Caribou Diocese. A dreaded call from the bishop announced the sad news. "We're selling the Home. We don't have a choice."

At least the bishop was allowing their residents a little dignity by keeping the doors open until the last one passed on to heaven. Approaching the elders, Father Joe thought about how many the Home of the Little Flower had served throughout the years. Kerr Bird Song had deeded his 25,000-square-foot mansion to the chapel, and the Home, as it came to be known, cared for many of Birdsong's local residents.

"What do you want to hear first?" Father Joe sighed as he stood before the elders. "The good news or the bad?"

"What did you break now, Father?" the woman asked.

"Nothing, Mary. I just knocked over a small table."

"Just another little thing for me to clean up," she replied, shaking her head.

"What will it be? The good or the bad?" Father Joe glanced over at the woman. "Mary?"

"Let's get the bad over with," she replied.

"The bad it is. Our recreational director just quit. The good . . ." His eyes trailed upward and into the heavens. "The diocese is sending a temporary administrator to replace the one who resigned last month. But only part-time."

"Let's face it, Father," the bald man said. "We're a sinking ship. Part-time *is* probably better than *no* time."

They all laughed.

The bald man added, "Now we only need the person heaven is sending us. Two for the price of one would be a winner for all."

A squall of Artic air along with a burst of snow blasted into the chapel. A woman, looking raggedy and forlorn, almost fell to her knees. Grabbing onto the back pew for support, she grinned over at them. Fighting with her feet for balance, the woman turned around and pushed the door shut. She wore blue jeans and a heavy coat. Shaking her head, the snow fell around her to the floor. As she dusted off her coat, her eyes widened.

"I'm sorry. I didn't mean to interrupt," the raggedy woman said, dusting off her legs. "My car broke down. I'm in your parking lot. Is that's okay?"

To Father Joe, the woman resembled a lost puppy. "Why, yes, my dear. Perfectly fine." Father Joe hesitated for only a moment. "Are you Catholic? . . . Not that it matters. All are welcomed here." Glancing into the heaven as if hoping for an answer, he sighed. "I'm Father Joe, and you are?"

"Hello, Father Joe," the woman said, grinning. "I'm Angie, Angie Pantera." Angie took a step toward the small group. Snow fell to the floor.

Father Joe chuckled. "Are you here on business or pleasure, Angie?"

"Both." Taking two more steps, more snow fell. "I decided to make Birdsong my home. Looking for a job. Bookkeeping. I'm a bookkeeper." Again, more snow fell around her.

The elders glared at each other.

"I was raised a Catholic." Angie took several more steps and reached out.

Father Joe grabbed onto her cold hand and smiled. "Welcome, Angie, welcome." Pointing to the elders, he chuckled. "This is Matthew, and this is Mark and Luke and John."

Looking at the wispy-haired woman, Angie mused, "And you're Mary?"

"Why, yes," Mary answered. "How did you know?"

"What else could it be?" Angie laughed, and her face turned bright red.

"Gets them every time," Matthew replied.

Glancing up at the Little Flower statue, Angie frowned. "I really should be on my way. But my car broke down in your parking lot. Could anyone give me a ride to the hotel?"

No one replied.

"I'll have my car towed tomorrow. I promise. Know of a good mechanic?"

"Jared's Garage," Mark said, his eyes wide. "But sorry, no ride."

Angie tilted her head and frowned.

Pushing his glasses up higher on his nose, John said, "The Holiday Inn closed. Had a kitchen fire just this mornin'."

"Must've missed that email." Angie sat in the pew across from the small group. "Is there another hotel or motel around?"

"Maybe we can help," Father Joe said, glaring down at his small congregation. "Maybe in more ways than one."

Angie tilted her head. "How so, Father?"

The elders glanced up at the statue of Saint Therese. Was Angie the answer to their nine-day novena?

"No, Father!" Mary stood. "She's not the one."

Father Joe winked over at Mary. "It's okay. Please sit down."

Turning to Angie, he grinned. "You see . . . we need an employee. A recreational director for the Home of the Little Flower. Doesn't pay much. Three hundred a week. Gives you the use of the caretaker's cottage. You can move right in. And you can eat all your meals at the Home." After clearing his throat, Father Joe added, "You'll have to distribute Holy

Communion to the eight residents for me. They're in their nineties. Just three times a week. Would that be a problem?"

Angie shook her head as if disoriented.

"I'll be out for a few weeks." Father Joe pointed to his braced leg. "Knee surgery and rehab."

Angie nodded.

"The diocese is short on priests right now. None available to say Mass while I'm away. We're basically shut down. Temporarily, I might add."

Angie's eyes widened. "Oh, I don't know, Father. I –"

"If you have your heart set on a bookkeeping job, I hate to be the bearer of bad news, but jobs are a bit scarce up here. We're still fighting our way out of a recession. What if you give it a try? Let's say, for a few months or so while you pursue other options."

"It's not the position that concerns me." Angie lowered her eyes.

"Then what is it?"

"I appreciate your offer and all, but—"

"But what?"

"It's the Communion part," she replied.

"You *did* say you were Catholic?"

"I am, Father, but . . ." Angie stared down at the floor. "I'm recently divorced and I haven't been much of a churchgoer lately."

"See!" Mary said, standing again.

Father Joe raised his hand, motioning her to sit back down. "How long *have* you been divorced, Angie?"

"Only a few months."

"Did you request the divorce, or did he?"

"I guess you could say I was forced into it," she replied. "By my husband. I mean, ex-husband—"

Father Joe grinned. "I had a feeling you were the innocent one. You will make confession and be just fine, my child, to receive and distribute Our Lord as a commissioned Eucharistic minister."

Angie's eyes widened.

"I'll see to it," Father Joe said, glancing over at Mary and winking.

Angie stared into her hands.

"Great meals at the Home," he said. "A warm, dry place to sleep. And new friends."

Jumping to her feet, Angie stood tall and firm. "Okay, Father Joe. I accept!"

The men smiled. Mary frowned. Father Joe chuckled, understanding that Mary always expected the worse.

The small white cottage stood alone behind the rectory. Normally, it was just a short walk from the chapel. That night, however, heavy snow and wind made Angie feel as if she was walking to another state. Pulling her collar closer around her neck, she shivered. Staring at the high snow drifts, her feet ached. Grabbing onto her suitcases and bag, her frozen fingers cramped from the bitterness.

At least it's a warm place to sleep.

Angie trudged through the snow toward the cozy looking cabin. As she pushed it open, the old front door squeaked. Angie's heart warmed. The small living room had a fireplace. Stepping inside, she shivered, again. Glancing around, a large lamp grabbed her attention. She clicked it on and sighed.

Where's the thermostat? Please, God, let there be heat.

Glancing into the kitchenette, she frowned at the rusted sink. She laughed when she walked into the bedroom—only a single bed. A full shower, though. That would be a wonderful treat after she unpacked. Still shivering, Angie searched for the heat. She pulled back a curtain and sighed with relief. A thermostat. Moving the dial to eighty, she breathed when the sound of the gas ignited.

While unpacking, a knock at the door startled her. Pulling her sweater tighter around her chest, Angie glanced out the window. Mary stood solemnly in the freezing cold as if it were a warm summer day. Shaking her head, Angie opened the door.

"I brought you something to eat," Mary said.

"Thank you." Staring at the cardboard box, Angie's stomach growled.

"I'll put it in the kitchen." After placing the food on the table, Mary walked back out the door without a word. Closing the door, Angie trembled. Not so much from the cold of the night, but from the person who had just left.

Peeking into the box, Angie gasped. Inside was a homemade chicken casserole, a whole pie, and a beaker of something hot. The sourdough bread, butter, and orange juice she would leave for breakfast.

Thank you, Elder Mary.

Angie giggled as she devoured the casserole and a slice of apple pie. Her favorite. While making the bed, the pie rested heavily on her mind. When would she start her so-called diet? Maybe she should have left some food for tomorrow's dinner. *Nah, I'll start the diet in a day or two.* Sitting down at the table, Angie poured a cup of coffee from the beaker. Taking another bite of pie, Angie texted her daughter.

Angie: *Hi Maddie hope all is well*

Maddie: *With you too*

Angie: *On my feet in Birdsong. Cute place. Got a job! Exhausted. Will call soon. Luv U*

Maddie: *Was worried. Glad you're good! Talk soon. Luv U2*

With a good night's sleep, Angie was ready for that hot shower she'd promised herself. Stepping into the warm water, another prayer was miraculously answered. The bathroom was stocked with shampoo, soap, and towels.

As she nibbled on three slices of extra-buttered sourdough toast, the broken-down car sitting in front of the chapel filled her mind. Grabbing her cellphone, she checked her messages. Nothing from that Jared's Garage. So much for mentioning the elders and Father Joe as referrals.

Stepping outside, the cold air nudged her. Walking through the deep snow toward the chapel, she stared at the bleakness. A dusting of snow and gentle snowflakes swirled through the air. The parking lot was empty. Her silver Honda had been towed.

Angie stepped up to the rectory and pressed on the doorbell. After a few minutes, she heard him shouting.

"Jesus, Mary and Joseph!"

Is he swearing?

The door flung open and a frantic-looking man stared out at her. "Good morning, Angie." Father Joe balanced himself on his crutches. "Hope you had a good night's sleep."

"I did, thank you, Father. The cottage is comfy. Mary stopped by last night with some food."

He chuckled. "Good woman, that Mary. My right arm most days. Means well. I thought you might like the cottage. Served others in the past."

Following Father Joe into his office, Angie maneuvered around the shards of broken glass. "I see you had a little accident."

He pointed to a large gold frame facing a wall. A torn wire seemed to be the culprit.

"Strangest thing. Turned my back and the portrait of Saint Therese just fell to the floor. I swear I had nothing to do with it." He looked over and smiled. "Of course, Mary won't believe me. Just another thing for her to complain about."

"I believe you. I'll take care of it. Where's the broom?"

While Angie swept, Father Joe moved the portrait into a storage room. After finishing her first chore of the day, Angie sat beside his desk.

"I'm really glad you accepted the recreational position."

With hands resting in her lap, she smiled. "So am I, Father."

"Since Kerr Bird Song donated his mansion to the chapel, we sheltered many under our wings." Lowering his eyes, he sighed. "Are you familiar with the history of Kerr Bird Song?"

"Yes, Father. I read up on him before I left Philly."

"We thrived through the years. Until recently, that is. Our dwindling numbers have left us little choice but to fold into the financial care of the Caribou Diocese. We recently received word from the bishop that the Home will be sold to the University of Maine. Nothing will change for now. That is, until the last resident has moved on to heaven. Only eight remain in the Home. All in their nineties."

Leaning forward, Angie frowned.

"But enough about me and my problems. We're here to talk about you."

Angie spent the next hour in conversation with Father Joe about her previous life. Her marriage, divorce, children, and faith. Afterword, feeling like a child making her first Holy Communion, she sheepishly followed Father Joe along a snowy path leading to the rear of the sacristy. They entered the small chapel. The dark wood pressed in on her as if challenging her right to stand in God's presence. The ancient aroma, and the glow from the stained-glass windows, nudged the memories buried in her soul. Glancing up at the hanging Jesus, she lowered her head. Her heart pounded.

Sitting across from Father Joe, Angie confessed her sins. Emotionally raw from bearing her soul, she forgot the words to the act of contrition. It'd been so long.

"I'm not worthy, Father."

It was a prayer of penance. And for Angie's penance, Father Joe handed her a blue crystal rosary. "Pray and meditate. I'll be back in an hour. We'll talk more."

With her knees on the pew's kneelers, Angie arched her back and made the sign of the cross. Gripping the beads with both hands, she mouthed a prayer while moving her hands down each side of the smooth surface. The silver crucifix dangling against her legs sent chills through her. She hadn't held a rosary in years. As she stared up at the wooden crucifix that filled her view, Jesus glared down as if searching through her private thoughts.

Blasts of wind howled eerily through the overhead beams. Drifting in and out with playful thought of years gone by, Angie giggled. The statues of Mary and St. Therese stared down.

Some words of wisdom would be good about now.

Angie lost track of her prayers just like she did as a child. She forced herself to concentrate, but her knees protested at her weight. Sitting back on the pew, the rosary dangling at her side, she thought back to when she was just a young child and smiled. The sweet perfume from her mother's bouffant hair hovered over her. So fresh and clear, it was as if her mother were sitting right next to her again. The words came back as if freshly spoken. "Wake up, Angie. You must get ready for church." Every Sunday morning her mother greeted her with the same words. And every Sunday morning Angie protested, "Mommy, can't I just sleep a little longer. Please?"

At the foot of her bed her mother would leave her fancy Sunday dress with a pair of buckled Mary Janes that were either white or black depending on the season. She always had two pairs—one for church and one to be worn with her parochial uniform.

Cringing, Angie remembered what she hated the most about Mass. Those darn ribbon bonnets with the rubber-band straps that pinched just below her jawline—the type of thing little boys pulled and snapped at every chance. Those were times she was glad she didn't have a brother or pain-in-the-neck sister around. Back then, everyone in Philly attended church and thought it a major sin if they slept through Mass.

For her first Holy Communion, Angie chose her frilly white dress. The store racks were filled with all different types. Her dress had to twirl big-time, something she could show off to the neighbors and cousins. A year later at age ten, she wore that same white dress when she received the Holy Spirit in Confirmation. Angie laughed remembering that her mom had to lower it by two inches. She had received so much money from relatives. *Too bad those funds are gone,* she thought.

Away at college, Sunday mornings arrived with a hangover. Angie skipped Mass to sleep in and nurse her hangovers, believing she'd made up for it all the years before.

For her parents' sake, she followed the Catholic practices and rituals by getting married in their neighborhood church. She even had the twins baptized. She and Jay rarely prayed. As the twins grew, the family stopped attending church altogether, except for Christmas and Easter, the two times a year when a person arrived early to find a seat.

She sighed. She had become a dwindling parishioner—one of those Catholics in name only. Her twenty-fifth wedding anniversary and renewed wedding vows were supposed to be a return to the faith and a fresh start for their marriage. Instead, everything crumbled.

When Father Joe returned, her atonement was over. Discussing the recreational position didn't take long. There wasn't much to it.

"Your hours are nine to three," he explained. "One day off a week. Your choosing."

"A bonus, Father?" Angie mused.

His smile faded. "I know the money isn't much. Make the position your own and have fun. Get to know the town and the people. I think you'll like it here."

"I plan on doing just that. Both the job and the town."

She looked forward to meeting the residents, especially Jakie, the only nurse, and Walter Heron, the Home's cook. Forgetting the name of the temporary administrator the diocese was sending over, she smiled. She'd meet her soon enough.

"When's your operation, again?"

"Thursday. I leave for Boston tomorrow. Let's discuss your role as Eucharistic minister. I think you'll find it rewarding."

With Father Joe in the lead, Angie cautiously approached the altar. A gold-plated tabernacle caught her eye. With her religious education slowly returning, she remembered that the consecrated hosts were kept under lock and key. Ready to take notes, Angie pulled out her cellphone.

Father Joe described the reverence associated with each consecrated host. Carrying the body of Jesus Christ was a huge responsibility.

"It's imperative," Father Joe explained, "should one of the residents not take Communion that you return the host back here." He showed her how to dispose of the host properly in a small, water-filled container next to the tabernacle. "First, pray the Our Father. Then say, 'This is the Lamb of God who takes away the sins of the world. Happy are those who are called to His Supper. Lord, I am not worthy to receive You, but only say the word and my soul shall be healed.' That's the old version. The church has introduced a new version. Sometimes our residents forget and recite the old. Just follow their lead." Father spoke the responses both ways again, a little slower so she could take her notes.

Nodding, Angie typed as fast as she could into her cellphone. *Communion every other day. Place Communion into gold pyx, then into black burse worn around neck. Purify after.*

Father Joe blessed Angie with a special commissioning prayer and gave her Holy Communion.

"I don't feel any different," Angie said.

"Maybe not on the outside, my dear, but on the inside your soul is rejoicing. Trust me."

"Thank you, Father."

They walked to the chapel's double doors. The ones she almost flew through the previous night.

"I see that Jared towed your car to his shop. It's almost noon. Mary should be here any minute. Can I give you a lift to the Home?"

The apple pie screamed through the tight feel of her pants. "Thank you, Father. But I think I'll walk."

"You sure? It's pretty steep to the Home." He frowned.

"I'm sure. Need exercise."

With a wink, he said, "I have the utmost faith in you, Angie. In more ways than one. Good luck."

"Good luck with the surgery, Father."

Snowflakes fell, clinging to her hair as she walked across the parking lot. Glancing down the straight road, she followed the line, which soon went almost straight up. The walk would be steep. She cursed herself for eating that apple pie. Cold and chilled, Angie pulled out her woolen hat and gloves.

The road, shouldered with snow banks and evergreens, showed no signs of hazards. Recently plowed, it wasn't too slippery. Angie started up the hill. Surrounded by a gentle stillness, light flakes continued from the darkening sky. Her boots gripped firmly to the road. Each step left behind an impression.

The walk was easy at first. But as she trudged uphill, her breathing became labored. Out of shape and thirty pounds overweight, her heart pounded as sweat rolled down her cheeks. Shoving her hat and gloves back into her pockets, she unbuttoned her coat. Finding respite against a tall evergreen, the thought of turning back and accepting that drive Father Joe offered tickled at her conscience.

Keep going. You can do this. Stop babying yourself!

Halfway up the road, Angie rested again. Dissecting her recent discussion with Father Joe about her marriage and divorce, she dwelled on her life and what was important. Maddie and Kevin were the best parts, the only good thing at that moment. Raising fraternal twins wasn't easy, but it was worth every sleepless night and worry. Remembering the happy and trying times, a heartwarming smile creased her face. She found pride and solace within her twin's independence.

Then, Jay's face flashed across her vision. She frowned. Father Joe said not to blame herself for her failed marriage. Nonetheless, she did. She shivered now more from the pain that she carried than from the cold.

She'd been blindsided. Her love for Jay was so strong that she never doubted the permanence of their relationship. She'd even thought about forgiving him and taking him back. But he never gave her a chance to forgive him. He was with someone else now. Bitterness eclipsed her melancholy.

After being released from the hospital, Angie had confronted him. Instead of a soft answer, his monotone and uncaring voice slashed her heart into pieces. He said he had simply stopped loving her. Their marriage was nothing more than empty motions. She was to sign the papers and walk away. Two minutes and a few signatures was all it took to flush away twenty-five years of marriage.

Angie sobered and concentrated on the difficulty of her snowy ascent. Each pound of her boots against the snow-packed asphalt sent daggers through her. Tears flowed down her cheeks—droplets of frustration, rejection and fatigue.

Catching her breath, Angie stood in front of the large, red, ornate door of the Home of the Little Flower. Glancing at her watch, she gasped.

"An hour and fifteen minutes! Not a short walk."

Chapter 3

Kerr Bird Song's home was a stately grayish stone mansion. Enormous bushes were wrapped in burlap to protect them from Maine's frigid winter. The building was about 25,000 square feet, on 150 acres. The grand estate had been converted into a nursing home that now looked as withered as its inhabitants.

Angie pushed open the door. Pulling a white handkerchief out of her pocket, she wiped her eyes and blew her nose. Proud for not giving up on the tough walk, she smiled. As she entered the white-marble lobby, a dark-skinned woman wearing nursing scrubs glanced over at her. Her black hair, styled short and tight to her scalp, gave her aging face an aura of grace.

Extending her right hand, the woman smiled. "Hi. You must be Angie. I'm Jakie Sterling, the nurse. Father Joe said you were on your way."

"Nice to meet you." Angie again blew her ice-cold nose and wiped the tears forming as warmth softened her eyes.

"I too cried the first time I tried to walk that half mile." Jakie giggled before placing her hands together. "Never do that again."

Angie laughed. "Car broke down. Thought it be a good time to start exercising." She glanced over at the marble staircase with dark railings that rose toward the coffered ceiling.

"Ever thought of joining a gym?" Jakie's laugh echoed off the bright, cream-colored walls.

Angie giggled. "You're right. I may have to rethink this exercise stuff."

Jakie pointed to the doors behind the oak counter. "You can hang your coat in the closet. A powder room's just to the left."

After pulling herself together in the lady's room, Angie found Jakie waiting for her in the grand lobby. Pausing next to the counter, Angie peered through an open door before following Jakie. It looked to be an office. *The administrator's office?* Father Joe mentioned a woman from the diocese would be part-time as well as temporary. Angie almost stumbled when Jakie suddenly stopped to describe the different areas of the Home.

"The residents' rooms are behind the stairs," Jakie explained. "Nobody lives upstairs except for me." She pointed to a set of double glass doors sealed with transparent film. "Through these doors there's a beautiful garden." Jakie laughed. "In the summer, of course. To our left is the dining area. Serves as a rec room, too. Looks like they're just finishing lunch. Apart from their rooms, our residents spend most of their time in here." Jakie stopped walking and glanced through a viewing window. "These doors open by pressing this button here." Jakie pointed to a large white button. "It's on both sides. Primarily for the residents. These doors are heavy."

Angie tilted her head.

"Our residents do not have the strength to open them."

Wanting a peek at the residents, Angie frowned because her view was blocked by Jakie.

"Walter's our cook," Jakie added. "He owns the Rose Petals restaurant in town. Check it out when you get a chance. Has an enormous rose garden out back. Never seen so many colors. I love to eat there. Especially in the summertime. Inside, the ambiance is nice, too." Jakie took in a deep breath and closed her eyes. Letting it out slowly, she smiled. "Walter's a doll. He comes in every morning before sunrise and preps our meals. Leaves behind enough for us employees to eat. Saves on the food bills."

"That's nice." Angie nodded. "I'll be sure to stop at his restaurant and introduce myself." With all the talk about food, Angie's stomach rumbled.

Jakie laughed. "Guess you need to eat, huh? Especially after that torture of a walk."

"I am a little hungry." Angie grinned.

"Let me introduce you to the residents and then I'll get you something. How about a tuna sandwich and some tea?"

"That would be wonderful."

"We can't have you working on an empty stomach."

"When is the new administrator starting?" Angie asked.

"Tomorrow."

Angie couldn't remember the woman's name. It had slipped her mind. Since Jakie didn't offer, Angie didn't ask.

Her thoughts shifted back to the residents. Walking behind Jakie like a duckling following its mother, Angie smiled at the small group sitting at the tables. The sunlight seeping through the white sheers cast a solemn stillness across the room. It was still a gloomy day outside with flurries floating around. The viewing windows showcased the snow-covered grounds that stopped at the evergreens in the distance.

The creamy décor with neutral carpets and ornate high ceilings made the place feel sterile. Eight round tables with blue tablecloths provided the only color. The room even had a cream-colored fireplace. Off to one side, a box of holiday decorations sat quietly next to two parked walkers. Scanning the room, her eyes landed on the four women and four men. Elderly and frail, they sat at the tables sipping on beverages and picking at what looked like cherry pie.

A smiling Angie cringed as eight pairs of eyes landed on her.

"Well—" Jakie clasped her hands together. "I bet you're all wondering who this is."

"You got that right," replied a dark-skinned man sitting in a wheelchair. With a bald crown and flowing gray hair that fell past his shoulders, he leaned forward. "She's not from the state, is she? Not here to take something else away."

"Spanks!" Jakie scolded. "I expect more from you. And no. This lovely lady is not from the state. She's your new recreational director."

Looking over at the others, she grinned. "With Father Joe away for a bit, Angie will be giving you Communion."

"I want to play bingo now," Spanks said.

Jakie glared at him. "Spanks, please. May I introduce her first?"

"Fine." Spanks pushed his uneaten pie into the center of the table. "No shirt off my back."

The small group giggled.

Extending her hands toward Angie, Jakie said, "This is Angie Pantera. Please give her a nice welcome."

The residents either said hi or waved.

Waving back, Angie stretched her smile as far as she could. "It's my pleasure to meet you. I look forward to playing games and bringing you Holy Communion."

"You've already met Roy Spankler," Jakie said. "We call him, Spanks."

Taking a couple of steps closer, Angie reached out her hand. "Hi, Spanks. Very nice to meet you."

Spanks's eyes jumped over to Jakie and then back to Angie. "I still want to play bingo."

Angie giggled. "I think I can arrange that."

"Good," Spanks said, folding his arms across his chest without accepting her hand.

"This is Rose Maquire," Jakie added. "And this here is Theodore Chumley. But we call him Teddy."

Shaking Rose's hand, a large emerald ring dug into her fingers.

"Nice to meet you, Rose," Angie said, flinching only slightly.

The woman, dressed to the hilt in a burgundy wool suit and costume jewelry, sat erect and firm. Not a single hair of her pearly white updo looked out of place. Bright-red lipstick distracted a person's gaze from the severity of her deeply wrinkled pale face.

"Likewise, Angie," Rose said.

With a head full of thick and tousled gray hair, Teddy, dressed comfortably and casually in a red flannel shirt and jeans, reminded Angie of a good ol' country man.

"Nice to meet you, Teddy."

"Same here, Angie," he replied. His smile looked more honest and genuine than Rose's.

At the next table a man with copper skin stared at her. He also had a full head of gray hair, and he presented himself in a genteel manner by standing up and holding out his hand. Angie held back a giggle as she noticed his hearing aids dangling from his ears.

"Hello, Angie, I'm Karun Nambeeson."

"Nice to meet you," Angie said, shaking his hand.

Sitting next to Karun were two very frail-looking women who looked related.

Jakie said, "This is Adelaide and Trudy Simmons. They're sisters."

Wearing long pink dresses that looked two sizes too big, they reached out with tiny, child-sized hands and laughed. Angie gently shook their hands and smiled back.

Standing near the last table, Jakie nodded. "This is Eliza Finney."

A heavy woman wearing jeans and a jean shirt nodded. Her white hair, streaked with blonde, was pulled tightly into a restricting bun. Shaking her hand, Angie took in a strong whiff of perfume.

"Nice to meet you, Eliza." The scent reminded Angie of something, but she couldn't say what exactly.

"I like your *Pantera* name." Eliza smiled. "It means panther."

"Thank you." Angie cringed. It was a name she wanted to erase from her life.

Next to Eliza sat a thin man wearing blue rectangular readers. Ghostly in color with coarse white hair to match, his head seemed large. He reminded Angie of a cartoon character, Casper, that Maddie and Kevin watched as toddlers. Flooding her thoughts with the past, the old theme song played through her mind. *Casper, the friendly ghost. The friendliest ghost you know . . .*

"This is Peter Peter," Jakie said.

Spanks recited, "Peter Peter, pumpkin eater . . ." He stopped chanting as soon as Jakie cleared her throat.

Extending her hand, Angie nodded. "Nice to meet you, Peter Peter."

Silent and uncaring, Peter stared down at the tablecloth and barely touched Angie's hand. He seemed withdrawn and almost pitiful.

"Nice to meet you, Peter," Angie said, a little louder. This time she left off his last name.

Still ignoring her, Peter retracted his hand, refusing to make eye contact.

"Well then," Jakie said, clasping her hands together. "Now that you've met everyone, the floor is all yours." Jakie took several steps back.

"Thank you," Angie replied, glancing at each of them. "I'll be here from nine to three daily, six days a week. We'll play fun games. Get to know each other."

"Goody," Eliza said, clapping.

Smiling over at her, Angie added, "Father Joe commissioned me as a Eucharistic minister. I'll distribute Holy Communion three days a week. All on alternating days. I'll start tomorrow morning."

"They'll be in their rooms right after breakfast," Jakie replied.

"Wonderful. I'll find you as soon as I arrive." No sooner did the words come out than her cellphone vibrated in her pocket. Praying it was about her car, Angie excused herself. "I'll be right back and we'll play bingo."

"Good," Spanks said with his arms still folded across his chest. "I need to win some socks."

Angie laughed.

Angie stepped outside the room to take the call. It was a local number based on the area code—probably Jared's Garage, she figured.

"What? Are you kidding me. Eighteen hundred dollars?" Angie's voice reverberated through the huge white lobby.

"Yes ma'am," the voice on the other end replied. "That's what the repairs will cost."

Taking in a huge breath, Angie frowned. "Don't do anything until I get there."

Angie composed herself and stepped back into the room. Handing out the bingo cards and chips to the residents, her stomach growled again. Knowing Jakie would be back momentarily with that tuna sandwich and tea she promised, she ran her hand across her mouth.

"You have a tiger in your tank, missy?" Spanks said, lining up his bingo cards.

Eliza Finney giggled. "We heard ya yelling."

Several pairs of new socks later, Spanks stuffed his prizes into his pockets and smirked. "See ya'll at dinner." Pressing the button at the door, he winked before rolling into the lobby.

The sisters, Adelaide and Trudy, waved goodbye at Spanks and gathered their belongings. Peter leaned against his walker and glared at Spanks. Teddy paid no attention as he seemed to be hovering over Rose. Eliza and Karun walked away together discussing the heavy snow shower outside.

Placing the lid back onto the bingo game, Angie glanced up at Jakie. "Spanks was the big winner today. Won several pairs of men's socks."

Jakie leaned over and whispered, "Didn't you see him cheating? Some are beginning to complain."

Grinning, Angie laughed. "Maybe . . . just a little." Glancing at her watch, she shook her head. "I think I'll head out. Need to stop by Jared's Garage before going home. Thanks for your help and for the lunch."

"You're welcome. That garage is all the way across town. Plan on walking?" She pointed to the window, where thick flakes blanked out the world outside. "I'm on break. Be happy to drive you."

Angie's legs still felt like limp noodles. "That would be wonderful. Thank you."

The sign over the door read, *Jared's Garage Depot*. Angie walked in. The jumbled space filled with cars and trucks, new and old in various stages of repair made her stiffen. *Eighteen hundred dollars? My ass! Jared's probably ripping them off, too.*

The place seemed unusually quiet for a car repair shop. Unfortunately, her silver Honda was nowhere to be found. The oil-stained concrete floor made her nervous. It was as if the lifeblood of previous vehicles had left their mark before passing away forever. Glancing over at a large metal sign, she laughed.

> *YOU HAVE ENTERED THE HOME OF THE*
> *FAIREST REPAIRS IN TOWN GUARANTEED*

"That's why my car is eighteen hundred dollars?" she whispered.

"Ms. Pantera?" a man's deep voice bellowed from behind her.

Although she recognized the voice from the phone calls, Angie still jumped. Turning around, she stared at the middle-aged man, tall and rugged with messy blond hair streaked with oil. He wore an untucked blue flannel shirt. A strong aroma of gas and oil tickled her nose.

"Yes, I'm Angie Pantera, and you must be Jared?"

He sniffed a few times before pulling out a dirty cloth from his pocket. Wiping his greasy hands, he nodded. "I'm Tom. Tom Jared."

Relieved when he didn't offer her his greasy hand, Angie sighed. "Mr. Jared. What could possibly have gone wrong with my car that it's going to cost eighteen hundred dollars? Not to mention the tax."

"Good question, Ms. Pantera. If you'd asked on the phone, I could've saved you the trip. Let's see. Where do I start?" With a calmer demeanor, he grinned down at her. "Your tires are bald. No traction. No traction, no stopping. No stopping, accident or a ticket from Chief Bertrand. Needs a new timing belt, alternator, and . . . when was the last time you changed the oil? It was thicker than my momma's molasses."

Angie couldn't answer. Instead she just stood there and stared at him.

"Dirty oil gummed everything up. Gotta replace gaskets and seals. If you'd kept driving, your engine could've blown. Perhaps start a fire."

When *was* the last time she changed the oil in her decade-old car? With Jay around, she never worried about such things. But he stopped caring and doing things for her a long time ago.

Pulling out an oil-stained piece of paper from his pocket, he handed her the invoice. Angie read down the discounts he was offering on the parts.

"I'm only charging half my normal labor. Because of Father Joe and the elders and all. Didn't even charge for the tow." He smiled at her, again. "Tell ya what. I'll throw in a bonus. You pay cash, I add no tax."

Clinging to the long bill, Angie frowned. Tom's voice murmured through her ears as her heart pounded. With her stomach tightening and her face hot, her hands shook.

"I don't even know how your car made it here in one piece," he said. "Father Joe said you came all the way from Philly. Really? Hey, I'm guaranteeing you the best service and cost in town. When I'm done, your car will be as good as new."

"Can anything be done for a fraction of the cost? Maybe just get it out the door?"

Tom's eyes trailed from her head to her toes. "Obviously you know nothing about cars. Unfortunately, no. Your car's ready for the junkyard unless I fix it."

Angie glanced over at the oil-stained floor again.

"You're welcome to have it towed outta here if you don't want me working on it."

"Can't do any better on the cost?" she asked. "I really have no money."

"I already did. I'm giving you the big discounts because of Father Joe. Take it or leave it." As her blood pressure rose, his voice softened. "Look, I'll put you on a payment plan. Let's say, a hundred a week?"

Running the amount through her mind, Angie replied, "Will you take a hundred up front and fifty a week?"

"Fifty?"

"Best I can do."

"Okay. But don't leave town until this bill is paid in full. You gotta promise me that."

Angie nodded. "I just got here. Can't leave anytime soon. Besides, you've got my car. How long to fix?"

"Two weeks."

"Two weeks? Are you kidding?"

Shaking his head, he raised his hands. "I just gave you a real sweet deal because of Father Joe. Take it or leave it. I don't care either way. As you can see, I'm a bit shorthanded."

He kept mentioning Father Joe. Not wanting to hear that name again, Angie frowned. "Fine."

Still shaking his head, Tom walked away without another word.

Not very friendly, is he? Ugh! Guess I'm walking for now.

With a little over an hour of daylight left and the falling snow finally showing signs of slowing, Angie strolled along Main Street. Browsing past the store windows, the charming shops of Birdsong gave her a warm feeling inside. The locals either smiled or nodded at her. Returning the nods, her heart felt full for the first time in months.

Eavesdropping on town maintenance workers taking down the holiday lights, she learned that bad wiring from past renovations most likely caused the kitchen fire at the Holiday Inn. Turned out good for her, but she prayed no one was hurt.

As she walked by a floral shop, large pompom-sized dandelions caught her eye. A great idea for a fun game popped into her head. Angie stepped inside. The various flowery scents filled her with longing. From behind a refrigerated case overflowing with colorful arrangements, a young woman with choppy, short pink hair stepped out.

"How may I help you?"

Glancing at the pink-flower tattoos on her wrists that ran up to her elbows, Angie grinned.

"Those pompom-like flowers in the window. The ones that look like elephant-sized dandelions." She pointed over to them. "How much? I'd need eight."

"They're unique, aren't they?" The young woman walked over to them. "Received two dozen by accident. They're from South America. Foothills of the Andes." Raising her eyebrows and lowering her voice, she stepped closer to Angie. "Grown by monks. I'm told they have spiritual and magical powers."

"Magical powers? Really?" Angie laughed. "Any discount if I buy eight? They're for my seniors at the nursing home. You know, up on the ridge?" Extending her right hand, she grinned. "I'm Angie, by the way. The new recreational director."

Shaking her hand, the young woman offered a crooked smiled. "I'm Ronnie. I own this joint. Welcome to Birdsong. Would you like those arranged with other flowers? I'd have to spray them if I do. Fragile."

"No, just the eight dandelions. How much?"

"They won't last long. Tell ya what—since they're for the residents, I'll give you all eight for twenty." Ronnie narrowed her eyes. "The spiritual magic is free, by the way."

Angie was more of a realist, believing in dictating her own circumstances rather than the arbitrariness of magic. "Works for me," Angie said, pulling out a twenty.

Angie watched as Ronnie packaged the eight fist-sized flowers carefully in a huge white box that looked like something Christmas bulbs would be stored in.

"Gotta be careful with this. I'll seal the box up, but no shaking it around."

Angie nodded. "Where can I find craft products?"

"The Hobby Shoppe. Just up the block."

Cradling the large box in her arms, Angie said goodbye and headed for the next store. With her creative thoughts flowing, she decided on a free-standing white poster board to showcase her idea. After choosing different colors of tissue paper, she grabbed several markers. Finishing with white index cards, she headed for the checkout counter when a small, floral box grabbed her attention. With a curved lid and a generous slit to stuff paper through, it was perfect. Just what she needed—a treasure box.

"I'll take this as well," she said to the young girl at the counter.

Spending twenty dollars on the elephant-sized dandelions, then another twenty-five on the crafts and treasure box, Angie prayed that Father Joe would reimburse her. She placed the receipts into her wallet. Towing two large shopping bags and one large box through the deep snow wasn't easy. She stopped at the Rose Petals restaurant and glanced at the carved wooden sign. Swirling rose petals beckoned her to enter. Not quite hungry yet, she still wanted to stop by and say hi to Walter, the cook. With him leaving before she arrived in the mornings, their paths most likely would never cross.

Then again, maybe takeout would not be such a bad idea.

As the heavy oak door closed behind her, Angie stepped into the waiting area. Framed art on the walls was complimented with a busy community board. Beyond an empty check-in counter, a large rectangular bar and white covered tables greeted her. Floor-to-ceiling glass french doors framed the outside courtyard, which was bordered with dozens of burlap wraps. *Those must be the rose bushes Jakie told me about.*

The restaurant's gaudy Christmas decorations were probably left up for the Epiphany, which was just a couple of days away. The Epiphany celebrated the visit of the magi after Jesus's birth and the revelation of his future destiny as Savior. Maybe Father Joe was rubbing off on her after all. Glancing at a flyer on the community board, she read, *COME CELEBRATE THE EPIPHANY SATURDAY, JANUARY 6TH NOON, TOWN PARADE.* Angie frowned. Today was the ninth. She'd missed it.

Not quite dinner time, the restaurant was empty. Angie grabbed two bar stools, one for her large box and one for her.

Within minutes, a middle-aged woman with spiked red hair walked through the swinging doors wearing a black dress decorated with long pearls. She smiled.

"Oh, hi. Didn't know anyone was here. Hope you haven't waited long."

"Not long. "

"Want a menu?"

"Actually, just want take out. Is Walter here?"

"In the kitchen. I'm Nancy, his wife."

"Nice to meet you. I'm Angie Pantera, the new rec person at the Home. Walter's gone by the time I get there. Thought I'd stop by and say hi."

Nancy grinned. "I'll let him know you're here."

A large man both in girth and height and about age forty waddled through the doors. He definitely looked the part of a gourmet chef, almost like Mario Batali without the beard.

With a big smile, he reached out his hand. "Hi, Angie. Welcome aboard. Big bags from the hobby store? Those residents need some fun." Laughing, Walter added, "Especially that Spanks."

Shaking his hand, Angie laughed. "Oh yes. I met Spanks."

"So, what brings you to Birdsong?"

"A wish and a feather."

"A wish and a feather?" Walter laughed. "I hope it was granted."

They exchanged small talk while Angie's food cooked. She shared her car troubles with him and her experience with Tom.

"Good man, that Tom. Know 'im well. Your car's in good hands."

Remembering her last words with Tom, she frowned. He could've been a little friendlier.

Walter insisted on her having the night's special, beef short ribs, without charge, making her feel welcomed. "I cook extra at the Home every day. Make sure you eat."

"I'll do that," Angie replied.

Walking through the darkening afternoon, Angie towed three bags and a large white box.

To my cottage home. Angie smiled at the thought. Home.

The day had been good—except for the repair bill. Looking forward to dinner, Angie thought about her special project for the residents. *They'll have so much fun with those ginormous dandelions. Spiritual magic?* Angie laughed.

Chapter 4

The following morning, Angie fumbled with the keys as she slid one into the sacristy door. After a loud *click*, the knob turned. Holding the shopping bags and cradling the large white box, she stepped inside.

Father had said to look for a closet. She glanced around.

Knowing the door straight ahead led to the chapel, she picked the door on the right. With a fifty-fifty chance and two keys left, she slid one into the keyhole. Nothing. Trying the other key, the lock clicked. Angie opened the door and saw a little gold-hinged box sitting alone on the closet shelf. Father Joe referred to it as the *pyx*. After placing her bags and box on the floor, she stepped up to the small cabinet. Slowly, she reached to touch the cold metal. A shiver ran up her arm and down her back.

Am I worthy? Father Joe's words echoed through her mind. *"I have the utmost of faith in you."*

Taking in a deep breath, Angie grabbed the box and hugged the small container close to her chest. Sitting farther back on the shelf was the burse, a black pouch with a long strap that held the pyx for Communion. She placed the strap over her head and relocked the closet. She frowned. Being a Catholic in name only sometimes wasn't a good thing.

With a knot growing inside her stomach, Angie opened the chapel door. The room, with its long, dark wood and stone structures, seemed eerily silent and even more ominous than before. Standing guard, the hanging crucifix of Jesus and the statues of Mary and Saint Therese stared down at her. Angie took in another deep breath and stepped forward. Were they judging her?

The golden dome-shaped tabernacle shone from behind the altar. Each step echoed through the large room, reminding her of where she was and what she was being paid to do. Angie clasped her hands together in prayer. Kneeling and making the sign of the cross, she whispered the "Our Father" prayer.

Saint Therese glared at her through uncaring eyes. "I have permission to be here," Angie said, to the statue. And to Jesus she added, "From Father Joe."

Stepping onto the platform, she counted her steps. Three to reach the shiny golden tabernacle. She used the last key to open the golden container. Reaching for the chalice-shaped ciborium, she counted out eight consecrated hosts. Placing the pyx back into the black pouch, Angie sighed. She was following Father Joe's instructions to the letter. So why were these saints judging her?

Having collected the hosts for the Home residents, Angie walked in the direction of Ridge Road, balancing the shopping bags and large box. She stared at the packed black snow and the dark sky as heavy gusts pushed her along. After several minutes, Angie felt as if she would perish from cold and exhaustion. A car revved behind her. After several beeps, the SUV slowed as the window rolled down.

Jakie, sitting on the passenger side, leaned forward. The young driver ignored Angie and stared straight ahead. Grinning, Jakie giggled. "You still don't like gyms, do you?"

Angie sighed. "My car's in the shop for another two weeks."

"Hop in," Jakie said. "Lucky for you, we're going your way."

The young driver reached behind him and opened the back door.

"Thanks," Angie said, sliding the box in first.

"This is my son, Michael."

"Hi, Michael."

Michael didn't respond.

"Walter covered for me this morning," Jakie said. "Yearly medical checkup. He stayed long enough to serve the residents their breakfast."

"Stopped into Rose Petals yesterday," Angie replied. "Walter insisted on giving me dinner at no charge."

Jakie laughed. "Told you. Walter's awesome." She glanced at Angie's large bags. "What ya got?"

"Games and flowers for the residents."

"I'll have to come and watch."

The drive to the Home was short. Jakie kissed Michael on the cheek and jumped out. "See you soon." Looking embarrassed, Michael said nothing.

Angie gathered her things and stepped out. "Thank you. Nice meeting you, Michael."

"You're welcome."

Stepping into the lobby, Angie glanced around. "Are they in their rooms? I have Communion to distribute."

"They are. In addition to my nursing duties, I'm also barber and hairdresser."

Angie laughed. "You're amazing."

"Thanks. I try."

After hanging their coats and scarves in the closet, Jakie walked away. "See you in passing."

Angie watched as Jakie walked toward the residents' quarters.

Picking up her two shopping bags and large box, she glanced at the administrator's office. *Still not here yet.* She walked into the dining room and dropped the bags on the floor. The box she carefully placed on the table. With plenty of time to set up, Angie slowed. Looking forward to the little game, she tapped the burse that rested against her chest. *It's Communion time.*

Drawn in by the grandeur of the Kerr Bird Song mansion, Angie stared at the ornate staircase. Around the corner was the entrance to the private living quarters. Only seven rooms were being used. Jakie's medicine cart sat silently in the center of the hallway. Lively music from the 1940s filled the air through the overhead speakers. With the apartment doors closed, Angie walked the gamut from one end of the hallway to the other, peeking over at the displays of World War II photos. A hanging American flag gave her reason to pause. Tilting her head from side to side, Angie stared at a few old-fashioned cleaning utensils and washboards sitting inside a glass display case. She laughed at a hand-cranked wringer washing machine and rusted old irons.

Touching the black pouch, she sighed. She'd have to visit each resident individually. Locating them wouldn't be difficult since the floral door hangers announced the occupied rooms.

Stepping up to the first door, Angie read off the brass plate: *One – Rose Maguire.* Flush against the wall, a glass shadow box displayed old black-and-white photos. As a young woman, Rose wore elegant gowns and her hair styled high. A handsome older man in a tuxedo stood next to her. Several of her fashionable friends smiled elegantly at the camera.

After a light knock, Rose's voice sang through the door. "Come in."

"Hi, Rose. I have Holy Communion for you."

Rose wore a black knit suit with pearl earrings and matching necklace. Rose sat at her oak dressing table, tracing her lips with bright-red lipstick. The mirror, wrapped in a white sheet, made Angie stare. The softer light lessened Rose's deep facial lines. With her pearly white hair combed out long and straight, the woman didn't look quite finished.

"Thought you were Jakie. Suppose to pin my hair a while ago."

"I'm sure she'll be here soon." Angie glanced around the room. Antiques and portraits of faraway places adorned the walls. "It's cozy in here."

"I guess I have time for Communion before Jakie gets to me," Rose said.

Holding onto Rose's hands, Angie winced. The large emerald ring again dug into her fingers. Loosening her grip, she grinned. They prayed the Our Father just as Father Joe instructed. Angie allowed Rose to lead with whichever response she wanted. Rose spoke the older version.

Placing the host on Rose's tongue, Angie whispered, "Body of Christ."

"Amen," Rose replied.

Glaring at the sheet covering the mirror, Angie asked, "Is your mirror broken?"

"Can't stand looking at myself." Rose sighed. "All these damn wrinkles. Was stunning in my day. Just a wrinkly old hag now."

"I think you're still stunning."

"Easy for you to say," Rose replied. "You're young. Aren't wrinkly yet."

Angie smiled. "See you later, Rose."

"Tell Jakie I'm still waiting."

"Will do."

Walking to room three, she read off the name. *Theodore Chumley.* Staring at the photos in the shadow box, Angie giggled. A handsome young man with the same thick head of dark hair posed as an outdoorsman with hunting, fly fishing, and camping scenes. A color photo of a woman at a campsite captured her interest. *Wife? Children maybe?*

She knocked and Jakie's voice reverberated through the thick wood. "Come in."

Peering around the door, Angie smiled.

Jakie was leaning over and trimming Teddy's bushy white eyebrows. "Almost done. Can give him Communion in a minute."

With his walker by his side, the man wore the same red flannel shirt and jeans from yesterday. "Hi, Angie. Nice to see you again."

"Hi, Teddy. You're looking handsome today. Have a special date or something in the works?"

"I wish," Teddy said.

Glancing around his room, Angie thought it looked rather sparse. Just a single unkempt bed, dresser, and TV that rested on a wobbly stand. A couple of flowery portraits hung on the otherwise empty walls.

"By the way, Jakie, Rose is waiting for you to pin up her hair."
Teddy's groomed eyebrows arched.

"Ya, ya. I'll head there as soon as I'm finished here." Jakie frowned. "That woman needs some patience."

Angie giggled. When Teddy stepped into the bathroom, Jakie vacuumed the floor with a hand-held model. Mumbling under her breath, Jakie said, "He has the hots for Rose. But she won't look his way." Still carrying the vacuum, Jakie nodded as she closed the door behind her.

"I'm ready," Teddy said, sitting down at the small table. Angie placed her hands over Teddy's. Together, they prayed. Teddy used the old prayer and took Holy Communion on his tongue. Smiling, he said, "Thank you, Angie. You made my day."

"As you made mine."

Adelaide and Trudy Simmons showcased themselves as dancers and teachers. In black-and-white photos, two dark-haired women posed with a dozen or so middle-grade girls. The sisters looked not much older than their students. They smiled broadly while standing under a large overhead sign that read, *Simmons Dance Academy*.

Angie found Adelaide dressing Trudy. A couple of framed landscapes decorated the barren walls. Near a curtained window sat a small table with two chairs.

"Hi, ladies," Angie said. "I have Holy Communion for you."

"Hi," the sisters replied together.

Adjusting the ribbon on Trudy's blue dress, Adelaide shook her head. "Trudy spilled coffee at breakfast."

Angie smiled. The dress looked to be about two sizes too big for the small woman.

"Little out of sorts this morning," Trudy whispered before looking away.

"That happens sometimes," Angie replied.

Angie stepped up to Adelaide first, since she seemed the oldest and seemed to take charge.

"Done," Adelaide said, smiling.

Standing in the middle of the room and holding hands, they prayed. Angie held back a giggle. They reminded her of a game—Ring Around the Rosie. Adelaide walked Trudy to her bed. After sitting, they leaned forward as Angie placed the host on their tongues. They, too, spoke the old response.

"Amen," Adelaide whispered.

Trudy remained silent.

With wide eyes and rosy cheeks, they reminded Angie of small children. "We're done," Angie said.

"Thank you," Adelaide replied.

Trudy smiled.

"Hope your day gets better," Angie said.

"Thanks," Trudy replied.

Standing in the hallway, Angie reviewed her notes. *No other residents on this side of the building.* Walking through the empty corridor, the silence overwhelmed her. Soon this magnificent place would be sold to the university. It seemed odd how much life changed over time.

"I'll start with the furthest room on my right before working my way forward," she said to the empty hallway.

Knocking on room fourteen, Angie glanced over at Peter's shadow box. Only one item was inside: a magazine cutout. With his arms and legs outstretched in quest of knowledge, Da Vinci's *The Vitruvian Man* seemed a little out of place. Knocking several times, she waited. No response. After a few more knocks, Angie poked her head into the room. Sitting at a table near the window, Peter wrote passionately inside a large folder. With his blue rectangular readers down low on his nose, his pale complexion faded against the white-washed walls. The melody of *Casper the Friendly Ghost* flew through her mind.

"Good morning, Peter," Angie said.

Head down, he gave no response. Angie's stomach tightened. She watched as he used a black marker to trace out a large number nine. Then, in no particular order and on the same page, he printed the numbers zero to eight. Glancing around, she saw a pile of construction folders on the floor next to his walker. Apart from a single bed, dresser and lamp, and several shelves overstuffed with intellectual-type books, his room was empty. No TV that she saw. *What is he doing with all those folders?*

"I'm here with Holy Communion," Angie said.

Closing the folder, Peter stared at the table. "Good morning."

Angie sat down across from him. His lips moved, but barely a sound escaped. Believing that Peter had agreed, Angie prayed the Our Father. With his eyes closed, Peter stuck out his tongue.

"Amen," she said almost jumping from her chair. "Goodbye, Peter. See you later."

Standing in the silent hallway, Angie sighed. *How awkward was that?*

Karun Nambeeson lived three doors down from Peter. Hoping Karun would be a little friendlier, Angie loitered at his shadow box before knocking. It overflowed with discolored black-and-white photos. With a strong family resemblance to most, only one was in full-color. An older woman with red hair stood next to a younger Karun. Fascinated, Angie studied the other photos in detail. In a large black-and-white, a smiling younger man dressed as a chauffeur stood in front of an antique Rolls Royce. In the distance appeared to be a palace. *Could that be an old photo of Karun?* The side door was open and a young Indian woman sat solemnly inside. Draped in a chiffon sari adorned with pearls and a small, shiny bindi, the woman looked sad.

Angie knocked on room eleven. Opening the door, Karun smiled. With a thick Indian accent, he said, "Welcome, Angie. Come in."

"I bring Holy Communion."

Karun rushed to turn off his large TV. Angie glanced around his modest room. Two wing-back chairs separated by a small table with a lamp faced the flat-screen. A single bed snuggled near a far wall looked very comfortable. Several colorful pictures hanging on the wall brightened up the room.

"I was admiring your photos outside," Angie said.

"Oh, thank you."

"Who's the young woman in the sari?"

His face lit as he smiled. "Ah, the princess." He looked up. "Very beautiful woman."

"Tell me about her," Angie said, sitting in one of the winged chairs.

"I was just nineteen," he said. "Chauffeur to the maharajah's daughter. Princess Aruna was one year older than me."

Karun explained how the maharajah sent an aide to Karun's village church asking for help. The head priest recommended Karun. The job would last a year. Karun spoke of the honor he brought to his lower-class family. How he cared for the new Rolls Royce Phantom that was assigned to him personally by the maharajah. He had trained with a pistol in order to protect Princess Aruna.

"I drove her everywhere," he said. "I cherished each day with the princess. We became good friends, discussed much. She insisted I call her Aruna." Pointing at Angie, he grinned. "Only when we were alone."

Listening to the fascinating story, Angie forgot about the Communion. As he spoke, her heart warmed.

"She said I was the most wonderful listener, her only confidant. Very sad day when she married Prince Anand. Everyone in my village knew how cruel the man was." His eyes glistened as he spoke. "She cried every day about him. Said her life was doomed. But I made her laugh." He sighed. "That is all I could do for her."

"What a story, Karun."

"I will never love anyone as much as I loved Aruna." Tears welled in his eyes. "It had to be so for my entire life."

Holding back her own tears, Angie whispered, "I'm sorry, Karun.

Did you ever tell her how you felt about her?"

"Absolutely not!" he stated. "I would have been beheaded. My family disgraced."

"So, what did you do?"

"After she married Prince Anand, I wept every day in sadness for her. Not wanting my secret revealed, I left my village for good. Spared my family the embarrassment. I traveled to Africa. Met a widow named Diana." He grinned.

The redhead?

"We became companions," he said. "Ended up here in America." Sitting in the other wing chair, Karun held tightly onto Angie's hand.

"Such a love story. Communion?" Glancing at his dangling hearing aids, Angie spoke loudly. His lips moved with the old response.

After receiving, Karun shouted, "Amen!"

Angie laughed.

At Eliza Finney's shadow box, Angie couldn't help but stare. Appearing not much younger in the color photos, Eliza was feeding cuts of meat to several big cats. Angie studied the lions, tigers, and jaguars. To one side sat a single black panther.

Knocking, Angie pondered Eliza's zookeeper job. Angie wouldn't want her hands anywhere near those cats' sharp teeth.

"Well, well. Come in, panther lady." Eliza's hair was pulled back and she was dressed in jeans and a bulky sweater. Strong—*and familiar*—perfume encased her.

"Hi, Eliza," Angie said. "I have Communion for you."

"Please, take a seat."

Angie followed her to a small couch and glanced over at a single bed covered in white gingham. On the nightstand was a perfume bottle with its name blocked by a photo of an older woman.

Taking Eliza's hands into hers, they prayed. Eliza led with the new response. "Lord, I am not worthy that You should enter under my roof, but only say the word and my soul shall be healed." After receiving, Eliza sat back.

"Guess you're the only one paying attention to Father Joe," Angie said.

"Pay attention to a lot of stuff around here."

"You were a zookeeper?" Angie asked.

"More like a big cat keeper. Worked for a reserve in Florida. Saved rejects from circuses, TV shows, and old movie sets. And from the stupids that bought them illegally for pets." She laughed. "Those we'd get after the cat tried to bite off their heads."

"You weren't afraid of 'em?"

"Nah, my cats were like my children. Loved 'em all. My favorite was Lucy. She was old. Hurtin' when she came to us. A bankrupt circus. She lived for about five years . . . Now, *she* was special."

Standing, Angie tried to see the name of the perfume, but it was still blocked by the framed picture.

"On your nightstand, that—"

"That's a picture of my sister, Sherry," Eliza said. "After the reserve went bankrupt, the state took over and let me go. Came to Birdsong to live with Sherry. She never married either. After she died, Father Joe brought me here. This is my only family now."

Angie nodded. "See you soon." She needed to finish up Communion; she would leave discovering the name of the perfume until later.

Angie studied Roy Spankler's two photos. On the top shelf was a black-and-white photo of a younger Spanks in military uniform holding the waist of a beautiful young black woman. Her shoulder-length, wavy hair gave her a seductive look. An old color photo on the lower shelf showed an older and balding Spanks standing next to an attractive middle-aged blonde. She was smiling and he smirking. Before Angie could knock, the door flew open.

"Stop complaining," Jakie said. "Your hair looks great."

Finding their banter amusing, Angie remained quiet.

"Told you take off just a little," he yelled. "Took off my whole head of hair. Now I'm bald!"

Stepping into the hallway, Jakie sniped, "You were bald to begin with, old man."

Spanks pushed his wheelchair into the doorway. He wasn't giving up. "Wasn't that bald when you started! And who're you calling old, missy?"

Angie giggled.

Jakie nodded to Angie. "Gonna put my cart away. I'll gather the others into the dining room for some rec time."

"Sounds good. I'm done after Spanks." As she stepped in front of his wheelchair, Spanks looked up at her. "Your haircut looks good on you."

Folding his arms, Spanks frowned. "Maybe."

"Would you like to receive this morning?"

"I'll have Communion right here. Don't want anybody in my room."

"You let Jakie in."

"She barges in . . . all the time."

Angie laughed. "I'm sure it's to take care of you."

"Maybe."

Not wanting to argue, Angie proceeded with the Communion while standing at the door. Her thoughts drifted to what Eliza had said earlier—the residents were her only family now. *Is that how the others feel?* Uncurling his arms, Spanks followed her lead with the new, sticking out his tongue. She placed the host in Spanks's mouth.

"Amen," Spanks said.

Chapter 5

Before setting up her poster and dandelions, Angie detoured into the kitchen. She took a quick glance around the spacious and professional stainless-steel room. It appeared to be fitted with everything a gourmet cook would need or want. Copper pots and pans hung from a ceiling rack. The large burner stove along with a massive refrigerator occupied one wall.

Walter's meals for lunch and dinner sat warming in the wall oven. Chocolate desserts and salads sealed in plastic wrap waited for the residents on the counter. Angie's stomach growled. The two slices of toast with butter and coffee she gulped down for breakfast were calling for reinforcements.

Angie stood before a deep sink and wished she had one of these when she was married. Life would have been so much easier. But that ship sailed months ago. Angie's smile disappeared.

It was purification time. *What did Father Joe say? Add tap water, swirl it around, and then drink it. The pyx may contain traces of the Holy Communion hosts, so wipe it clean with the purification cloth.*

Since she left the purification cloth in the chapel's closet, she needed something else. After drinking the few drops of water, she used a paper towel. *I apologize, Little Flower.* Angie's eyes raised to the heavens as she gave a little prayer for forgiveness.

Not allowed to wear the pouch after giving Communion, Angie tucked the dry set into her pocket. Angie kicked a small bowl as she turned to leave. Water ran freely across the kitchen tile floor. Using the same paper towel, Angie wiped up the floor. The bowl resembled one that a house cat or small dog would use, but Jakie never mentioned a pet. *Did Walter let in a stray?* Tossing the paper towel into the trash, she sighed. Time to get busy.

The eight enormous white dandelions preserved inside their special box sat on one of the tables. Angie placed the treasure box and index cards next to it. Picking up the large bag from the craft store, Angie pulled out a free-standing poster and stared at it. The darn thing took her hours to make—kept her up until past midnight. Her grin said it all as she gave her work a big thumbs-up. On the poster, with a blue-gray background, was the silhouette of a young girl blowing on a dandelion, the little puffs swirling around her. Silvery flowers and floating stars surrounded the girl. Near her mouth, the words accentuated the child's thrill: *DANDELION PUFFS AWAY, MAKE MY WISH COME TRUE ONE DAY!*

She took several steps back, and the outline of the little girl almost jumped off the poster. Angie reveled in her work. She read the large words under the silhouette:

THE HOME OF THE LITTLE FLOWER IS
GRANTING YOUR WISH!
Every Week, One Lucky Resident Will Have
Their Dream Come True. What Will You Wish For?

"I wonder what my residents will want?" Glancing at the instructions, Angie's finger trailed through the lines:

1. Write one real wish on the card.
2. Close your eyes and make the WISH!
3. Place the card in the Treasure Box.
4. Seal your WISH for it to come True!

Teddy grunted as he pushed his walker toward her. "What do you have, Angie?"

"You're gonna have a fun morning, Teddy. I promise."

Teddy placed his walker against a wall before taking the seat closest to her. He studied the poster. The doors flew open and in walked Adelaide and Trudy. Of course, Adelaide held Trudy's hand. Eliza was right behind them.

Maneuvering around the sisters, Eliza said, "Sorry, ladies. Gotta see what Angie's got here." Stepping up to the poster, Eliza leaned in. "Got the perfect wish for you, Angie."

"That's great, "Angie replied.

Glancing away and ignoring the poster, the sisters walked past, talking to each other and then taking a seat. It was as if no one else existed.

Humming, Karun walked up to Eliza. "What kind of a wish can I make? Can it be anything at all?"

"Think of something fun," Angie replied.

Eliza laughed. "You heard the lady. Something fun, not old and boring."

"Glad you two are enjoying this." Angie giggled.

Karun sat across from Adelaide and Trudy. Eliza sat at the next table, alone. Paying no attention to the idle chatter, Peter pushed his walker into the room. Stepping past Angie and the poster, he parked next to Teddy.

"Hey, Peter," Eliza said.

Peter mumbled something.

Jakie pushed Spanks toward the tables in his wheelchair.

"What is this?" Spanks asked. "I want to see."

"You'll love it," Angie said, nodding to Spanks.

"Doubt it," he said.

While Spanks read from the poster, Angie counted heads. "Just waiting on Rose."

Jakie whispered, "Rose is always the last to arrive. She usually rushes in at the last moment. Teddy will pull out her chair with a silly grin on his face. He does this three-seven."

"Three-seven?" Angie asked.

"Three times a day. Breakfast, lunch, and dinner. Seven days a week." She waved her right hand through the air. "Rose does this before sitting down. Always saying the same thing: 'Why thank you, Theodore. You're such a gentleman.'" Jakie dramatically batted her eyes as she and Angie giggled.

"I'll keep an eye out," Angie said.

"She insists on calling him Theodore. He's a man of patience dealing with her."

The photos from Teddy's shadow box flashed through Angie's mind. He'd have to have patience since his life flourished around fishing and gaming.

"Just one wish?" Spanks asked. "What fun is that?"

"A lot," Angie replied. "I promise."

Pulling him from the display, Jakie parked Spanks at Teddy's table. "I have to go make a call," Jakie said. "Spanks, you hush your mouth now."

As Jakie pulled the door open, Rose walked in and skirted past Angie. Angie's eyes followed her to Teddy's table. As promised, the scenario played just as Jakie described. No one paid any attention, though. Smiling, Angie remembered what Jakie had said earlier, that he had the hots for Rose and she refused to look his way.

Clearing her throat, Angie said, "Now that everyone is here, let's begin." She pointed to the girl on the poster. "You're probably wondering what this is all about."

"You got that right, missy," Spanks smirked.

With all eyes focused on her, Angie wondered why no one asked about the dandelions or their enormous size. *They probably think they're fake.*

"We're going to play a wishing game," Angie said, handing each resident a blank index card and a pen.

Peter pushed his away.

"Think of something you want," Angie said, holding up a blank card. "Anything you want. Write it down and sign your name at the bottom."

Adelaide grabbed Trudy's index card from her hand and began scribbling on it. One at a time, each resident lowered their head and scribbled on their cards. Even Peter jumped in. Eliza, the first to finish, flipped hers over and sat back, beaming. Rose, of course, took her time.

Walking around the tables, Angie rubbed her hands together. "When you're finished, fold your card in half. Don't want anyone to see what you wrote down."

Grinning from ear to ear, Teddy and Karun held up their cards. Adelaide handed the card back to Trudy, who glanced at it before folding it in half.

"Close your eyes," Angie whispered. "Make a wish." With their eyes closed, Angie picked up the treasure box. "Okay. Now open your eyes. As I come around, place your card into this little box." As the last card dropped into the little container, Angie grinned. "And now, the fun part."

"There's more?" Teddy asked.

"You bet there's more." Angie replied. "We're going to seal your wish so it comes true." Carefully, she pulled out one of the large dandelions from the special box. "Don't breathe on these. Just hold them." She handed one to Spanks.

"What do you expect me to do with this thing?"

"Just hold it. Carefully. When everyone has one, I'll explain."

Pulling out the next flower, Angie's stomach tightened. *What if they don't have the lung capacity to blow?* Her mind filtered through the possibilities. Grinning, she handed a flower to Teddy. *I'll blow it for them while they make their wish if I have to.*

"And now for the pièce de résistance." Angie handed Eliza the last dandelion.

"This is so big," Eliza said, turning the fluffy white sphere in her hand.

"Please, hold it still," Angie said. "Okay, close your eyes and think of your wish. The one that's written on the card that's in the treasure box. Got that in your mind? Yes? Then open your eyes and blow on your dandelion. Blow as hard as you can."

"Huh?" Spanks stared at her.

"Blow on your dandelion so your wish will come true. Now, blow, and I'll pick the first winner out of the treasure box."

Interested now, they sat up straighter. Bringing the huge white puffs closer to their faces, they blew. Some made the attempt with their mouths opened wide. Others just pursed their lips. No white puffs scattered.

"The dandelions are from the foothills of the Andes Mountains," Angie said. "Grown by the monks themselves. It's said the puffs have special spiritual and magical powers."

"Really?" Rose asked. "But the puffs won't blow away."

"Let's find out." Raising her arms as if she were conducting an orchestra, Angie yelled out, "*Blow!* Blow now! As hard as you can!"

Together the ninety-something men and women filled their lungs with air and blew with all their strength. Their faces turned shades of pink and red.

As they huffed, Angie recited the silhouette's verse. "Dandelion puffs away, make my wish come true one day!"

Opening the small box, Angie took out a card. Holding it in her right hand, she waited. She glanced over her shoulder and saw Jakie leaning against the back wall.

Eyes bulging, Spanks blew. His white puffs floated up toward the ceiling. Rose's and Teddy's flew up next. With wide eyes and large grins, Karun, Adelaide, Trudy, Eliza and Peter blew. More puffs swirled through the room. As they stared upward, their mouths hung open. The puffs swirled and swirled, refusing to come back down.

Jakie darted over to Angie. "What's going on?"

Angie shook her head. She could only stare. Instead of floating to the ground like snowflakes, the puffs churned through the air, taking on the shape of flying birds. Swarming together, the white puffs made the first pass over their heads. Again and again, the murmuring puffs dipped and soared through the room. Each time, they seemed to multiply, doubling in size—no, tripling. There were more.

Angie's heart raced. *Is a window or vent open somewhere?*

Jakie gasped. "What in the world?"

With her mouth open and eyes wide, Angie flailed her arms to protect the residents. Rose and Teddy laughed and clapped. As the puff swarm grew, the others laughed, too.

Twisting and turning, the swirl above took on the shape of a giant white wave. Karun jumped up to grab an armful. But as they swooped down toward his hands, they soared right past him. The more the swarm teased, the more Karun jumped up. Playing like young children, the sisters bounced up and down. Eliza climbed onto her chair to reach the soaring puffs. The swirling mass continued to rise and fall, eluding them all.

Peter stepped onto his chair and Jakie grabbed his leg.

"Peter," she yelled. "Sit back down! You'll fall."

He pushed her away as the puffs aimed straight for him. Reaching forward, Peter swiped his hand through the white dust. Just crusting his fingertips, the puffs swirled and split and swirled together again.

"Ooooh!" the residents chanted.

Spanks clapped, yelling, "More! More! More!"

Teddy helped Rose out of her seat. Pulling her in close, he twirled her around. As they danced to a tune only they could hear, Rose laughed excitedly.

"Why, Theodore. I never would have guessed you were such a good dancer."

"Lot you don't know about me, Rose," Theodore replied.

Jakie stood vigilantly next to Peter.

"What should I do?" Angie yelled. "This shouldn't be happening."

"Look at 'em." Jakie screeched. "Never seen 'em happier. They're just like little kids. You hit a home run, Angie."

The double white doors flew open with a thunderous bang. A loud screech filled the air.

"Ms. Pantera! What in the world is going on in here?"

Everything stopped. The puffs rained down around them, missing their heads. The swirling white flakes blanketed the carpet and tabletops.

It was as if the snow outside had visited them personally. Even Angie's display table wasn't spared from the white dust. A stern-looking woman stood at the double doors with her hands planted firmly on her hips. If this was the new part-time administrator, Angie wished she could remember her name.

The dining room doors slammed behind the angry woman. She glanced out at the white mess covering the room. Her eyes darted past Angie and Jakie to the residents still standing on their chairs.

"Residents," she ordered. "Take your seats, now!" The angry administrator charged into the middle of the room. "I'm Ms. Fettore from the diocese. I order you to clean this place up, immediately."

The residents slowly took their seats. Watching her every move, they remained silent. Angie's stomach tightened.

Extending her hand, Jakie said, "Ms. Fettore. We've been expecting you."

Ms. Fettore glared at Jakie, who stood looking guilty in her nurse's scrubs. "Just in time, I see. Nurse Sterling, is it?"

Placing the folded index card into her pants pocket, Angie stepped forward and extended her hand as well. "Ms. Fettore? I'm—"

"I know who you are, Ms. Pantera. Father Joe informed the diocese of your hiring."

"The game we're playing took a turn—"

"Right now, I'm only interested in our residents' safety." She frowned at Angie's poster.

"As their nurse and caretaker," Jakie said, "I can assure you they're perfectly fine. They were all having a lovely time with the game Angie was playing."

Nodding at Jakie, Angie added, "Yes, they were. In fact, I still need to announce the first winner."

Ignoring Angie's comment, the administrator glared at Jakie. "Nurse Sterling, take the residents directly to their rooms. Lunch will be served there and not here. The dining area must be cleaned first." She glared at Angie. "What is this white stuff, anyway?"

"Dandelion puffs," Angie replied.

Jakie whispered into Angie's ear. "There's a commercial vacuum in the storage room off the kitchen."

Ms. Fettore frowned again before adding, "Ms. Pantera, announce your first winner. Then bring the other wishes directly to my office."

After reading Spanks's wish, Angie worried about what the others wrote. Spanks was probably just being Spanks and thought this was all a big joke.

"Spanks is our first winner," Angie said, placing his wish back into the treasure box.

"Lucky me," Spanks said. "I'm glad I'm not you right now." Smiling, he gave Angie a thumbs-up.

Ms. Fettore glared one last time at Angie before leaving the room. As the doors closed, Angie sighed.

"That's the best you can expect from Spanks," Jakie said.

"What do you mean that's the best you can expect from me?" Spanks repeated.

Angie knew Ms. Fettore was beyond mad. Laughing, Teddy and Rose walked up to Angie. Teddy held onto his walker.

"You know how to throw a good party." Teddy winked.

"That's the most fun I've had in a long time," Rose said. "Thank you, Angie."

"You're welcome. Glad you enjoyed it."

Grabbing and shaking her hand, Karun's grin warmed Angie's heart. "Thank you. Much fun."

"You're welcome, Karun."

Adelaide and Trudy gingerly stepped forward. "Enjoyed it," Adelaide said. "Can't wait 'til tomorrow. See what else you have for us."

"Glad you enjoyed it," Angie replied.

Pushing his walker, Peter stuttered. He wrapped his arms around Angie and held tightly.

"You're welcome, Peter."

He lowered his head and grabbed his walker again. Mumbling

something about researching the Andes Mountains, monks, and dandelions, he scooted away.

Eliza stood a few feet away with a huge grin. "Angie, you're the best rec person we've ever had." Stepping forward, she whispered, "Don't change. This new administrator is an old fart. Promise me you won't change. I'm lookin' forward to every day with you."

"Thank you, Eliza," Angie whispered back. "I promise not to change."

After spending almost two hours vacuuming the dining room, Angie sat in the kitchen nibbling on her lunch.

Jakie's laugh filled the room as she entered. "You've been summoned, Ms. Pantera. Ms. Fettore wishes to speak with you as soon as you're done."

Angie sighed. "What's so funny?"

"Oh, just everything," Jakie replied. "You made my day. I bet everyone else's, too. Except for Ms. Fettore's. We haven't laughed that hard in ages." She laughed again.

"Thanks, I guess." Angie would have to forgo the chocolate cake. Talking to Ms. Fettore would probably ruin the flavor anyway.

Angie handed the treasure box to Ms. Fettore. Sitting in front of her, Angie felt twelve years old again. It was as if she'd been summoned to the principal's office. Laid out on the desk were the eight index cards printed with the wishes that she promised to fulfill.

Ms. Fettore glared menacingly. "They are *all* unrealistic wishes."

"I asked for a real wish on my poster. I explained it that way, too."

"Guess they didn't understand your instructions, Ms. Pantera. You now have a problem."

Angie stared at the stern principal. Her brown hair, tightly arranged into a bun, pulled her face into a constant fake smile. No makeup on a round, smooth, pale complexion. Angie thought the woman looked like a throwback from the twenties in her dark-blue suit with a hint of white peeking out near her neck. Angie couldn't begin to guess this woman's age.

Sitting up straighter, Angie swallowed. "How unrealistic can they be?" she giggled. "I'm sure I can meet their wishes in some fashion."

"Oh really?" The woman moved her nameplate to one side. Picking up a card, Ms. Fettore read aloud, "Rose Maguire. My wish is to look young again and not have any wrinkles on my face." Glancing at Angie, she frowned. "Oh, there's more . . . Then, I want to dance and party as I once did when I was younger."

Leaning forward, Angie said, "I can—"

"Let me finish, Ms. Pantera." She handed Rose's card to Angie. "Peter Peter. Is that his real name?"

Angie nodded.

Ms. Fettore shrugged and continued. "Peter wrote that he wishes to know the true meaning of life and the universe." She handed the card to Angie, who placed it on top of Rose's. "Karun Nambeeson wishes to drive Princess Aruna around one more time in his Phantom." Glaring at Angie, she added, "Whatever that means. What is a Phantom?"

"It's a car."

"A car! Great. Oh, this one will be easy. I guess that Teddy Chumley listened to you. He wrote down that his utmost wish is to go on a date with Rose Maguire. "

Angie held back a snicker. She knew exactly what Teddy had wished for before Ms. Fettore read it aloud.

"I wouldn't smile if I were you."

Angie sighed.

Holding up two cards, the woman snickered. "Adelaide and Trudy Simmons. They must have colluded in their answer because the handwriting's the same on both cards. They wish to be young dancers again. They want to go back to Simmons Dance Academy."

Angie had watched Adelaide write on Trudy's card.

"Eliza Finney wishes to take a bubble bath with Lucy." Looking at Angie, she chuckled. "And who, pray tell, is this Lucy?"

"A cat."

"She has a cat. Here in her room?" Raising her hand, she added, "As if cats like water. Who in their right mind . . ."

Angie added Eliza's card to her pile.

"And the winner for the wishes is . . ." Ms. Fettore laughed. "Roy Spanks Spankler. He wishes to have dinner and spend the night with both of his wives, Linette and Michelle."

Angie stared at the floor, suppressing a grin.

"I'm assuming they're deceased?"

Angie nodded. "Yes, they are."

"And how, pray tell, do you plan on meeting these wishes?"

"I don't know just yet. But—"

"Good day, Ms. Pantera." Ms. Fettore handed Angie the treasure box. "We're done. I dare say that the residents have had enough excitement for one day. I trust that you'll keep me informed of your future follies?"

Angie nodded. Feeling ever the student that was dismissed early, her heart pounded. At least she didn't have detention—or worse, expulsion.

In the kitchen, Angie packed up a plate of chicken for dinner. Slicing off a piece of chocolate cake, her mind ran back through the residents' wishes. How would she ever fulfill them? Leaving a thank-you note for Walter on the counter, she flipped off the lights.

"You coming back tomorrow?" Jakie asked, leaning against the kitchen door.

"Yes."

"Should be interesting." Jakie smiled. "Know how you'll answer the wishes?"

Angie shook her head.

"See you tomorrow then."

"See you tomorrow," Angie repeated.

On a table in the dining room, Angie left behind the wishing poster of the little girl blowing on her dandelion. In front of it she sat the treasure box with the cards.

She bundled up and stepped into Maine's wintery bluster. Angie stayed to the snowy grass, finding it easier to keep her balance there on the icy walk home. The road was just too slick and steep. Carrying one of the shopping bags and cradling her evening meal, Angie thought about how she was going to grant Spanks's wish on Friday. As she contemplated her choices, Maddie flashed through her mind. What would she think about the magical dandelion puffs? Would she even believe her?

Chapter 6

Walter leaned against the counter in the Home's kitchen. Reading the note from Angie, he smiled.

Walter,

Thank you for the most delicious meal I ever had.
Look forward to more here and at Rose Petals.

Take care,
Angie Pantera

Walter dropped the note on the counter. Swinging the back door open, his eyes darted across the snow-covered brick leading to the parking lot. A fat, orange tabby sat alone near the recently plowed street. It stared up at him.

"Where have you been, Jellybean? You scoundrel."

Concerned over his furry friend's three-day absence, Walter sighed with relief. Enjoying the mornings with this silly stray had become the highlight of his days. He named the feline after his favorite candy—orange jellybeans. With an angora tail waving high, Jellybean walked nonchalantly past Walter and into the kitchen. Rubbing himself between Walter's legs, he meowed once.

"Ya, ya. I forgive you." Lifting Jellybean, Walter cradled him against his large chest. "I was worried. Thought something happened to you. Guess you'd rather be with the ladies than with me." He laughed.

Jellybean purred. Jumping out of Walter's arms, Jellybean stood patiently by his small bowl. Walter brushed the cat hair off his flannel shirt with a wet paper towel.

"You're shedding." Kneeling down, he petted the stray. As his ponytail swung forward, Walter whispered, "You came back cuz I've spoiled you. An ordinary house mouse just won't do anymore."

Glancing up, Jellybean responded with another *meow*.

"Yes, yes. I know exactly what you want, my friend."

On the counter, a chuck roast waited for Walter to prepare. Tonight's dinner would be his signature dish. A boeuf bourguignon stew with carrots and white potatoes. Fresh mushrooms sat alone on one end of the counter. This was one of the residents' favorites. For lunch, he planned on tuna salad and leafy greens. Several slices of apple and blueberry pie would wrap it up for an epicurean meal.

Rubbing against his legs again, the cat meowed, demanding to be fed. Cutting off a small wedge of the meat, Walter minced it into smaller pieces.

"For easy digestion, my friend." He glanced down at the nervous cat.

Sitting the dish on the floor, he picked up the empty bowl and refilled it with fresh water. He placed it next to Jellybean and pet him again. Walter wished he could run his life like a cat—wild and free of restrictions and obligations. Pulling out his cellphone, he searched for the saved number. It was time to place the restaurant and nursing home's food orders for the coming week.

Dialing his wholesaler, he wiped his brow and stared at the glistening back of his hand. His mind wandered as his heart pounded. Maybe his deep, dark secret was taking a toll on him after all.

Now settled in his hospital room, Father Joe's spirits rose. Any minute now, his nurse would prep him for his knee surgery. He stared out at the city skyline, where the sun barely crested the tallest buildings. Anticipating the nurse scurrying in like a whirlwind, he chuckled. Since checking in yesterday, he was ready to get this over with.

Since he had recently celebrated his seventieth birthday, his primary doctor in Birdsong thought it best to have the surgery at the medical center. The surgeon, already here and gone, said everything should go smoothly.

"Father Joe, you'll remain with us for at least five days before transferring to the rehab facility next door."

"I'm in good hands, Doc." Father Joe had pointed his finger upward.

"Yes, yes, of course."

Now, a middle-aged nurse rushed in.

"Good morning, Father," she said, a little out of breath. "How're we doing this morning?"

"Good, and you? Your patients keeping you on your toes?"

"Busier than usual," she replied. "You might have a roommate when you return."

"Good. Never did like being alone."

The nurse was finishing up when John Leland entered. "Mornin', Father."

"Morning, John." Father Joe turned his attention back to the nurse. John waited at the end of the bed.

"Are you Catholic, my dear?" Father Joe asked the nurse.

Adjusting the blanket, she stopped. "Does that matter to you, Father?"

Laughing, he replied, "Not really." He winked.

Rose Marie frowned.

"He gets them every time with that line," Elder John said, pushing against his round spectacles.

"What if I was to tell you that I am Catholic? Been so my whole life," the nurse said. "Not that it matters."

"Then, thanks for being on our side." Father Joe laughed.

Grinning, she replied, "You're welcome." Looking over at John, she added, "You have him for a couple minutes before I come back and get him."

Being good friends for the last twenty-some years, Father Joe and John played Scrabble twice a week. Tuesday and Thursday evenings the two sat across from each other accusing the other of cheating. While Father Joe was recuperating, John would board at St. Aloysius Rectory. He planned on remaining present throughout Father Joe's recovery. John's wife and dogs would have to survive the several weeks without him.

"How's the rectory?" Father Joe asked.

"Good."

"And Father Francis?"

"Good. He sends his regards along with hopes for a speedy recovery."

"Ask him to stop by," Father Joe said, tugging on his blankets.

"Will do."

"Sleep okay at the rectory?"

"Yup." John glanced out the window.

"Susan will miss you not sleeping next to her."

"Nah, she has the dogs to keep her company. Good timin', your surgery. Her sister's comin' to visit." John chuckled. "Best time to be away."

Father Joe glanced at the door. "Any news from the diocese or Mary?"

"None."

Knowing that Mary, his right arm, would contact him if there were any news, Father Joe replied, "No news is good news then." He smiled when the nurse returned.

"It's time, Father," she said. "I'll take your glasses now. You'll get them back in recovery."

Grinning, he replied, "They're my only pair."

"How many times have I heard that one?" she said.

Following them into the hallway, Elder John grinned as the two bantered. He waved at Father Joe. "See you in recovery."

Father Joe gave a thumbs-up.

Although Father Joe had reassured him that the surgery was routine, John's gut just didn't feel right this morning. The hard mattress at the rectory kept him up all night. His home mattress was more on the mushy side.

His gut feeling, never wrong, worried him. Married for fifty years, his wife would attest to his premonitions. John Leland prayed, *Take care of him, Jesus. We need him back.*

Putting the final touches in place in the dining room, Angie refreshed her memory with Spanks's exact words. *I wish to have dinner and spend the night with both of my wives, Linette and Michelle.* Preparing dinner for two ghosts would not be easy.

Angie glanced at the grand fireplace. Elder Luke knelt in front of the hearth and lit the fire. A warm glow now filled the room. Angie imagined the incredible heyday of this place—how grand the parties Kerr Bird Song held on cold snowy evenings must have been. Private moments, good and bad, that were now forgotten in time. She hoped the Home's last elderly residents lived to be one hundred or more to delay the inevitable.

"Luke, I can't thank you enough," Angie said. "Now there's ambiance." Privately, Angie had nicknamed him Christmas Bulb. All because of his bulbous red nose.

Luke stoked the baby flames. "You're welcome, Angie. Anything else before I leave?"

"This'll do. Wasn't sure which of you would handle my request. I just asked Jakie for some help."

"I take care of cleaning and other things around here. Mark is groundskeeper. Matthew is always fixing something." He chuckled. "We do the best we can. This place. The chapel. The rectory, your cottage, and the cemetery. Never seems enough for the diocese. Guess that's why they're selling the place."

"I heard," Angie replied.

"Fire should hold you for a while. Be back tomorrow to clean it out."

"Thanks again, Luke." Angie watched as he walked through the large double doors. "Lights dimmed, check." She crossed off the items on her to-do list. "Fireplace lit, check, dinner table set, check."

Smiling, Angie looked at her table setting. *Lovely.* Jakie had helped by bringing in her family heirloom china and sterling serving pieces, not to mention the fancy candleholders. Angie found some treasure in the storage room—a long white tablecloth and napkins.

Glancing at the covered warming tray, she sighed. "Filet mignon dinner, check." Spanks's favorite, ordered by Angie and delivered from Rose Petals.

Dinner was easy. But ensuring that Linette and Michelle's ghosts show up was a little harder. However, Angie took care of that. Sort of.

"Linette and Michelle, check."

The two photos in Spanks's shadow box worked perfectly. Angie had the ladies' headshots enlarged. The Photo Shoppe colorized Linette's face from the black-and-white photo. Placed into frames, they sat on opposite ends of the table. Angie smiled, hoping Spanks would be pleased. After picking them up, she had run home to change into a black evening dress that was way too tight. Totaling her expenses to date, the rectory owed her about ninety dollars. Angie ran into Mary outside the rectory and accepted a ride back to the Home.

Nosy Mary wanted to know everything. Why was she dressed up? What was going on? What, what, what. Dodging as many questions as she could, Angie had counted the minutes until Mary stopped in front of the mansion.

The residents had teased Spanks all through lunch. With him waiting in his room for his special dinner with Angie, Jakie hurried the remaining residents through their dinner. Now, it was time to check on them before retiring. If she didn't, they would surely summon her by pushing the emergency call buttons they wore around their necks. Feeling exceptionally tired, Jakie hoped they'd sleep throughout the night.

To hold Spanks over until dinner, she carried a small tray of cheese and crackers to his room.

"Have fun tonight," Jakie said, placing the tray on his small table.

"I plan on it. Thanks for the snack. I hope I get more food later."

"Oh, you will." Jakie laughed, knowing what Angie had in store for him.

Jakie dragged her legs up the staircase to the second floor. Her room was the first on the right. Another thirteen rooms remained vacant. Her position here, working with the residents, was a dream job come true. Once a month, Doctor Bolton volunteered his time at the Home, updating their medications among other things. He was also Jakie's personal physician. Attributing her recent ailments to her workload, he requested bloodwork and advised her to work less. After all, in four months she would turn sixty-five.

Her son, Michael, had pestered her to retire. This put a thin wedge between them. She loved her son and his family, but she was happy here.

Jakie lay on her bed and stared at the ceiling. She thought about the residents, pushing Michael from her mind. They were in pretty good shape. Better than her. Mobile for the most part—except for Spanks. After he turned ninety-one, she watched him lose his mobility. Switching him from a walker to a wheelchair bothered her.

Sitting up, she popped a pill, downing it with a glass of water. *Will Spanks's wish come true tonight? I hope so.*

Angie knocked on room number eight.

"Come in," Spanks said.

Dressed in an old-fashioned striped suit and a dingy white shirt that Angie suspected accompanied him on too many previous life occasions, Spanks smiled. "You look nice, Angie. Really nice."

"Think so?" Her dress, sticking tightly to her curves, was anything but comfortable. Angie tugged on it.

Holding a burgundy-striped bowtie, he sighed. "Can you help? My fingers are a bit numb tonight."

Angie knew how to fix a bowtie. Memories of Jay flooded back and touched her soul. Since their first Christmas together, Angie had always tied Jay's Christmas bowtie. Each time, she'd whisper in his ear, "You're the best Christmas present ever."

Taking a step back, Angie looked at her handiwork. "It's perfect, Spanks."

"I hope so. Wouldn't want to look bad in front of my wives."

As Angie pushed Spanks down the hallway, no words were spoken. In the dining room, the dancing candlelight bounced off the china.

"Fancy smancy," Spanks said. He scanned the glowing embers and gentle flames radiating from the other side. "Lived here all these years and never been in here when there was a fire. Didn't think that thing worked."

Concerned Spanks wasn't his usual snarky self, Angie searched for the right words. "Hope you like everything." She glanced between Spanks and the photos, her heart pounding.

Staring at the enlarged photos of his wives, Spanks whispered, "Linny looks good. How'd you get a color picture?"

"The photo place colorized it for me."

"Can I keep 'em?"

"They're yours." Angie smiled.

Staring at the table, Spanks cleared his throat. "What'd I do to deserve all of this?"

"Your name was picked for the wish. Hope you're pleased."

He put up both thumbs.

"Wow. Two thumbs-up. You're very welcome, Spanks. I have your favorite meal, filet mignon with mashies."

"Whoo-wee. My stomach's growling already. All I had were some stale crackers and dried-out old cheese."

Angie laughed; her old Spanks was back. "Then you've come to the right place."

After placing the food in front of Spanks, Angie sat and helped fill his plate.

"Could never love anyone like I did Linette," Spanks said once his plate was full. Picking up a fork, he added, "Michelle helped me when I didn't want help from anyone. She understood me."

Pouring him some water, Angie nodded. She remained quiet, not wanting to interrupt his memories.

"At seventeen, signed up with the Navy. Right after Pearl Harbor and all. Nothin' left for me in Mobile after Momma died. Wanted to see the world. Maybe serve my country." He sighed. "Assigned to the Indianapolis. Twelve of us black boys. They kept us separated from the whites." He frowned.

Angie put down her fork and knife. She studied Spanks's face.

"Started out scrubbin' and peelin' potatoes 'til my fingers bled. Day in an' day out 'til I had to jump in to cover for one of the cooks. He was so drunk. Hoo boy!" Spanks laughed.

Angie grinned.

"Did me a favor by getting too drunk. Loved cookin' with Momma. Always did. She taught me a lot. Never went back to peeling those potatoes. Nope, worked as a cook from then on. And for most of my life." Angie watched as he put down his fork and knife. Staring at his plate, he added, "Remember it like it was yesterday. We were sailin' in the Pacific ready to meet up with another carrier. It was after midnight. I was playin' cards. Cards kept my mind off things." Spanks stopped talking. Raising his arms he yelled, "*Boom!*"

Angie flinched.

"Torpedoes were soaring every which way. Broke our Indy into two pieces. We sunk fast. Real fast. I passed out from the heat and smoke. Woke up to cold water fillin' me lungs. Found myself a floating life vest I did. A lot of us were in the water. Some hurt real bad."

"Oh my, Spanks!" Angie's eyes widened.

Looking up, he stared out way beyond her. "Before long, some friends joined us. The bad kind—sharks. First, they ate the dead. But soon they wanted more. They wanted us living ones. We hung together the best we could. Those bastards came up from under us. Nudged and nudged until they got us, one by one." Spanks's eyes tightened as he shook his head. "Funny how we weren't segregated anymore after that. Funny how some stupid fish can suddenly make everyone equal."

Angie's heart raced. Glued to his every word, she leaned forward, wanting to hold his hand, but she didn't.

Taking in a deeper breath, Spanks added, "Four days before they rescued us. Four days of pure hell. And that's when that son of a bitch finally got me. I was helping another by punching them off."

He made a fist and punched the air. He stuck out his leg with half the calf missing. She gazed at the large scar.

"Spanks," Angie gasped. "What you've been through. I can't begin to imagine."

"Lost blood. Lots of blood. Don't remember 'em pulling me out. When I came to, thought I had done died and gone to heaven. The most beautiful woman I'd ever seen was hovering over me." He picked up Linette's photo. Staring at it, he smiled. "Was in Guam. She was my nurse and angel. Come to find out she was from my neck of the woods. Mobile and N'awlins, not that far apart. After we got married, a doc said she had a bad ticker."

Spanks put down her photo. Tears welled. "She died five years later. Best years of my life with that woman."

"I'm so sorry, Spanks," Angie said, putting her hand over his.

"I was never the same," he whispered. "Worked around the country as a cook. Worked up north and down south. Then went west before going out east. Met up with Michelle in Boston in the late sixties. I was a short-order cook in a breakfast place. She was a divorced waitress. White folk didn't like us black men with their women back then." Spanks leaned back and pulled his hand away.

Angie remained quiet.

"Heard about this place called Birdsong where people looked at blacks the same as they looked at whites. Got married after a while. Found some peace and friends here. She died twenty years back of breast cancer." He paused. "She was a good woman. Took real good care of me. Father Joe helped us. After she died, he brought me up here. Didn't have much to my name by that point. Didn't really want to be around anymore. After a while, this place became my family. More folks were living here back then. All supported by the father."

"What a life you've lived," Angie said. "Thank you for sharing it.

"Got any more of that filet mignon and mashies?" he asked.

She wheeled Spanks back to his room. The hallway remained silent. Spanks refused to let her go any further than the doorway. In his lap rested the two portraits. Smiling, he reached for her hand.

"Thank you for the best night I've had in a long time."

Bending down, Angie kissed him on the check. "You're welcome, Spanks. I had a wonderful night, too." Angie patted his shoulder. "Get some sleep. I'll see you Sunday morning. Tomorrow's my day off. Night."

"Night, Angie."

Feeling elated, Angie walked back to the dining room. She needed to tidy up and let Jakie know the evening went wonderfully. Spanks had given her two thumbs-up. With a full moon lighting the way, Angie looked forward to her long walk home. And tomorrow, a bonus: she'd sleep in.

Spanks watched Angie disappear down the hallway. He held tightly to the two photos as he turned the doorknob. After wheeling himself in, he pushed the door closed and switched on the light. His body went numb. On his single brass bed sat two women, Linette and Michelle. Michelle looked younger than he remembered.

"Hello, Roy," Linette said in her sultry Southern drawl.

There was no doubt that this was in fact the real Linette. He remembered her pearly white smile and svelte figure. She always called him *Roy.*

Patient as always, Michelle sat smiling. "Hi, Spanks. I've seen you looking better."

Michelle was just as attractive as he remembered. The women patted the space between them on the bed.

"Come join us," they said, together.

The photos fell from his lap, shattering across the tiled floor. His entire body numb, he tried to reach for the button hanging around his neck. But his right arm refused to move. It fell lifelessly toward the floor.

Not wanting to put up with Jakie or Angie anymore, he stood. He pushed the wheelchair away with his foot and walked with a slight bounce toward the bed, his arm dangling. It was time to enjoy his ladies. He'd missed them both for so long. Feeling young and full of energy, Spanks yelled, "This is the best night ever. Thank you, Lord." He glanced into the heavens.

The beautiful ladies smiled.

Chapter 7

Jakie found Spanks unresponsive, his skin blue and cold. There was nothing she could do for him. He'd been deceased for hours, slumped over his wheelchair, the photos of his wives shattered near his feet. Jackie stared at his frozen grin. Since he didn't summon her in the middle of the night, he obviously didn't suffer.

Closing Spanks's eyes, Jakie cried.

"Hope you had a good evening, my dear friend. I'll miss you, Spanks. Knew you a long time, twenty years."

Jackie dialed 911 and then Elder Mary's number.

After four rings, Mary answered. "Hello?"

"Mary. It's Jakie. Spanks is dead."

"When?"

"Sometime during the night. Police are on their way as well as the coroner."

Still sounding groggy, Mary replied, "I'll let Father Joe know. If there's anything you need, don't hesitate to call."

"Thank you, Mary."

Officer Raines arrived fresh faced and cheery. Standing outside Spanks's room, he covered the formalities with Jakie. "Coroner's on her way." He stepped into room number eight.

Jakie stood guard. Rose, Teddy, and Eliza learned of the news first. They loitered, talking about Spanks and how much fun he was when no one was around. After several minutes, Officer Raines stepped back out. Glancing over at the residents, he pulled out a notepad and pen.

"Spanks's full name?" Officer Raines said.

"Roy Spankler," Jakie whispered. "We just called him Spanks."

He spied the correct spelling of the name on the door plaque. "Age?"

"Ninety-one."

"Relatives?"

Karun, Adelaide, and Trudy joined the others.

"They're right here, Officer," Jakie said, staring over at their saddened faces.

He wrote down, *None*.

Peter walked by and frowned.

As he approached from the end of the hallway, Walter waved at Spanks's room. "Heard the commotion."

"It's Spanks," Jakie replied. "He passed away last night."

"Sorry to hear that." Glancing at the officer, he added, "Be happy to serve 'em breakfast. I see you're needed here."

"Appreciate it. I'll be down as soon as I can."

Officer Raines's eyes darted from Walter's head down to the orange Crocs. "And what's your relationship with the deceased?"

"I'm Walter Heron," he replied. "I'm here every morning to prep the meals for the day. I also own Rose Petals."

Officer Raines smiled. "My wife and I are new here. Been wanting to stop by for dinner."

"Gonna start running some specials soon." Walter grinned. "Let me know when you come in. We'll take good care of you."

"Thanks." Officer Raines went back to writing in his notebook. Looking over at Jakie, he asked, "Who was the last person to see Mr. Spankler?"

"That would be Angie Pantera." Jakie said, nodding to Walter. "She texted me about ten last night. She was on her way out. All seemed fine. Didn't think I needed to check on him."

Officer Raines jotted more onto his pad.

"If there was an issue," Jakie said, "Spanks would have been able to reach me with the emergency button. All the residents wear one. I sleep on the second floor. Spanks never pressed it."

He looked up at her. "What was Ms. Pantera's relationship with the deceased?"

"She's our new recreational director. Spanks was the first one to win the wishing contest."

His eyebrows raised. "Wishing contest?"

"Yes. Angie is granting each resident a wish. Last night was Spanks's turn."

"And that was?"

With her stomach tightening, Jakie replied, "To have dinner with his deceased wives."

"You mean the shattered photos on the floor?"

"Yes." Jakie held her breath.

"Since it was his final meal, I hope he enjoyed it." He changed the subject. "Can I see that text from Ms. Pantera?"

"Of course." Pulling out her phone, she retrieved the message. Jakie handed her phone to Officer Raines.

10:01 PM

Angie: Hi Jakie all went super! Had a great evening with Spanks. Think he did as well, got 2 thumbs up. Dropped him off a half hour ago at his door, wouldn't let me go any further.
Thanx for all your help. Left your stuff in the kitchen.

5:40 AM

Jakie: You're welcome! Glad all went well.

Officer Raines handed her cellphone back. "So, you didn't check on Mr. Spankler last night after Ms. Pantera dropped him off. Is that correct?"

"No reason to," she replied. "Spanks didn't request any assistance."

"Was Mr. Spankler seriously ill?"

"At ninety-one?" Jakie raised her eyebrows. "Not really. Just medication for high blood pressure. And he used a wheelchair." She glanced away. "He was not terminally ill."

"I'll need to speak to Ms. Pantera. Where can I find her?"

"Today's her day off. I'll call her. She lives in the church cottage."

Coroner Dr. Lizette Humpries arrived with two of her staff. They entered Spanks's room. Jakie redialed Mary. It was time to bring Angie in to see Officer Raines.

Putting on her reading glasses, Mary phoned the hospital. This early in the morning, all calls had to be screened.

"This is Elder Mary Mead. I must speak to Father Joe Methuen. Room two thirty-two. It's an emergency."

A sleepy Father Joe answered on the third ring. "What's the bad news, Mary?"

"How'd you know it was me?"

"Who else would be calling this early?"

"Spanks died last night." Mary sighed. "Jakie has it under control. Police are there with the coroner."

"Good man, that Spanks. I'll miss him."

"As we all will," Mary replied.

"I need you to get over there. It's too late for Spanks to receive the sacrament of the Anointing of the Sick." He paused. "I wasn't aware of any serious illness."

"I think this was sudden."

"Yes, yes, natural causes. What I need for you to do as a layperson is pray the prayers of the dying."

"I thought that's what you'd want me to do."

"I feel better knowing that Angie gave him our Lord and Savior in Communion. Once you hear from the coroner, we'll discuss burial service."

"How are you holding up?"

"Didn't get much sleep last night." He sighed. "I'm in pain even with the meds. They're moving and twisting my knee around like a pretzel."

"Just do what they tell you to do. That way you'll be on the mend."

"Ah, breakfast," he said. "You know what to do, Mary."

"Yes. I do."

Flashes of Angie Pantera came to mind as Mary pulled out a navy-blue dress and large cross to wear around her neck. Buttering her toast, Mary's unpleasant thoughts ran wild. *Spanks got his wish and now he's dead. Father's out of his mind. A recent divorcee and now a Eucharistic minister—unheard of.*

Mary would keep those thoughts to herself—for now, anyway. Her house phone rang. "Hello. Yes, it will be my pleasure to bring Ms. Pantera in to speak with Officer Raines."

Angie answered her cellphone. With her lovely dream still fresh in her mind, Jakie's fast-talking confused her.

"Is Spanks okay?" Angie yawned.

"He died last night."

Angie sat up. "Did you just say that Spanks is dead?"

"Yes. The police and coroner need to speak with you. You were the last to see him alive. Mary's on her way to pick you up."

Angie jumped from her bed and pulled on her jeans and a black sweater. Feeling sick, her stomach turned. Spanks was just fine last night. What in the world happened after she left? Stepping outside, the cold air sliced through her heart. Shivering, she wrapped her scarf closer around her neck. Dark clouds overhead signaled more snow. No sooner did she think it than snowflakes dotted her coat.

Mary's old Buick sputtered as it pulled up. Angie tugged on the door and it slowly budged open. The strong odor of motor oil made Angie wince.

"Thank you for picking me up," Angie said. Bracing for a slew of unwanted questions, she stared straight ahead.

"You're welcome."

Angie was sure that Mary wanted to know more. Driving no faster than five miles an hour, Mary's foot barely reached the pedal. Angie could walk faster than this car could go.

"The police asked to speak with you. Being that you were the last person and all." Mary's voice oozed with sweetness. "You two had dinner together last night, right?"

Still staring straight ahead, Angie replied, "Father Joe said to have fun with my job. I had each resident write down a private wish. Each week I planned on picking a winner. Spanks was the first. Had dinner and we discussed his wives." Angie watched as a tree slowly crept by. She laughed to herself. At this pace, they just might arrive by tomorrow around lunchtime. "When I took him back to his room, he looked fine."

Before Angie could tell the story about the magical dandelions, Mary floored the gas pedal. Sputtering at first, the car roared like a rocket before skidding to a stop at the red door of the old mansion.

"It's still got some kick." Mary laughed. "See you inside. I must say the last prayers over Spanks."

Mary Mead walked somberly up to room number eight. Nodding at Jakie, she stared at the police officer. She stepped inside room number eight and closed the door behind her.

Pulling his notepad from his back pocket, Officer Raines glanced up at Angie as she approached. "Ms. Pantera?"

Angie nodded.

"Did Spanks seem ill to you last night?"

"No, not at all. In fact, he was in good spirits."

"Did he wear that burgundy-striped bow tie?" Jakie asked. "Only one he owned. I've tied it for him so many times." She smiled and a tear ran down her cheek.

"Yes, he did. Asked me—" Angie stared into the shadows. Rubbing her hands against her pants, she frowned. "He asked me to tie it for him because he said his fingers felt numb."

The officer scribbled on his notepad.

Spanks's door opened. A man dressed in white stepped out pushing a covered gurney. He nodded before taking Spanks through the long hallway. Then Dr. Humpries and Mary stood in the doorway and frowned.

Nodding at the officer, Dr. Humpries turned to Jakie. "Who was the deceased's physician?"

"Dr. Bolton," Jakie replied. "Visits us once a month to check on the residents."

"Know him well," Dr. Humpries replied. "When did he last see the deceased?"

"Two weeks ago."

"Ms. Pantera mentioned that Mr. Spankler's fingers felt numb last night," Officer Raines said to the coroner.

"Good to know. Everything is just a formality now," she said. Turning to Mary, she added, "I'll be in touch. I should be able to release the body tomorrow."

"I'll let Father Joe know." Mary replied.

Dr. Humpries nodded. "Thank you." She headed down the hall.

Officer Raines closed his notepad. "I'm done. Thank you for your time." Entering the lobby, he hollered, "Lizette, hold up."

"Jakie, do you have any idea what caused Spanks's death?" Angie asked.

Jakie sighed. "He was slumped over in his wheelchair with a huge smile. His fingers felt numb? Maybe he suffered a stroke. If so, then he died instantly."

Angie groaned. "He made me stay outside. If he wasn't feeling well, I would've called you. If I had, maybe Spanks would still be alive."

Jakie put her arm around Angie. "Don't blame yourself. That was just Spanks's way. Anyway, if the stroke was that massive, I wouldn't have been able to do anything. I'm sure you gave him the best night he's had in a long time."

Glaring at them, Mary remained speechless.

Walter pushed a tummy-content but sleepy Jellybean out the door. "Sorry, my friend. Saturday's my busiest day. Gotta get back to the restaurant."

Although running a little behind, he was happy to help Jakie. Leaving Jakie and Angie in the dining room, he had to laugh. Jakie handed out meds while Angie played bingo to honor Spanks's memory. When she handed a pair of socks to Adelaide, he held back a snicker. He liked Spanks, always did. In fact, he liked anyone who appreciated his cooking.

As Walter rinsed out the water bowl, Jellybean jumped onto the outside windowsill. Walter ignored the tabby's cries for attention. Instead, he thought of the paperwork left on his desk from the previous night, mostly overdue bills. The restaurant business was a little sketchy thanks to the slow economy. When people were financially stressed, eating out was usually the first to go. Some blamed a slow business on the cold or the snow. No, it always had to do with money.

Locking the kitchen door, Walter watched as Jellybean jumped down and rubbed up against his leg. He reached down and brushed the cat away. "I'll see you bright and early. Don't stay up too late with the ladies, now." Jellybean scaled the brick wall and stared down at him. Walter shook his head.

After parking his SUV on the backside of Rose Petals, Walter entered through the kitchen. Maybe he should hire entertainment on Friday and Saturday nights. But if he did, he could just hear Nancy: "Entertainment? Are you kidding? It'll cost us big!"

Walter made an executive decision. Drastic times called for drastic measures. He would spruce up the food menu, add something new and exotic, adjust the prices, and run ads in the town flyers. Pulling up one of his ads on his laptop, he stared at it.

Maybe these changes would help in the short run. He didn't want to let go of any staff. Not yet, anyway.

While answering the ringing phone, Elder John took his eyes off his seven little tiles. Scrabble had always been his game of choice. Annoyed at being disturbed, he sighed before answering. "Hello?" After a few seconds, he handed the handset to Father Joe. "It's Mary." His eyes flashed back to the scrambled letters. Ahead by five points. He glanced over at the backs of Father Joe's tiles. On the verge of placing six tiles with a high-point objective, John was sure to win. He leaned over the board and listened to Father Joe's one-sided conversation.

"That's good, Mary. Call Roger Tempe from the funeral home. They'll give us a good price." Father Joe glanced at his tiles. "I'll need the funeral home to hold Spanks until I return. I owe Spanks a proper service. We'll bury him next to his wife Michelle."

"What about his other wife, Linette?" Mary's voice echoed.

Pulling the phone away from his ear, Father Joe shook his head. "Spanks and I discussed it over a year ago. Linette's buried in New Orleans. No room for Spanks in the family space. In fact, Spanks said it was already crowded in there." Father Joe laughed. "Her cousins . . . Okay, Mary. Thank you." Handing the phone back to John, Father Joe sat back and grinned.

After hanging up, John laid six tiles on the board.

"Time for brunch . . . and that's fifty-five."

Glancing over at John and then back at his tiles, Father Joe snickered.

"Oh, I see it now." Slowly, he placed his seven tiles onto the board. As John updated the score sheet, he shrugged.

"How many wins is that now, Father?"

"Lost count." Father Joe's eyes brightened.

"Another round?"

"Nah. Think I'll close my eyes a bit before dinner. Feeling tired."

On the way to the cafeteria, John stopped by the nurse's desk. "Father Joe's lookin' a lot paler since yesterday."

"You're keeping a good eye on the father," the nurse replied. "I'll let the doctor know."

"Thank you." John walked away with a knot tightening in his stomach.

Wanting to tell her daughter about Spanks, Angie tapped Maddie's number. The voicemail answered.

"Hey, honey. It's Mom. Hope all is well. Call me. Love you."

Although Saturday was supposed to be her day off, she was glad she had stayed with the residents. They played various board games and reminisced about Spanks. Made her feel better. *Maybe I'll take tomorrow off. Better yet, I'll have dinner at Rose Petals tonight.*

Angie found that walking cleared her head, and that evening the exercise justified the slice of chocolate cake she was about to have for dessert. Grabbing the last seat at the far end of the bar in Rose Petals, Angie ordered a glass of red wine. She silently toasted Spanks as Tom Jared and a woman entered and sat at a table. They wore almost-matching dark-leather jackets. *Probably his wife.* Not that she cared.

Still owing Tom a payment for his auto repair, Angie scooted closer to the couple next to her to hide from him.

With her chocolate craving satisfied, Angie started the long walk back to her cottage. The light snow had changed; it was coming down harder and faster. "Blinding snow storm" took on real meaning. She couldn't see a thing. Startled by a few car beeps, Angie turned around, hoping it was Mary and her old Buick. With the snow accumulating and blocking her way, she would gladly answer any of the elder's nosy questions in exchange for a ride home.

A black pickup truck with a massive snowplow pulled to a stop next to her. Its headlights heavily covered in snow, the vehicle produced only a faint glimmer on the sparkling road. The passenger door sprang open. As the snow fell away from the door, Angie read the words:

JARED'S GARAGE DEPOT
GUARANTEED BEST REPAIR COSTS
333-1234

Angie stepped up to the passenger side.

"Hop in, Ms. Pantera," Tom Jared said. "Unless you'd like to become roadkill. Town's plow coming through any minute now." Staring down at her, he shook his head. "They'd never see you. Think you were a snowman or something."

Watching her step, Angie climbed in.

"Where to?" he asked.

"The cottage behind the rectory, thanks." Her mind whirled as she prayed he'd not mention the missing payment.

"Saw you at Rose Petals," Tom said.

"Oh? You were there?" Angie grinned but refused to look at him. His laughter filled the truck making her cringe.

"Saw you hiding in the corner. Didn't want to say hello to me?"

Angie frowned. "As blunt as ever. It's not that. I owe you a hundred dollars. Just embarrassed to see you since I agreed to the payment plan." She giggled.

"I trust ya."

The truck came to a stop in front of the cottage, and Angie opened her door. "Thank you. I'll get that hundred to you."

"I'm going to need another week."

"Are you kidding?"

"I never kid," he replied.

"I'm walking everywhere. Now you're telling me you need more time?"

"Look at it this way." He chuckled. "A great way to lose weight."

Angie slammed the door. With a red face and huge frown, she mumbled, "Now he's calling me fat. And where'd that wife of his go? Does he tell her that she's fat, too? She looked rail-thin to me."

Her cellphone vibrated inside her coat pocket. Looking at the small screen, she smiled. It was Maddie.

Chapter 8

It was a Tuesday afternoon when Administrator Fettore strolled into the Home's lobby wearing a long, gray coat. She stepped up to Angie and glared at Jakie.

"The diocese informed me of Spanks's passing. I'm sure you have everything under control."

"We're good," Jakie replied. "Looks like a stroke. Spanks didn't suffer."

Turning toward Angie, Ms. Fettore asked, "How are you doing, Ms. Pantera?"

"I'm fine," Angie replied.

"Carry on, then," Ms. Fettore said, walking away.

Jakie left Angie standing alone in the lobby. Watching Ms. Fettore walk back to her office, Angie wondered why the woman didn't say anything about the other wishes. Ms. Fettore turned on the office lights and shut the door behind her. Thankful to have only run into the woman once today, Angie turned her thoughts back to Spanks. She was tired, and it was time to go home. She pulled her coat from the closet and walked past the office door, smiling as she wondered who the next winner would be.

Angie delivered Holy Communion to the residents for a second time that week. After lunch, she stood in front of the residents and proudly pulled a card from the treasure box. Reading it, she smiled.

My wish is to look young again and not to have any wrinkles on my face. Then, I want to dance and party as I did when I was younger.

Rose Maguire

"Rose. Congratulations."

The residents clapped. Teddy clapped the loudest.

With a big smile, Rose sat up. "Oh my. I'm so thrilled. I never win anything."

Teddy placed his hand over Rose's. "You're always a winner in my book. Congratulations, my dear."

"Thank you, Theodore." Rose pulled away her veiny hand.

"You're welcome, Rose," Teddy said.

Walter offered to prepare the dinner after Jakie informed him of Rose's love of all things French. He planned on making coq au vin— braised chicken with thyme and red wine—and agreed to leave a bottle of Veuve Clicquot Champagne in the kitchen fridge. Jakie passed this promise on to Angie.

"You have my permission to give her a glass of champagne. But only one."

"How many am I allowed?" Angie mused.

"As many as you like. You're still carless."

Angie frowned. "For at least an additional week."

"Ouch. Sounds like a sore subject."

"Don't even get me started."

"Don't get you started on what, Ms. Pantera?"

Startled, Jakie and Angie turned around at the same time and stared at a stern-looking Ms. Fettore.

"We're talking about Rose," Angie replied. "She's our next winner."

"Speaking of wishes," Ms. Fettore said, "come to my office before you leave today."

"Sure," Angie said, with her stomach churning.

Ms. Fettore was quite cordial about Angie's plans for Rose. She even wished her good luck. On her way home, Angie stopped at the local drugstore. It was important to give Rose the appearance that she'd had a facelift. Hopefully, they'd have something cement-like she could use.

Friday evening soon arrived. Wearing the same black evening dress she wore a week earlier for Spanks, Angie admired herself in the Home's bathroom mirror. To her surprise, the dress wasn't as tight.

Entering Rose's room with a barrage of facial products, Angie smiled. Buying these products added another fifty dollars to her hopefully reimbursable expense bill for the Home. She had spent almost half-a-week's pay on the residents.

Sitting at her dressing table, adorned in a light-blue evening gown and costume jewelry, Rose resembled a Hollywood siren from bygone days.

"Hi, Angie. I'm going to look young again." Her face lit with excitement.

"Yes, you are, Rose." Angie rolled her eyes heavenward. *We can only hope.*

Standing near the covered mirror, Angie went to work. She'd received tips from an informed source—an older female employee at the cosmetics counter. "When I need to look ten years younger for a special night, this always works for me," the woman had said.

Lightly pulling on Rose's sagging skin, Angie secured it with invisible face-lifting tape. With all the pulling and taping, Angie felt as if she were wrapping a mummy. Angie arranged Rose's silky white hair to conceal the so-called invisible tape. She had completely hidden her magic. Angie carefully applied a clear cement fill. Rose sat patiently, holding her breath. Working feverishly like an artist in the final throes of a masterpiece, Angie moved on to the final step—the foundation. A fine beige powder that was guaranteed to camouflage any facial lines by reflecting light. She applied it with a soft pad.

After applying eye shadow, mascara, and blush, Angie was almost finished. She had saved Rose's signature red lips for last. Finally, she removed the makeup collar and stood back.

"Wow, you look amazing, Rose."

"Can I look?"

"You'll have to use your mirror," Angie replied.

"Can't wait anymore." Rose closed her eyes. "Let me know when it's okay to look."

"Okay . . . look!"

Opening one eye and then the other, Rose leaned forward. Staring at herself in the mirror, she frowned. "Oh my!"

She hates it. "I'm sorry, Rose, if you're unhappy with the results—"

"Unhappy? Heck no, my dear. I haven't looked this good in fifty years." Turning her head from side to side, Rose's eyes remained glued to her reflection. "You took away my wrinkles. Exactly what I wished for."

"You have to stop crying or you'll smear your mascara." Grabbing a tissue from the dresser, Angie patted around Rose's large blue eyes. "You look timeless."

"I do, don't I?" Sitting up, she posed for a selfie on Angie's phone.

Leaving the bedroom, they marched arm in arm to the dining room. Overhead, the speaker played Sinatra's "The Way You Look Tonight."

Swaying her hand in rhythmic motion, Rose hummed. "I haven't felt this happy in ages."

Angie expected Teddy to pop out from somewhere at any moment to see a vibrant Rose. But he was probably too much of a gentleman to intrude on Rose's special wish-night. If Spanks were still here, he'd no doubt be leering from his doorway in that funny Spanks fashion.

Angie pressed the button to the dining room and the doors swung open. She extended her right arm. "*Voila! Entre, Madame Maguire. Si vous plait.*"

Rose giggled at Angie's attempt at speaking French.

Guided by Angie, Rose strolled in. A glowing fire, thanks to Christmas-bulb Elder Luke, warmed the room. Fine china and crystal goblets surrounded the candelabra. A dozen red roses tied with a white ribbon sat next to Rose's plate. Jakie's help, again.

Rose glanced over at the champagne chilling in the ice bucket. "I'm speechless, Angie."

"I'm happy that you're happy." Angie helped her into her seat. "Walter made you coq au vin. Only the best for Rose." Angie sensed Rose's previous lifestyle must have afforded her all the finer things in life.

Angie tucked her cellphone playing Sinatra music near a potted plant. It took a community to put this wish together, and Rose was appreciating every ounce of it. Popping the cork, Angie poured the champagne into the glasses.

"Are you sure you're old enough to drink this bubbly, young lady?"

Rose laughed.

Clinking crystal officialized their cheers. Rose sipped from her glass. "French champagne has always been my favorite."

Angie still smacked her lips. "I can certainly see why." As she served the meal, Rose reflected on her life.

"The Depression hit the Midwest hard. I was just a toddler. Mama and Papa always did the best they could with the little they had. They called me their little princess." Rose's eyes darted upward as if she was privately thanking them.

"Were you an only child?" Angie asked.

Rose laughed. "Momma and Poppa said I was a handful." Rose paused, taking a bite of chicken. "I met Wendall when I was twenty-one. We were at the lunch counter in the Five & Dime. I worked as a secretary for an insurance company. He was a widower, eighteen years my senior. Some bigshot at a New York City bank. Was on business in my town and the rest was history."

Angie listened, taking little sips of her champagne.

She called her Wendall "the Cary Grant type" and said they had married in their local church. "The grandest reception followed at the fanciest hotel in town." She paused and stared into nothing. "I wore the most beautiful wedding gown anybody ever had. Wendall paid for everything. Mama and Papa were so proud that he chose me. Goodness, we were the talk of the town." She looked into the heavens again. "Wendall took good care of them. All the way until their end."

Rose stared at her plate. "After our marriage, we moved to New York City. We lived in the grandest apartment on Park Avenue. We had a maid, too. Always entertaining, we made the society pages of the paper at least once a week."

Angie couldn't fathom such a lavish lifestyle. Hers was basic—graduated college, marriage, kids.

"Never had children. Wendall didn't want any. When he retired, we traveled around the world. I had the perfect life, Angie." Rose blew her nose.

"Are you okay?" Angie asked.

"Yes." Rose pushed her food around her plate. "Wendall was a good man. I know he loved me. Wanted me to be happy. But he left me penniless." She sighed. "After he died, I found out that we were broke. Borrowed from his friends for years. They had signed notes to prove it. Everything we owned had to be sold. My furs. My jewelry. Even my wedding diamonds. They allowed me to keep a few furniture pieces and, of course, my clothes. I hid my emerald ring from them."

"I'm so sorry, Rose," Angie said.

"Turns out they weren't my friends after all. My good times were over. I was back to being the pauper from whence I came. Once a pauper always a pauper, I guess."

Angie put her hand over Rose's and her one genuine emerald stone. "You were never a pauper, Rose. You were always loved. And you're loved here." Angie thought about bringing up Teddy's affection for her but decided to wait.

"Yes. It was Father Joe who saved me. I took Wendall's car before they took that from me. I just drove and drove. No idea where I was going or what was the day. I drove until I ran out of gas. Managed to pull into the chapel's parking lot. Went inside and saw beautiful red roses everywhere. Cried and cried so loud that Father Joe heard me. That was twenty years ago. And you know what?"

"What, Rose?"

"I'm good and hungry now."

"Well then, eat up." Feeling a little braver, Angie added, "Rose, may I ask you a personal question?"

"Ask away."

"You do know that Teddy has the hots for you."

Rose laughed. "Theodore has the hots for me? All this time I thought he was just being nice to an old-looking hag." She paused. "He's not my type."

"You mean the Cary Grant type? Does it really matter?"

Rose didn't respond. *Perhaps it is best to let it go—for now, anyway.*

Carrying the flowers, Angie walked Rose to her room. After Spanks's untimely death, she lingered to help Rose dress for bed.

With the red roses on her dresser, Rose doted on herself in the mirror. She insisted on wearing her fancy chiffon gown to bed and refused to wash her face. Rose lay down on her bed and Angie removed her blue slippers.

Rose grabbed Angie's hand. "Thank you for granting my wish."

"You're very welcome. I wish we had danced a little."

"I shall dance in my dreams."

"Pleasant dreams then, Rose. I'll see you tomorrow."

After closing the bedroom door, Angie texted Jakie: *Hi Jakie, A really good night with Rose. Left her good & healthy. She insisted on sleeping in her evening gown and makeup. See you in the AM.*

Feeling a little woozy from the champagne, Rose drifted off to sleep. She opened her eyes to the sound of an orchestra playing. Rose stood. Far off in the distance, music enticed her to dance. A manicured hand held out a single red rose. She stared at it for only a moment before taking it. Lifting it to her face, she took in a deep breath. The sweetness filled her with a longing she hadn't felt in a long time.

"A rose for my Rose," the familiar voice said. "May I have this dance?"

Rose took hold of the strong hand. Waves of emotions flooded through her, making her gasp.

"Have I told you how lovely you look?"

Rose smiled as she stared into the familiar eyes. "Wendall."

After reading Angie's text, Jakie fell asleep. Rose was in good hands. *No need to check on her until morning.* As she tossed and turned throughout the night, the recurring argument with her son played through her mind.

"Ma. Don't you think it's time to start taking it a little easier?" Michael had argued. "Retire and come live with us." Jakie knew his wife was on board; otherwise, he wouldn't be pushing so hard. When all else failed, he threw in the granddaughters. "What, you don't want more time with the girls?"

Jakie loved being gramma to five-year-old Tamara and two-year-old Lila. Conflicted, she gave her usual spiel. "Of course I do, but I enjoy my independence."

Her real reason centered around a recent conversation with her primary physician, Dr. Bolton—a medical condition she was determined to hold back from her son.

Jakie woke up tired and much later than usual. Now running behind with the residents' med distribution, Jakie changed the rotation. Peter was first and Eliza second. She saved Rose for third, knowing that Rose would keep her busy with fixing her hair and other needs.

Waking up happy and content, Angie's first thought was of how much Rose enjoyed the evening. Concerned about her sleeping with the heavy makeup, Angie wanted to arrive to work early to help Rose freshen up.

Angie finished off her instant oatmeal and mint tea and pulled on her woolen pants and a black sweater. The cloudy skies and chilled morning air made her shiver. Tucking her collar closer to her neck, Angie braced against the wind swirling through the massive evergreens. Hands inside her pockets, her strides now longer and easier, she only required an occasional stop to catch her breath. Over the last week, she'd cut her time by a quarter. As she walked up the last curve in the road, Angie couldn't wait to see Rose.

Jakie knocked on room number one. "Rose?"

No response.

She's probably still sleeping. Stepping into the room, Jakie grinned. Just as expected, Rose's eyes were shut. A single red rose rested on her pillow next to her head.

"Wake up, sleepyhead," Jakie whispered.

Rose didn't move.

"Too much of that French champagne?" she mused. "I told Angie to give you only one glass."

She stared at Rose. Beautifully coiffed, she looked peaceful with closed eyes and a sweet smile. The fake jewelry shimmered against her glass-smooth skin. As she leaned in a little closer, Jakie's heart pounded. Rose wasn't breathing. Checking for a pulse, she gasped. No pulse. Rose's hand felt cold and clammy. Jakie almost didn't recognize the woman whose hand she held so tightly.

"Angie did some job on you," she whispered. Jakie's mind whirled. "What in the hell is going on with these wishes?"

Following protocol, Jakie dialed 911. She sighed after she hung up, and, staring at her cellphone, she tapped Mary Mead's name.

"Hello?" Mary said, chewing loudly.

"Morning, Mary. Jakie here. Rose Maquire is dead."

Mary coughed. "Not again. How?"

"Looks like natural causes. She had dinner with Angie. Her turn for a wish."

"I'll be there shortly to pray over her," Mary sighed.

After several minutes of banging on the cottage door, Mary's knuckles ached. "Angie Pantera!" she yelled out. "You need to wake up."

Angie wasn't answering her cellphone, and the cottage didn't have a houseline. Mary peeked through a window. Three windows later, there was still no sign of Angie. Mary hustled back to the old Buick. She would call Father Joe and give him the news after she prayed over Rose.

Driving to the Home as fast as her old car would go, Mary's mind ran through the questions. *Where is that woman? Another dinner and another wish-winner dead?*

Father Joe trusted her, and now two residents were dead. And only a week apart. Flooring the gas petal, Mary worked herself into a frenzy.

"That woman probably skipped town," Mary yelled out. "I bet she killed Rose. Maybe she killed them both."

Feeling something inside her boot, Angie sat down on a large rock. As she shook out a pebble, a police siren blared through the thin, cold air. A police cruiser flew by seconds later. Angie's breakfast churned deep inside. Jumping to her feet, she darted for the Home.

"Please don't let it be— Anybody but Rose."

Angie ran fast. Her heart raced. She unbuttoned her coat, the cool air feeling good against her flushed skin. Panting in front of the red door, Angie's hands shook. She pushed the red door open and stepped into the lobby. Coughing, she tried to catch her breath. The lobby seemed quiet. Too quiet. Darting past the staircase and directly into the residents' hallway, she glanced around. No one. All was quiet. *Maybe it's just a slight emergency.* Angie knocked on door number one.

"Come in, Mary."

Hearing Jakie's voice, Angie relaxed a little. *Maybe she's helping Rose out of her gown.* Angie entered with a smile. Officer Raines and Jakie stood near the bed. Her knees buckling, Angie sat down in the closest chair.

"Thought you were Mary," Jakie said. "Rose died sometime during the night."

"Oh my God!" Angie whimpered. "She was fine when I texted you."

Officer Raines glared over at Angie. "Please wait outside, Ms. Pantera. I'll speak with you in a moment."

With one last look at Rose, Angie nodded. Rose was smiling. Angie cringed. She wanted to stay. Rose was a woman she considered as a friend. As she hesitated, Officer Raines waved for her to leave.

Mary stood on the other side of the door when she opened it. The elder wore wide eyes and a huge frown.

"I was just looking for you at the cottage," Mary stated firmly.

"I was up early." Angie walked past her and into the hallway.

Pacing, Angie's stomach hurt. When Jakie finally stepped out of the room, she was about to explode into a gush of emotion.

Jakie wrapped her arm around Angie. "I'm sure Rose died of natural causes. It just seems weird. I mean . . . another contest winner. What a coincidence. Officer Raines's going to ask you some questions. I'm sure they'll be checking the food."

Angie glared at Jakie. "Checking the food?"

"Is there any champagne left?" Jakie asked. "They'll need to check that as well."

"I gave Rose only one glass. I had one, too. Stuck the bottle in the fridge."

"Sorry, Angie," Jakie whispered. "Didn't mean for it to sound as if—"

"It's okay. You're upset. All this death stuff is so new to me. I'm not sure how to act."

Jakie excused herself. She needed to talk with Walter. He'd have to package the leftovers from last night's dinner, as well as the French champagne.

Angie watched as Jakie walked away. The coroner's staff entered the hallway pushing a stretcher. Doctor Humpries trailed in behind them, looking somber as usual.

Angie glanced away. Soon the residents would be awake and asking questions. All Angie could think about was Teddy, who always tucked Rose in for breakfast. Now he'd never see her alive again.

Angie knocked. As the door opened, her heart pounded. Staring into Teddy's sleepy eyes, Angie held back tears.

"Morning, Teddy."

"You delivering Communion?" he asked.

"Something else," Angie said, trying to stay calm.

Teddy's eyebrows raised. "Did Rose get her wish granted?"

"Yes, and she looked as beautiful as ever."

"Well, she always looks beautiful to me."

"I'm afraid I have some bad news." Angie looked down at the floor. "Rose died sometime during the night."

Stepping back into his room, Teddy sat and stared at the wall, tears flowing.

"She'll never know how I felt about her," he whispered. "So stupid. I should have told her a long time ago." He pulled out a handkerchief and wiped his eyes.

Angie touched his hand. "I told her how you felt."

"What do you mean?" He pulled away his hand.

"I told her how you felt last night at dinner." Searching for the right words, Angie added, "That you have the hots for her."

His lips curled. "I couldn't have said it better myself. Thank you. What did she say?"

Knowing his heart was already breaking, Angie lied. "She was quite open to it."

He slapped his right knee. "If only." Teddy smiled before lowering his eyes.

Seeing that her lie brought him a little happiness, Angie kept the truth to herself.

Removing Father Joe's breakfast tray from the rolling table, Elder John set out the Scrabble game. Tests were ordered after the priest complained of headaches and blurred vision. The results came back normal, but John still worried about his close friend, who now complained about ringing ears.

"This place is homier than that hospital room," John said, reaching into a pouch to grab some tiles.

"Not bad." Father Joe adjusted his leg on a pillow.

Pleased with his tiles, John arranged the letters on the track. "How's the knee?"

"I'm gonna need some pain meds soon. After yesterday's session, it's hurting more."

"Takes time, Father. Takes time." The ringing phone startled John. It was Mary.

"And a good mornin' to you, too, Mary." Frowning, he handed the receiver to Father Joe and scooted closer to the bed to eavesdrop.

"Who died?" Father Joe asked.

"Rose!" Mary's voice was loud enough for John to hear. "It's Rose Maguire this time."

"This time?" Father Joe repeated with a serene calmness. "People die all the time from natural causes. Especially at their age. . . . I understand, Mary. Two deaths and only a week apart. First Spanks and now Rose."

"They won a contest that Angie Pantera manipulated. She's granting their wishes, and now they're dead."

"Contest or no contest, they were not young. Thank you for praying over Rose. Sweet lady. I'm sure she received Communion from Angie. Ask Roger to keep her until I return so I can administer the burial Mass. Mary . . ." Father Joe rolled his eyes. "There's nothing sketchy going on at the Home. Your imagination is taking you for a ride. Call me when you hear from Roger. And, Mary, try and have a good day." Handing John the phone, Father Joe smiled. "Rose Maguire was welcomed home by Our Father last night."

"I heard," Elder John responded.

Adjusting his leg, Father Joe reached for the pouch. "She thinks Angie had something to do with it." He frowned.

"Mary means well. Just lookin' out for our residents' welfare."

"That's the problem, John. That's always the problem. Woman drives me crazy."

Excusing himself to use the restroom, John glanced back at the board. "Pick your tiles carefully, 'cuz I'm ahead. You've had the upper hand for way too long." He smiled warmly at his old friend.

Father Joe laughed. "You think so?"

"I know so." John said, closing the bathroom door.

Stepping back into Father Joe's room, John froze. Father Joe was slumped to one side, unconscious. In his right hand, John saw three tiles—Z, X, and M. Father Joe always did have good luck with picking the higher point tiles.

Chapter 9

Kneeling in the first pew, Mary stared up at the Little Flower. With her heart breaking, she searched her heart for answers.

"First Spanks," Mary whispered between tears. "Then Rose, and now Father Joe's in a coma." She clasped her hands. "You let us keep our father. You hear me? Don't you take that man home with you. Not yet."

After suffering a brain aneurysm and emergency surgery with a 50 percent chance of survival, Father Joe was on a respirator. Elder John agreed to stay by his side while Mary kept vigil every evening at six with prayers for Father Joe's recovery. As the news about his illness spread, parishioners flocked to the chapel. Mary hoped that their sudden rededication to the faith would become permanent.

The mood at the Home was rather somber. Although Spanks and Rose's deaths were ruled to be by natural causes by the coroner, Angie felt guilt stricken and refused to take any time off. She needed to console Teddy.

After hanging her coat in the closet, Angie glanced at Ms. Fettore, who glared from inside her office door. She didn't look happy.

"Morning, Ms. Fettore." Angie lowered her gaze.

"I heard about Rose and Father Joe's sudden decline," Ms. Fettore stated.

Angie was silent.

"Ms. Mead keeps the diocese abreast of all current news. How are you holding up, Ms. Pantera?"

"I'm good. I'm coping."

What she really wanted to say was that she felt horrible—that she had merely wanted to give the residents a fun time. News about Father Joe was depressing, too.

Ms. Fettore clasped her hands together and shook her head. "We are stronger than we think, Ms. Pantera. God does work in mysterious ways."

"I guess so."

Ms. Fettore closed her office door.

Feeling that the conversation was rather odd, Angie headed to the dining room. It was time for recreation. Thank goodness Ms. Fettore didn't mention her wish-granting sessions. Under the circumstances, Angie was going to cancel the other wishes anyway. For now, at least.

The TV was on a stand waiting for her. Jakie never let her down. Angie hoped that the residents would enjoy the movie *The Sound of Music*. It might just lift their spirits. It would definitely lift hers.

Karun was the first to arrive. "Morning, Angie."

"Hi, Karun."

Peter entered second, placing his walker against a wall.

"Hi, panther lady," Eliza said as she strolled into the room. "What do you have in store for us today?" She sat beside Peter.

"I thought a movie would be nice," Angie replied.

As usual, Adelaide and Trudy walked in together. Teddy chose a new spot at the table with Eliza and Peter.

"Before we watch the movie, I have an announcement." She glanced around at the expectant faces. "I've decided to stop granting your wishes. Under the circumstances, I'm sure you'll agree."

Eliza spoke up first. "Oh fudge." She glanced over at the others. "We thought you'd say something like this. Discussed it at breakfast. We all want our wishes granted."

Heads nodded.

"You sure?"

"Yes," Karun said.

"Yes," Peter added.

"I do, too," Adelaide said.

"Me too," Trudy added, speaking out for the first time.

Jakie walked into the room and leaned against the wall. She folded her arms.

"Rose died with a smile on her face," Teddy added. He glanced at Jakie, then back over at Angie. "Jakie told me that Rose looked beautiful and she must've been thinking of me."

Angie looked at Jakie, who shrugged. *Did Jakie also lie to Teddy about Rose's true feelings?*

"So did Spanks," Eliza said. "He had a smile, too. Please, Angie? Oh please." Eliza pointed to the table with the poster and treasure box. "Please grant our wishes."

Taking in a deep breath, Jakie sighed. "Go for it. Angie. They all want it."

Angie nodded. The heavy karma needed to change. Angie picked up the treasure box. Maybe if she picked a name today instead of Wednesday, and if she filled the wish on Thursday instead of Friday, maybe her luck would change. But first, she needed the administrator's blessing.

Sitting across from Ms. Fettore, Angie again felt chastised.

"I would have thought that after two deaths you'd have curtailed these events," Ms. Fettore sneered, her eyes wide and menacing.

"I wanted to, but—"

Ms. Fettore raised her right hand. "This one wish I thought was somewhat reasonable." Ms. Fettore held up the index card Angie had picked out of the treasure box. "But now I'm not so sure. Let me read it for you. From Teddy Chumley: *My utmost wish is to go on a date with Rose Maguire.* How do you plan on granting this wish?"

Angie remained silent.

"The woman is dead!" Ms. Fettore huffed. "Teddy cannot nor will I allow him to have dinner with a dead woman."

What was the chance of pulling Teddy's card out of the treasure chest? Karma was definitely going against Angie today.

Angie wanted an update on her car. Poking her head into the garage, she frowned. Several cars with their hoods up filled the greasy floor. Not a good sign. Hearing power tools, Angie yelled, "Hello? Mr. Jared?"

No response.

A man stepped out from under a hood. "Can I help you, ma'am?"

"I'm looking for Tom Jared."

"Out. On a job."

"Okay." Angie pulled out a white business envelope from her purse. "Can you make sure he gets this? Tell him it's from Angie Pantera?"

After wiping his hands, the man took the envelope. "I'll make sure he gets it."

"Thank you." Angie glanced around for her car. "Excuse me?"

The man under the hood looked up again.

"By any chance would you know the status of my silver Honda? Mr. Jared said it'd only take a couple of weeks."

"Uh, yeah . . ." He looked down at the engine. "We're working it."

"Thank you." Angie left hoping that was indeed the case.

The mechanic slipped the envelope under a black Mustang he had been working on. "You heard the lady," he said.

Tom Jared slid out from underneath. "Thanks, Havi. I owe you one. Just couldn't deal with her right now."

Tom hated hiding from Angie but felt he had no choice. He was working eighteen-hour days and still couldn't get caught up. Two new mechanics would start working for him in a week. Tom was the town's only full-service car repairman, and the town's harsh winters were hard on its aging fleet of vehicles. Right now, everything was on a priority basis only. Considering himself a nice guy, he didn't have the heart to tell Ms. Pantera that she wasn't on his VIP list.

Angie walked up Main Street and headed toward the Photo Shoppe. A light snow drifted across her path, making her shiver. Passing the thrift store, Yesterday's Tomorrows, she spied a tuxedo hanging in the window. *That'd be great for Teddy's wish dinner,* she thought. Even if Rose couldn't be there, the man should look the part. *About his size, too.*

Angie stepped into the warm shop. A woman folding clothes smiled.

"How much is the tuxedo and everything that goes with it?" Angie pointed toward the front window.

"Twenty dollars."

"I'll take it." Angie grinned. *Who says I can't turn Teddy into the Cary Grant type?*

Carrying the tuxedo over her arm, Angie stepped into the Photo Shoppe. A silver frame on the clearance table grabbed her attention. It'd be perfect for the photo of Teddy and Rose that Jakie had emailed her earlier.

This recent excursion added thirty dollars to her already high expenditures. Not wanting to ask Mary for money, Angie walked home praying for Father Joe's speedy recovery.

With the wet snow clinging to his flannel shirt, Walter dug a keychain out of his pocket. He shook his head, the flakes sticking firmly to his shoulders. He blinked a few times and fumbled with the keys. Locking the Home's kitchen door was always difficult.

"Gonna be a bad one," Walter said, glancing around. *Now where is that cat?*

With no Jellybean in sight, Walter dashed up the alleyway, aiming for his black SUV. He brushed off the snow before climbing in. Not wanting to think about his private issues, he headed for the restaurant.

Jellybean stared out at the snow through the Home's kitchen window, licking on his paw. The warmth from the stove always calmed him. Curling up in a corner, he purred a few times before falling asleep.

Carrying a shopping bag with Teddy's tuxedo and the framed photo, Angie stared out at the picture-perfect winter wonderland. *How beautiful! Like a postcard.* Stepping up to the red door, she paused to enjoy the falling snow.

She stepped into the warm lobby, where the snowflakes fell onto the shiny tile floor. Ms. Fettore glared over at her as she hung up her coat.

"Morning," Ms. Fettore said, before closing her office door.

"Morning to you, too," Angie replied to a now-empty foyer.

After placing her bag in the storage room, she found Jakie talking to Dr. Bolton in the hallway.

"Morning, Angie," Jakie said.

"Morning," Angie replied. "So, Dr. Bolton, how are my residents doing? Good, I hope."

"Yes," Dr. Bolton replied. "Everyone's alive and healthy."

Angie nodded. "Communion this morning."

"See you at lunch?" Jakie asked.

"Most definitely," Angie replied, knocking on Teddy's door. No answer.

Just after dark, Angie again knocked on Teddy's door.

"Teddy? It's Angie."

No response.

Angie knocked again. "Teddy?" she said a little louder. *He should be here!* Jakie had just finished prepping him for his special night. Feeling her stomach tighten, Angie tapped her foot. Before she could charge through the door, Teddy finally answered.

"Coming," he said. "Had to get my walker from the bathroom."

Teddy opened the door.

Angie put her hand to her mouth. Stepping back, she couldn't believe her eyes. Teddy's gray hair, usually tousled, was trimmed short and styled. Shaved and manicured, he wore the vintage black tuxedo with pride.

"Oh my!" Angie shrieked. "You are without a doubt Cary Grant tonight. I wish Rose could be here to see you."

Smiling, he whispered, "Thank you, Angie. That's what Jakie said . . . and, may I say, Angie, that you look lovely."

Angie smiled. Her black evening dress felt looser than ever. "Why, thank you, Teddy." She took his arm. "Leave your walker behind. Let's enjoy our evening without it. We're honoring Rose tonight."

With a light dance in his step, he replied, "I've been dreaming about tonight."

The walk down the dark hallway was anything but easy. Teddy's weight pushed against not only her body but her heart. With each step, his raspy breath sent chills all through her. How much longer would this man be in this world?

After she helped him sit at the candlelit table, Teddy squeezed Angie's hand. She sat and watched him take a bite of the venison dinner.

"Delicious." He scooped mashed potatoes onto his fork.

After wiping her mouth, Angie felt something brush her leg and looked under the tablecloth. Two glowing green eyes stared up at her.

"Who are you?" Angie giggled.

"Who's under there?" Teddy asked.

"I think this is Walter's stray cat. He feeds it." Angie reached out and picked up the orange tabby. He purred. "He must have snuck in."

"Maybe the cat would like a piece of venison." Teddy cut a small chunk from his plate.

At the sound of Teddy's deep voice, the cat sprang from Angie's arms and ran back into the kitchen.

"I must have scared him. Did he scratch you?"

"I'm good." Angie picked up the meat. "I'll be right back. Maybe he's hungry."

"Okay," Teddy said, taking a long drink of the dark-red cabernet from his crystal wineglass.

As the wine warmed his insides, Teddy listened to the Sinatra music playing from Angie's cellphone.

"Sinatra's your favorite, Rose," he said. "Wish I could share it with you." Gazing at the photo of them laughing together, he smiled. "Angie's nice, Rose. But she's not you."

Picking up the framed photo, Teddy studied the lines on Rose's face. All he saw was her beauty. Teddy raised his glass in a toast.

"I miss you." He took a sip.

With the room moving around him, he thought back to that day when he first saw Rose. A bachelor for most of his life, he felt more comfortable and in tune with the great outdoors. It was why his first marriage failed. The only woman displayed in his shadow box was his sister. Several years older than him, she lived with him in Birdsong until she passed on.

When he saw Rose for the first time, dressed in his favorite color of emerald green, she reminded him of the vast outdoors. She stirred something he'd not felt in a long time. Knowing that Rose was classes above him, he cultivated a close friendship, but longed for more.

Gazing upward, he searched for her. "I wish I told you from the start, Rose. I love you. I've loved you from the moment I laid my eyes on you."

"Come on kitty, kitty." Angie shook the piece of meat. Opening the back door, Angie tossed the food onto the snow. "Go get it, kitty."

Sitting in the middle of the kitchen, the cat stared at her.

Angie stood still, not wanting to frighten the animal. "Guess not, huh? I don't blame you. It's cold out there. You're kinda cute."

Using a heavy pot, she braced the door open and stepped into the freezing cold. Angie picked up the meat. "Can't blame you for not wanting to come out here. But you don't have a choice. I have to get back to Teddy."

As she balanced on the icy sidewalk, a gust of wind pushed against her. Taking a step, she fell backwards and hit the ground hard. The cat seized the opportunity. He lunged at the treat, hitting the copper pot with his back paw. The door slammed shut. The cat jumped onto the brick wall, the venison hanging from his mouth.

"You're welcome," she said. Seeing the bright-red ice glimmering in the lamplight, she sighed. "Oh damn. Ouch." She touched the bloody tear in her pantyhose.

Try as she might, Angie couldn't pull open the kitchen door. The blood on her fingers instantly froze when she touched the doorknob. Holding back a scream, she stomped her feet. Now she'd have to walk all the way around to the front door. With sleet pelting her every step, she tightly folded her arms. The pace was slow with no moonlight showing her the way. Taking several steps in the hardened snow, she winced. Her shoe crunched as it slid into a snow-hidden bush.

Teddy smiled when the dining room doors opened.

"What took you so long—" Not seeing anyone, Teddy stared into the darkness. "Why you coming back that way, Angie? I thought you were in the kitchen." The dining room remained quiet. "Jakie, is that you?"

"Theodore?" A familiar woman's voice echoed through the room. "I wish you'd told me sooner."

"Rose? Is it you?" Teddy's heart exploded with affection. Imagining only one possible scenario to explain what he was experiencing, he shook his head. "I'm dead."

"No." Rose smiled. "You're very much alive."

Wearing a blue chiffon evening gown and all dolled up, Rose walked sensually over to him. Teddy stood and pulled out a chair for her. Staring at the wrinkled woman he'd fallen in love with, Teddy took Rose's hand and kissed it.

"You're looking lovely tonight."

Rose giggled. "Why thank you, Theodore, or should I call you Cary Grant?"

With a feeling of weightlessness overpowering him, Teddy's heart pounded.

Rose waved her hand and sat. Picking up the framed picture, she tilted her head as she studied her reflection. She slapped the frame on the table.

"I hate the way I look in that photo." Rose sat back and pouted.

He gazed into her eyes. "You should never feel that way. You are always beautiful."

"You've always loved me? Not feeling sorry for this old hag, are you?"

Picking up her hands, he whispered, "I've always loved you, especially now. You were and always will be very beautiful to me, Rose Maguire. I love you with all my heart."

Rose glanced away. "I love you too, Theodore."

Serenity flowed through him. Picking up the wine, he poured some into a glass. Rose picked it up and took a sip. Together and alone, they dined on the venison, sipped on the red wine, and shared loving kisses. They danced to the timeless music by the glow of the roaring fire.

"Thank you for making my wish come true." Wanting this moment to go on for eternity, he prayed. "And thank you, Angie. Wherever you are."

Angie's knee throbbed as she trudged shivering through the packed snow. Slowly she made her way to the red door. The warmth of the lobby greeted her. With shaking hands, she wiped the blood from her leg. Needing to get back to Teddy, Angie darted through the dining room doors.

"Sorry, Teddy, I—"

Angie's legs turned to rubber. Teddy's face lay pale and smiling against the white tablecloth. His right hand held firmly to a single red rose. Three dinner plates sat where there were once only two. One was Teddy's and one was hers, but who ate off the other one? *And where did the rose come from?* Pushing the emergency button that hung around Teddy's neck, she prayed he was still alive.

"Please, dear God, please. Just be sleeping." Angie immediately called Jakie, who was there in minutes responding to the emergency button.

With Sinatra singing "I did it my way," Jakie worked to revive Teddy with the defibrillator at her side. She kept saying, "Come on, Teddy, wake up!"

Angie dialed 911. As she waited, her mind went blank. "I need an ambulance . . . The Home of the Little Flower. One of our resident's in cardiac arrest."

Jakie looked up and frowned. "He's gone, Angie."

As the phone fell from her grip, Angie's heart sank.

Jakie reached over and closed Teddy's eyes. "Sleep tight, sweet prince. May you meet up with Rose. Tell her how much you loved her."

Using a blue tablecloth, Angie covered Teddy's body. Tears slid down her cheeks.

"At least he went with a smile on his face," Jakie said.

Angie stood speechless, staring down at the covered body. *Here we go again. Another wish, and another dead body.*

Jakie said something, but Angie didn't hear the words. As their eyes met, Angie frowned.

"He probably died of a broken heart." Jakie glanced at the blood on Angie. "Why do you have blood on your hands? It's also on Teddy's shirt."

Angie pointed to her skinned knee. After explaining about the cat and accidently locking herself outside, she sat and cried.

Officer Raines walked into the dining room. Glaring down at Angie, he laughed. "Why am I not surprised you're here? Another wish winner, I suppose?"

Thursday was retro movie night at the Birdsong theatre. Sitting in the middle row, Sarah, Mary's cousin from Boston, chewed on her butter-flavored popcorn. As Mary sipped her soda, her phone vibrated inside her purse.

"I think that's you, Mary," Sarah whispered.

"Who'd be calling me now?" Mary said, raising her voice.

"Shhhh," a voice from behind sizzled out.

After glancing over her shoulder, Mary answered in a whisper. "Who's this?"

"Mary, it's Jakie. I'm sorry, but . . ."

Mary screamed, "What the hell!"

Cursing at the attendant who pushed her through the door, Mary stormed out of the theatre.

"This has to stop," she yelled from inside her car. "The woman's killing them off faster than God. Angie Pantera has got to go." Clenching her teeth and reminding herself of the plan, she whispered, "And it's working."

Chapter 10

Police Chief Woulfemere Bertrand was tough but fair. Reigning as chief for the past five years, he commanded a diverse force of a dozen officers, several of them military vets. His recent hire, Officer Raines, was back from a tour in Iraq. Raines poked his head into his office and smiled.

"Morning, Chief." Officer Raines leaned against his desk. "Got a minute?"

"What's up?"

"Have a situation."

"What kind of a situation?"

"Not sure."

"Care to fill me in?" Chief didn't like surprises, especially when it came to his officers. And Raines had a habit of beating around the bush instead of just stating the problem.

"Three deaths. Two weeks apart." Raines shifted to his other leg.

"I'm listening."

"Nursing home up on the ridge. They each died just after winning some wish dinner hosted by a newbie in town. Hired by Father Joe. Name's Angie Pantera. From Philly, I think. Took the rec job."

"What's Lizzy say?"

"Lizzy?" Raines repeated.

Shaking his head, the chief chuckled. "The coroner. Dr. Humpries?"

"Oh, yes. Sorry. She said from natural causes. The one from last night will be listed the same."

"Then what's the problem?"

"Just strange," Raines replied. "And Elder Mary's concerned. Doesn't think it's right."

"How old were they?"

"Ninetyish."

"Ninetyish?" Chief laughed while scratching his head of grays. "We all have to go sometime, right? Making it to ninety ain't so bad."

"I guess. But the weekly pattern's bothering me."

Needing a stretch and refill, Chief stood.

"Any insurance money involved?"

"None that I know of, Chief. They were all poor. Father Joe took 'em years ago."

"Any previous connection to this Angie woman?"

"No. Like I said, she just arrived in town several weeks ago with a broken-down car. She needed a job and a place to stay. Father Joe took her in."

"Sounds like Father Joe. Let me know if the pattern continues or something nefarious turns up; otherwise, don't waste my time," Chief said as he walked out the door.

For some, playing with herbs and spices was a chore. For Walter, it was paradise. Didn't matter where he was if what he was doing involved cooking. Standing in the Rose Petals kitchen, he felt a tap on his shoulder. He smiled at his wife, Nancy.

"Tonight's special is veal osso buco." He minced the herbs with the sharp blade, avoiding his fingertips—a method he'd learned years ago.

"Love it," Nancy replied. "You make it the best. Did you put our order in yet?"

No response.

"Walter? Did you put in our order? If not, I've got a few things to add."

Walter kept chopping.

"Walter? *Yoohoo,* you okay? Got some additions. Wrote it on the pad in the office. Can you add them to our order?"

"Sorry, hun. Mind's miles away. We lost another resident last night. Teddy Chumley. You remember Teddy?"

Nancy nodded. "That makes three this month."

"Yup." Walter grabbed a handful of herbs from a box.

"Pretty soon they're gonna analyze your cooking."

"Nah. If it was my cooking, Angie would be sick too."

"Guess you're right." She put her arms around his huge waist. Her slender hands barely made it to the front.

"Thanks, baby."

Backing toward the swinging doors, she laughed. "It's *my* cooking they should be worried about. Not yours. Never yours. Maybe today's specials will bring in a good crowd. Been a little slow lately." She sighed before walking out.

Married minds seemed to think alike. As he worked, Walter thought about his conversation with Jakie. Looking exhausted, Jakie asked about Jellybean. Angie had tried to put him out but locked herself out instead. Could Teddy's death be partly his fault because of that stray cat?

Needing to place next week's order, Walter picked up the office phone. "Larry? Walter Heron here." Hesitating, he thought about what Jakie said about needing less food now.

"Same order as usual?" the voice from the other end asked.

"No." Among the stack of bills, he read over Nancy's note. "I'm going to need a little more."

Magdalene Oquoque had lived in Maine her entire life. To her one remaining friend, she was Madge. To family dispersed around the world, she was Grandmum. But to Bishop Lansing and the other pastors she was simply *Mrs. O.* Pronouncing her French-Canadian name was just too difficult. Beloved by all, she was the only Caribou Diocese secretary.

At eighty-two, Mrs. O styled her strawberry-blonde hair in a bob. When her husband of forty-four years left her a widow, Mrs. O answered the diocese's ad in the *Caribou Daily.* She remembered that day as if it were yesterday. Running into the bishop right before her interview, she chewed his ear off asking for a blessing. Through the bishop's office door, she heard him say to his assistant priest that he didn't care if she was too old—qualified or not, she needed a job. Twenty years later, she still needed her job as a reason to get out of bed in the morning. With the bishop's busy schedule, he was away most of the time. Her plan was to stay put for as long as she could.

This morning had been extremely difficult. For some reason, her brain refused to work right. More and more, she was becoming forgetful. She'd often tell her friend, "My brain slipped on a banana."

Today it was her car keys and her shoes she couldn't find. Walking to work with bedroom slippers would have been just plain silly. The keys she had found in a cupboard, and her shoes in with the dirty clothes. Mrs. O just couldn't remember what she'd forgotten yesterday. But did that really matter?

Her journal was her constant companion. She wrote down everything to help her remember. Things like turning on her computer or making coffee. Mrs. O kept the journal on her desk and never forgot to take it home after work.

Startled by her ringing phone, she jumped. "Bishop Lansing's Office. Mrs. O speaking. How may I be of assistance?"

"Hello, Mrs. O," Mary said, her tone unfriendly as usual. "Please let the bishop and the administrator know of another passing." Mary sighed. "That makes three now. I'm waiting for Father Joe's return to hold the services."

Mrs. O shuffled several papers across her desk. "I'm sorry. Any improvement in Father Joe's condition? He always stopped by to chat when he visited the bishop. I do wish him a speedy recovery."

"As we all do, Mrs. O. There has been no change."

"I will let 'em know of the passing," Mrs. O replied.

Adelaide, Trudy, Eliza, and Karun sat at the dining room table enjoying shortbread and coffee. Peter, however, sipped on hot tea. Across from him, Angie sat staring out at nothing. Mourning for Teddy, Rose, and Spanks, her mind twirled. All she wanted was to bring them a little fun, and now they were dead.

No doubt Elder Mary had passed on the news of Teddy's passing to the bishop. Soon she'd be sitting in Ms. Fettore's office receiving her routine admonishment about the wish-grantings. Of course, everything would be over now.

Angie still couldn't figure out Mary. She seemed stoic when arriving the previous night to say prayers of the dying over Teddy. Maybe she was in shock, but weren't they all?

After reiterating the cat story to Officer Raines, Angie expected to repeat it again for Mary. As strange as it was, Mary didn't ask about it. She was way too cordial and sweet. Could nosy Mary be that desensitized? Or was she so concerned about Father Joe that the residents had become an afterthought? Glancing at the other table, Angie's heart warmed. Adelaide, Trudy, Karun, and Eliza were laughing. Did they not feel the same sadness she was feeling? After Teddy's sudden death, they probably wouldn't want their wishes granted. Looking at the poster and treasure box, Angie decided to remove them before the day's end.

Tugging on Angie's sleeve, Eliza whispered, "Angie, we know you're feeling sad about Teddy. But you need to trust us now."

During breakfast, Eliza had used the same words with the others. After breaking the news about Teddy, Jakie stepped outside to answer her phone. It was Eliza's only chance to spread the word.

"I know you're feeling sad about Teddy," Eliza had whispered to the small group. "But trust me now."

"Trust you about what, Eliza?" Karun asked. "Why are you whispering?"

"Shhhh," Eliza said, glancing at the closed doors. "I don't want Jakie to hear. Three deaths. Don't you think Angie will stop our wish-granting?"

"I think she should," Karun had replied.

"I don't think so." Eliza glared at them. "Hear me out. Don't know what Spanks, Rose, or Teddy wished for, but whatever it was, their wish was granted and it was spectacular."

The sisters didn't respond. Peter stared down at the table.

"How do you know that, Eliza?" Karun asked.

"Jakie said Teddy died happy. Spanks and Rose wore smiles to their graves. And I heard Jakie talking to Angie about that new administrator who said we wished for unrealistic things," Eliza said. Eliza had thought about her own wish: a bubble bath with Lucy. *If only. Could it be?* What she wished for was crazy. Did the others ask for one last chance at happiness, too? If she could just be with Lucy, she could truly be at peace.

Peter had looked up. "I don't want to die."

"Who said anything about dying? I'm talking about our wishes being granted." Eliza had softened her voice. "Wouldn't you want that? Remember those magical puffs? You were so fascinated?"

"Maybe."

"And what about you, Karun? And you, Adelaide and Trudy? Didn't you wish for something so special only a wish can bring?"

Karun had frowned. "I don't know about—"

"You want your wish to come true, don't you, Karun?"

Karun smiled and nodded.

"Good!" Eliza cheered.

Trudy glanced over at Adelaide and whispered, "I want my wish granted."

"I do too, Trudy." Eliza had reached over and touched Trudy's hand. "Since we're all thinking the same, I'll tell Angie. I'll tell her she can't say no to us."

They had watched as Eliza reached into the treasure box and pulled out a card. Holding it close to her chest, she prayed, silently. She would convince Angie, one way or the other, to grant the remaining wishes. Hoping her wish would be granted next, she squeezed the card between her fingers. Should it be, she would demand it so loudly the whole world would hear her.

"Trust you about what, Eliza?" Angie asked.

"We discussed everything, and we want our wishes granted."

"Under the circumstances, I don't believe that's such a good idea."

Eliza opened out her left palm. The folded card sprang halfway open. "We took care of the next name for you."

Angie stared at the folded index card.

"I didn't open it," Eliza said, frowning. "I swear. Picked it out with everyone watching. Been holding it tight ever since."

Angie shook her head.

"Please, Angie, open it. Pretty please?" Eliza pushed the card closer to Angie's face.

Angie stared up at Eliza. "Fine." Angie grabbed the card.

Eliza clapped.

"Oh my," Angie said after opening the folded card. "There are two folded together."

Eliza laughed. "Better odds in my favor that way."

Silently reading both wishes, Angie grinned.

I wish to drive Princess Aruna one more time in my Phantom. Karun Nambeeson.

In very small print, Peter had scribed one sentence: *I wish to know the true meaning of Life and the Universe.* On one end he traced out a crescent-shaped moon. On the other end, a five-pointed star.

Standing, Angie proudly announced, "Karun and Peter."

Karun smiled. Peter continued to stare down at the table.

"Damn." Eliza pouted. "Next time." Sitting next to Angie, she asked, "Who'll go first?"

Karun and Peter raised their hands.

"To speed things up, why don't you grant both wishes at the same time?" Eliza asked.

"Slow down," Angie said. "I need to think about this."

"What's going on?" Jakie asked, walking in. "I see a bunch of very excited faces."

"They're trying to convince me to continue with the wishes," Angie replied.

"I think you need to hear this," Jakie said. "Just got off the phone with the coroner's office."

They all sat up a little straighter.

"Teddy died of stress cardiomyopathy." Looking at their puzzled faces, Jakie added, "Teddy died of a broken heart. Just like I thought. Not unusual when one loves another the way Teddy loved Rose. He just didn't want to be here without her."

"That's a sign if ever I heard one." Eliza smiled. "What do you say now, Angie?"

Flashes of Ms. Fettore's dark eyes flew through her mind. Angie shook her head. "I'll let you know my decision by the end of the day."

Elder John sat across from Father Joe. John stared at his friend and priest, who was still attached to the endless wires and tubes. Father Joe was sleeping through his sixth day of a coma, showing no change. According to Dr. Yates, Father Joe still had a 50 percent chance of recovering. John banked on the positive side. John had read that people in a coma could hear everything going on around them. He kept the father updated about the other elders, the church, and the prayers for him from home. He also talked about the recent happenings in Birdsong and, of course, Mary's latest news about Teddy Chumley.

"We're doin' the same with Teddy as the others. We're keepin' him on ice until you return." He paused. "Accordin' to Nurse Jakie, Teddy loved Rose so much he died of a broken heart." His eyes welled with tears. "Come back to us, will ya, Father? We need you."

John glanced at his watch. Any moment now, Father Francis from St. Aloysius Church would be visiting. The visit was not a good one. Father Francis would be administering Father Joe's last rites—the sacrament of the dying.

Knowing that Teddy died of a broken heart, Angie felt a little better about things. It wasn't unusual for someone to die soon after a loved one. At the end of their rec session, Angie shared her thoughts about continuing to grant wishes.

"I've made my decision." Their eyes were glued on her. "I'll fill Karun's and Peter's wishes on Tuesday." If Ms. Fettore wanted to stop her, it'd be too late.

"Yeah," Eliza said, clapping. "And after you guys, I'll be next."

Neither Karun nor Peter seemed as excited as Eliza, although Karun grinned.

Chapter 11

Walking home, Angie was looking forward to some *alone time* on Saturday. After a long soak in the tub, she slept in late. She called Maddie, needing to clear her head of the past several days. Just the sound of her daughter's voice cheered her up. After she brought her daughter abreast of the unfortunate deaths, they discussed Maddie's job and her online dating connections.

"Mom," Maddie said, "you should try a dating site. Meet somebody new."

"Maybe someday." Angie frowned. "Not there yet."

Email with her son, Kevin, always proved distantly emotional. They exchanged small talk, which was mostly about their work. She didn't write about the deaths. That was more information than she cared to share. Kevin always replied with great news. He was looking forward to visiting Birdsong in the summer.

Tears flowed. Angie missed her children, and she felt alone. Angie thought about the dating sites. *No, too soon.* Maybe it was time to visit the movie theatre in town instead.

Stopping by the Garage Depot, she paid Tom another fifty dollars and was pleased to see her Honda on the greasy floor. *At least my car made it inside this place.*

"I'm on it," he replied.

"May I ask a question?"

"Fire away." Tom smiled.

"How much would it cost to rent a 1939 Phantom Rolls Royce for an hour?"

He laughed. "A 1939 Phantom Rolls Royce for an hour?"

"Yes." Angie nodded.

"Why that car?"

"I'm granting a wish. One of the residents drove a princess around in one once. And that's his wish. To drive her around again."

"To drive around again?"

"Actually, not drive. Maybe just sit in one."

"Color?"

Angie thought about that for a second. "I don't believe he ever mentioned a color." The photo of him standing next to his Phantom was in black and white. "What color Phantom would a maharajah likely own?"

"A maharajah?" Tom chuckled. "Probably a deep blue or black."

"Either, then."

"And when would you need this Phantom?"

"Tuesday."

Raising his eyebrows, Tom replied, "Could get a black Rolls Royce Phantom III from the south where they're on exhibition." Staring at her, he chuckled again. "Around three thousand. Should I order one for you?"

Not amused, she frowned. "Just hoping for the impossible. I thought an exotic car like that could be leased for a reasonable amount."

"Not the case."

"When can I have *my* car back?"

"As you can see, I'm working it." He walked away, leaving her standing there, alone.

Irritated by the three-thousand-dollar price tag, Angie walked out, wanting to get back to her relaxed mood. And perhaps to the theatre to see a movie.

Tom enjoyed the moment about the exotic cars; it was his dream to buy and sell them to the rich and famous. He could retire in the south and make a great living on just the commission. After Angie left, Tom had her Honda pushed back outside. He'd have to deal with her soon enough. Just not tonight.

Trying to forget about her car, Angie entered the theatre. *How can I grant Peter's wish?* Then it hit her. *Cut out several large numbers from zero to nine. What else?* She'd make it the residents' activity.

"Lee," Cy yelled. "Wake up."

Originally from Brooklyn, Cy spent his teen summers riding the famous Coney Island rollercoaster, the Cyclone. After that, the nickname Cyclone stuck. No longer a teen, everyone called him Cy.

His life had many ups and downs. At the moment, it was down. His haul en route from Palm Beach to Quebec was having engine problems. Heading up I-95, Cy was ahead of schedule. That was, until an odd detour took him off course. He hated driving the old country roads. Not sure why his truck's GPS was malfunctioning, he tried his cellphone. No signal. The detour brought him and his partner to some town named Birdsong. At least the northeast weather was cooperating. No snow.

"What's up?" Lee asked, rubbing his eyes.

"Only an hour away from Quebec and we're having problems," Cy said.

Lee sat up and looked around.

"What kind of problems?"

"Engine making noise."

"Hope someone in this town can patch us up. We have to get back on the road today."

With no cell service, Cy pulled over on Main Street. A man walking his dog directed him to Jared's Garage Depot.

The room remained quiet while the small group concentrated on cutting out stenciled numbers from zero to nine.

"Been meaning to toss these old things out for ages," Jakie said, snipping around a foot-long number one.

"You should never throw out magazines!" Eliza stated. She was flipping through a *People* magazine that was at least ten years old. "There's history in these pages."

Angie finished tracing out a number eight using a stencil. "We're almost done. Thank you, everybody."

Cutting out his number that had a forest background, Peter glanced over at her. Angie hoped this activity would help them cope with the recent deaths. If nothing else, they still had each other.

"Peter, why do you like to write out the numbers?"

"Because," he said, staring at her. "The universe is made of numbers. That's why."

"Okay," she whispered. Maybe she shouldn't have asked.

Ms. Fettore's dark eyes flew through her mind. Angie had been surprised by the normally threatening woman. Earlier that morning, Ms. Fettore only said, "Bless Teddy's poor broken heart." No lecture, no warning. Just a few kind words for an old man. Instead of hauling Angie into her office, Ms. Fettore looked Angie directly in her eyes and smiled. Then she wished her luck. How odd.

As he hung up his cellphone, Tom stared at one of the largest transporters he'd ever seen. Smoke spewed from its corners. When the air cleared, Jared read the colorful logo: *TEEEM*.

Two men jumped from the cab.

"Where you guys headed?" Tom asked.

"North," one of the men replied. "Short delivery date."

"What's with the TEEEM?"

"What?" the man glanced around. "Oh, stands for *The Exotic Express Experience Migration*."

Having no idea what the man was talking about, Tom dropped it. "Having problems?"

"Started acting up about twenty miles back."

"I'll get my guy right on it," Tom said, silently counting his profits.

"Appreciate it. I'm Cy." He extended a hand. "And this is my partner, Lee."

"Tom. Tom Jared." He shook their hands.

"Where's a good place to eat?" Cy asked.

"Rose Petals. Couple blocks up. Good lunch menu. Bit early, but tell 'em Jared sent you. Nancy'll take good care of ya." Wondering why such a strict timeframe, Jared added, "What ya hauling that's so hot?"

"Couple of Rolls Royces, and—"

"You wouldn't happen to have a 1939 Phantom III in there, would ya?"

With a puzzled look, Cy replied, "As a matter of fact, I do. Once owned by an Indian maharajah."

With a picnic basket in tow, Angie and Karun walked arm in arm through the Home's lobby. Karun talked about Princess Aruna as if he was on his way to meet up with her. As they stepped onto the front stoop, the winter wind pecked at their cheeks. The graying skies lifted their moods. Stepping into the carport, Angie was thankful for the groundskeeper keeping the driveway cleared of snow.

"Jakie's bringing her car around to the front. She's warming it up for us. You'll get to sit at the wheel and I'll sit behind you." Angie giggled. "Then you'll tell me about your life in India with the princess."

"I'm so happy right now," Karun said.

Handing Karun the small picnic basket, she patted his shoulder. She forgot to grab the princess's framed photo. "I'll be right back. Wait here."

Karun nodded.

"Your princess will return," she said, darting into the lobby.

Angie thought about the photo. She'd used the black-and-white of the princess, had it cropped and enlarged and changed into color. Although she still had a sad expression, the princess seemed to come to life. Dressed in an apricot chiffon sari adorned with white pearls and a diamond bindi, the woman looked beautiful. Angie had thought about buying a sari and placing an artificial stone on her forehead, but that would have been too cheesy.

Karun squinted as he stared into sunlight. His heart pounded. A black Rolls Royce Phantom III braked to a stop right in front of him.

A middle-aged man wearing dingy coveralls stepped out. Nodding, he smiled at Karun. "Hello. Where can I find Ms. Pantera?"

Karun's eyes remained glued to the Phantom. "She went inside." Karun pointed toward the red door.

"Thank you," the stranger replied, stepping onto the stoop.

Karun strolled around the black chassis. Warm memories overpowered him. Having no control, he slid his hand across the car's splendid contours and stood by the driver's door. The vehicle was exactly as he remembered.

He pulled open the door; the strong aroma of aging leather greeted him. Karun pulled out his handkerchief and wiped away some dirt. He frowned. Sliding onto the seat, his heart ached. Still holding onto the wicker strap, he placed the lunch basket next to him.

"Could it still be here?" he whispered.

Karun ran his fingers across a secret compartment known only to the maharajah and the chauffer. It held something special, something precious. A pistol. A weapon to protect the princess. Although he'd reached for the gun several times, he had never used it.

Popping the compartment open and reaching in, his hand brushed against the cold metal. It was still there, hidden from the whole world. He'd placed it there himself many years ago.

Karun pulled it out and lifted it to his nose. He longed for closure.

The deep love for the princess still resided in his heart. He took a deep breath. A dried-up rose resting by the pistol sent him back to the summer day when Princess Aruna handed it to him.

"I have something for you, Karun," she had whispered.

He had glanced in the rearview mirror. "And what would that be?" Her inner beauty always amazed him.

"Ah, you promised to call me Aruna."

"Yes, Aruna. What is your surprise?"

A white rose tickled the back of his ear. "I picked it myself."

"Thank you, Aruna, I shall cherish it forever."

With the memory fading, Karun glanced down when the familiar alluring fragrance tickled his senses. He was now staring at a healthy and recently clipped white rose. His mind fell blank.

From somewhere behind him, a soft voice whispered, "I'm happy you like it, Karun."

Karun blinked several times. Now dressed in his gray chauffer's suit, his hands on the mahogany steering wheel, he felt young and vibrant again. A handsome nineteen-year-old with deep-brown eyes stared back at him from the rearview mirror.

Suddenly, he pulled on the steering wheel to avoid a sacred cow. Karun was back in India. Transcending both time and space, he glided his Rolls Royce down a long dirt road. He was where he wanted to be—back with his beloved princess.

She was beyond beautiful. Her sparkling eyes stared at him through the mirror. Wearing an apricot chiffon sari adorned with creamy white pearls, the princess frowned at him.

"The cows are everywhere. People think they have right-of-way. They are a nuisance."

"Yes, Princess . . . I mean, Aruna."

"Are you okay? You are acting a bit strange."

"I feel that I have arrived in heaven."

"Heaven?" She laughed. "You know I have no heaven. I have only a hell. I am to marry a cruel man."

"I am so sorry, Pri . . . Aruna. I wish with all my heart I could change things for you." *And, if only, for myself.*

"That is why you are my best friend. I can be honest with you and know you shall honor my secrets." She sat quietly for several moments before adding, "I promised myself to clear my head of that monster today." Aruna pointed out the window. "Over there. Let us have our lunch hidden within the lychee trees. Away from the rest of the world. Just for today."

Hidden away from the rest of the world, Karun told his princess how he felt toward her. Smiling, she leaned into his warm embrace and they kissed each other, tenderly.

Chapter 12

Angie grabbed the photo of Princess Aruna from the table.

Adelaide tilted her head. "What games are we playing after lunch, Angie?"

"What?" Hugging the frame close to her chest, Angie paused.

"Are we playing games today?" Adelaide repeated.

"Uh, no," Angie said, shaking her head. "Not today."

"Oh darn," Adelaide replied.

Angie glanced at the sullen faces. "I'm sorry. But I have so much to do. Hanging the numbers and all. In fact, I need you all back in your rooms."

"What about dinner?" Eliza asked. "I hate eating alone in my room."

"Fine," Angie replied, tapping her foot. "Eat early and then go to your rooms."

Slapping his soup spoon against the table, Peter glared.

"It's your night, Peter," Angie said. "I'll come get you once they've eaten. You'll have a wonderful evening."

Hurrying through the double doors, Angie spotted Tom Jared standing in the lobby looking lost.

Tom waved. "Ms. Pantera, there you are."

"You brought me my car? How nice of you."

He shook his head.

"No! Then why are you here?"

"I brought you something better." His large grin almost revealed his surprise.

"Something better?"

Tom opened the red door. Angie's mouth dropped open. Stepping outside, she stared at the antique Rolls Royce parked only a few feet away.

"Is that thing real?"

"It's real. A 1939 Rolls Royce Phantom III. Once owned by an Indian maharajah." Tom seemed to be dancing on his toes.

"But how? How did you—" Angie's mouth refused to cooperate. "From where?"

"Exotic car transport broke down right in front me," he said, laughing. "So . . . I negotiated."

Glancing around, Angie froze. "Where's Karun? I left him out here."

"He was standing over there when I pulled up," Tom replied.

Darting for the shiny black vehicle, Angie almost tripped when she spotted Karun sitting behind the steering wheel, staring straight ahead. In his hand, he held a single white rose. Something didn't look right. Karun wasn't moving.

Angie knocked gently on the window. "Karun!" Angie yelled.

Karun slowly turned toward her and smiled. Tom opened the driver's door. Jumping out with vigor, Karun held tightly onto the fresh rose.

"Karun? You okay?" Angie asked.

Kissing both sides of Angie's face, he replied, "You have made my life complete. I can't thank you enough for granting my wish."

"It wasn't me," she replied. "Thank Mr. Jared here for this car."

Karun grabbed Tom's hand and vigorously shook it. "How did you know, Mr. Jared? How could you possibly know?"

"I'm sorry." Tom looked over at Angie and shrugged. "I don't understand."

"This is the *actual* Rolls Royce I drove as a teenager. Back in India." Karun grinned as a tear ran down his cheek.

"You're welcome. Mr. Karun," Tom replied. "Ms. Pantera asked about one just the other day."

"Is that for me?" Karun asked, pointing at the picture frame.

"Oh, yes." Angie handed it to him.

Clutching it to his heart, Karun closed his eyes. "Perfect. My life *is* complete now." Karun opened his eyes and stared at Angie. "I'll be in my room if you should need me." Karun stepped around the stunned onlookers and headed for the red door.

"Karun?" Angie yelled. "What about your lunch?"

Ignoring her, Karun disappeared behind the red door.

Tom opened the wicker basket. "Looks like he already ate."

"He must've been hungry," Angie replied. "He ate mine, too."

Tom laughed.

"How much for this unbelievable rental?" Angie asked. "And that rose was a nice touch. Thanks."

"An extra week's time to repair your car?" Tom tilted his head and smiled.

Taking in a deep breath, Angie laughed. "Deal."

As he started the car, Tom leaned out the window. "Hey."

"Yes?" Angie stepped forward.

"I didn't put a rose in here."

As the Phantom rolled down the long driveway, Angie shook her head. *If he didn't put it in there, where did it come from?*

Jakie's sedan squealed to a stop in front of Angie. "Sorry," Jakie said, jumping out. "Had problems getting it started. Running fine now." Jakie glanced over Angie's shoulder. "Where's Karun?"

After paying his bill, Cy handed Tom Jared his TEEEM business card.

"Cyclone?" Tom chuckled.

"Long story. One I'd share if you're ever in New Orleans. Besides, I owe you one. On time and with a discount."

"Call us even," Tom replied. "That Rolls did the trick. Have a safe trip, Cyclone."

They shook hands.

"Seriously, call me when you're in New Orleans." Cy said, climbing into his cab.

"Will do." Tom's late wife always wanted to visit New Orleans.

Eliza knocked on Karun's door.

Opening it only a crack, Karun peeked out. "Eliza?"

"Was your wish granted?" she asked.

"More than you will ever believe." Karun smiled.

Jakie stepped up holding Karun's dinner tray. "Curious are we, Eliza? Your dinner is being served right now in the dining room. Don't let it get cold."

"Thanks, Karun," Eliza whispered.

Karun winked at her.

Nodding to Jakie, Eliza said, "Just wanted to see how Karun was feeling."

"You wanted to know if his wish was granted. So, was it?"

"Yes, it was." Eliza darted down the hallway to tell the sisters and Peter the good news.

Placing Karun's dinner on the table, Jakie smiled. "May I check your vitals?"

"Again?" Karun asked, taking a bite. "That makes twice this afternoon."

Jakie pulled out a blood-pressure cuff from her pocket. She listened as Karun told his story to her for a second time—how the vehicle was the exact same Rolls Royce he once drove in India.

Leaving Karun's room, Jakie sighed. *No more deaths.* Karun was alive and healthy.

Angie glanced at the numbers hanging from the ceiling. The different sizes added a mystical feel. They shimmered like stars.

"It takes a village," Angie had said earlier when Jakie and Elder Luke climbed down from their ladders. "Thank you both. Peter will be so surprised when he sees this heavenly extravaganza."

Tonight, no fire blazed in the fireplace. Peter requested darkness. No fancy crystals or china. Walter's famous lobster mac and cheese worked better on regular dishes anyway. No Sinatra tunes tonight. Instead, a DVD of *The Universe on Steroids* waited patiently next to the television. Happy she didn't have to wear her black evening dress, Angie was comfortable wearing her work clothes. Peter was a simple man.

It was time to meet Peter, the simple man, in his room and escort him to dinner. Exiting through the large double doors, she almost tripped over him.

"Peter! You startled me."

Leaning against his walker, Peter stared down at the floor. He wore light khakis and a white shirt; once again, the ghostly image of Casper flew through her mind.

"Couldn't wait, huh?" Angie giggled.

"No," he said, still staring at the floor. "Eliza told me Karun's wish came true."

"Yes, it did." Angie gestured for him to enter the dining room. "Are you ready for your wish?"

Peter refused to move. "Is Karun okay?"

"I'm happy to say he's doing just fine. Jakie checked on him several times this afternoon."

Peter shuffled through the doors.

"Welcome to your wish," Angie said, prodding him along.

Squinting into the dark, Peter gazed up at the ceiling. "Wow, Angie. Nice. Really nice."

Numbers zero to nine made from colorful pictures dangled from long silver threads. Three hundred floated in the darkness.

"I knew you'd love it." Angie wrapped her arm around Peter's and helped him to his seat.

A single small white candle lit the table. Peter's favorite dinner awaited him. He seemed uninterested in talking. As Peter served himself, Angie hit the play button on the DVD player.

"Hope you like everything, Peter."

He nodded.

"It's everything you requested."

Peter nodded again.

Angie watched him take a bite. *What is wrong with him?* At this pace, dinner was going to take all night. Glancing around the table, Angie wanted to slap herself. She'd forgotten the beer Peter requested.

"I'll be right back," she said. "Need to get your dark stout from the fridge."

Peter ate as Angie disappeared through the kitchen door.

"Peter?" a soft voice called.

Peter glanced around. The shadows, dark and empty, didn't look right. Everything seemed fuzzy, as if a light mist had suddenly fallen.

"Peter?" the soft voice repeated.

Peter glanced around again. He was alone.

"Peter," the soft voice said a third time.

Peter heard his name loud and clear from the TV speakers. He wiped his lips with a paper napkin and walked to the TV. *The Vitruvian Man*, the same one from his shadow box, stared back at him. As he ran his fingers down the screen, a flash of white shot out. The sizzle traveled up his arm, and Peter's hair rose. He watched the spark travel down his legs, through his feet and out his toes.

Lifting his arms, Peter's body was no longer in his control. Taking on the appearance of the Vitruvian Man, Peter smiled and floated up. He danced with his numbers, swimming within the stars. As he dissolved into the universe, Peter's brain was now a human computer, compounding and inquiring about everything.

Angie was holding two beers between her fingers when one suddenly slipped and crashed onto the floor. The glass bottle shattered into pieces.

"Dammit!" Angie cursed.

Placing the unbroken bottle on the counter, she sighed. She swept up the pieces with a broom and dustpan. After what seemed like forever, the floor clean, Angie grabbed the remaining beer.

Entering the dining room, Angie found Peter standing in front of the TV. No movie was playing, just static. With his hand on the screen, Peter swayed in a silent dance, singing one of her favorite tunes.

"Fly me to the moon," Peter sang. "Let me play among the stars. Let me see what spring is like on a Jupiter and Mars . . ."

"Peter?" Angie's heart pounded. "You okay?"

Still swaying to a tune only Peter could hear, he continued to sing. "In other words . . . I did, I did!"

"Peter? You okay?"

Peter stopped dancing and turned to her. He chuckled. "Couldn't be better, Angie." Grabbing her arms, Peter stared straight into her eyes and whispered, "Thank you, Angie. Thank you for granting my wish."

Angie's mouth dropped open.

"This is only the start," he said, with a Cheshire-like grin. "There's more to come. And I can't wait."

"What are you talking about? You're not making any sense." Pushing herself away from his strong grip, she glared at him. "I'm calling Jakie."

Peter frowned. "I'm fine. I'll be in my room if you need me."

Angie pulled out her cellphone and hit Jakie's name.

Opening the doors with both hands, Peter sang out his song.

Following behind him, Angie yelled, "What about your walker?"

"Don't need it anymore," he yelled back, waving his arm through the air.

Angie watched as he sang and danced down the hallway. Stopping at the picture of *The Vitruvian Man* displayed in his shadow box, Peter saluted before disappearing into his room.

"Jakie!" Angie screamed. "It's Peter!"

"Is he dead?"

"No. He's not dead. Just acting strange. Went to get his beer from the fridge and when I returned his hand was on the TV. Instead of the movie, the screen was all static and snowy."

"Define strange," Jakie said. Obviously, she'd been sleeping.

"He sang and danced to his room. And he left his walker by the table."

"Excuse me? That is strange. Man can barely talk, let alone sing."

"Could he have gotten a shock by touching the TV?"

"It's possible. I'll check on him."

Jakie grabbed her stethoscope and scrambled down the staircase. Stepping up to the silent door, she knocked once.

"Peter? It's Jakie. May I talk to you for a minute?"

Peter opened the door. Grabbing onto her waist, he smiled. "Thank you for everything, Jakie."

Concerned about a possible electric shock, Jakie gently hugged him back. "You're welcome." She stepped back and studied his face. "Show me your hands." Peter held out his hands, turning them over for her. Nothing looked wrong. "How're you feeling?"

"Couldn't be better," he replied, bouncing back and forth on his feet.

"How so?"

"Saw a glimpse of the future." Peter placed his hand over his heart. "Can't wait."

"A glimpse of the future?"

"Actually, a glimpse of the truth." Peter smiled. "I'm not afraid anymore."

"Can we go inside and sit down? I need to listen to your heart."

Stepping into his room, Jakie felt as if she'd just walked through a portal into a different dimension. She listened to his heart. Peter seemed normal, but something wasn't right.

Peter arrived at the Home a decade earlier wearing flip-flops and tattered clothing. He said he was homeless. When she examined him back then, he refused to say where he was from. Never mentioned marriage or children. Gave no next of kin. The small-framed man with a full head of white hair only referred to himself as Peter Peter. Walter found Peter digging through his dumpster one night. Peter told Father Joe his home was an old refrigerator box on some street somewhere. Peter inherited room fourteen after a professor died there. The extensive collection of books remained on the shelfs. No one ever knew if Peter had read them. All he ever loved doing was writing down numbers—zero to nine.

Completing her exam, Jakie sighed. "Can't find anything wrong with you. But I want Doc Bolton to visit you tomorrow."

"I'm tired now," Peter replied.

"Lie down and rest. I'll check in on you again later."

Jakie entered the dining room. Angie sat at a table finishing her dinner. The nighttime starry transformation still glittered through the room.

"Looks amazing," Jakie said. "No wonder Peter's so happy."

Angie frowned. "I was worried about him."

"So far, so good," Jakie replied. "I'm calling Doc Bolton in the morning. I'll have him look at both Peter and Karun."

"The movie popped back on as soon as Peter left. Must've been a glitch of some kind." Angie grinned. "I couldn't have done this without you. Thank you."

"You're welcome." Yawning, Jakie giggled. "Maybe I will join you."

Feasting on the leftovers, the two women shared the warm beer and talked. The lobster mac and cheese was the best food Jakie had ever tasted. She felt closer to Angie than ever before.

"I was blindsided by my ex-husband," Angie said. "Jay left me for a younger woman. After twenty-five years, I thought we had something special. What a fool."

"My husband died many years ago," Jakie whispered. "Kidney failure. He was in his forties. We age and they age. Men seem to wonder more about their mortality than we do. Then, during the staleness of life, something new and exciting sparks something inside them. Something that's been sleeping. It's the same old story. The older woman is left behind for the fresh younger one. See it all the time these days. Nobody says life is fair. It's just life. Personally, I think that men revert back to scared little boys when reality hits."

"Words of wisdom, Jakie?" Angie frowned. "Thanks, but it still hurts. He just wanted me to disappear as if I never existed."

Sitting under the twinkling numbers, Jakie thought about her son. She wished only happiness for him.

It was rec time and Eliza was acting more of a pest than usual. Working on a group puzzle project, Eliza refused to stop prodding Karun and Peter.

"Just a little tidbit?" Eliza whined. "That's all I ask."

The men ignored her.

Something wasn't right. Karun kept smiling, and Peter wasn't acting like Peter anymore. He was charming and engaging, also empathetic—a real human being.

"Okay," Eliza said, with her arms folded. "What did you do with the *real* Peter?"

Peter laughed. Concentrating on placing a puzzle piece into place, he grinned.

"And you, Karun. You haven't stopped smiling since you walked in here." Eliza shook her head. "I'm starting to think you look better frowning."

"You'll find everything out for yourself when it's your turn," Karun replied, moving a few puzzle pieces around.

"Yes," Peter whispered. "When your time comes."

"Angie, can you pick names again?" Eliza yelled out. "I can't wait anymore. I want my wish granted now!"

Angie laughed. "Maybe after lunch."

Eliza stomped her foot and grunted.

Not wanting trouble, Angie nodded over to Eliza. "Fine. Pick a card. But don't read the name."

Eliza, beaming from ear to ear, stepped up to the little treasure box.

"There's only the three of you left," Angie said. "Since Trudy and Adelaide share a wish, you have a fifty-fifty chance of pulling your name."

"I know exactly what we can wear for our show," Trudy said.

Eliza frowned. "You haven't won yet."

"Eliza," Angie whispered. "Pull out a card."

Eliza shut her eyes and reached into the little treasure box. Hemming and hawing, she pulled out a folded index card. Staring at it, she handed it to Angie. "Here's the winner." Eliza took in a deep breath. "Hope it's me."

They watched as Angie read the card to herself first.

We both wish: To be young dancers and dance teachers once again at our Simmons Dance Academy.
Adelaide Simmons

"Sorry, Eliza," Angie glanced over at the sisters. "Adelaide and Trudy are next."

"Oh damn! I should have held onto the first one that dropped."

Knowing how much Eliza wanted it to be her, Angie replied, "You may be last, Eliza, but certainly not the least. I promise you."

Pouting, Eliza turned away, whispering to herself.

"Ladies, get your dancing shoes ready," Angie said. "It'll be a go this Friday evening."

Adelaide spoke up with a smile. "Angie, we have some requests."

"Okay. After all, it is your wish."

"We need a real stage," Adelaide replied.

"A real stage. Okay."

"And four different kinds of tea sandwiches and punch."

"Spiked or plain?" Eliza mused.

The sisters giggled as Angie frowned at her.

"And we want to invite everyone to our show."

Angie's mind swirled. Ms. Fettore wasn't going to like the stage idea, and Jakie would make comments about teas. Maybe it would be best if she consulted with Dr. Bolton about Karun and Peter prior to agreeing to anything. After all, the two men were still acting very odd.

Later that morning, Angie realized she hadn't seen Jakie since conveying the sisters' invitation. Usually, Angie ran into Jakie around every corner. Now, Jakie was nowhere to be found.

Then again, the timely and prompt Ms. Fettore hadn't shown up either. Maybe the predicted ice storm was keeping her away. Angie would ask for a ride home from Jakie later today. If Jakie ever showed up.

Chapter 13

The arrival of Groundhog Day didn't matter to Mainers. There would be more than six weeks of winter left no matter what Punxsutawney Phil saw. May always arrived before the benefits of spring. And not until mid-June would the roses bloom.

Angie entered the serenity of the chapel's sanctuary, sticking to her thrice weekly schedule. She nodded at the statue of the Little Flower. With three of the residents gone and Father Joe in a coma, there was a lot of uncertainty. Kneeling at the tabernacle, she thought about looking into that bookkeeping position she'd seen in the paper. Maybe even leaving Birdsong altogether. Had she made a mistake by following serendipity and moving here?

Making the sign of the cross, she prayed, *Help me out.* Angie said the Our Father several times for the safe return of Father Joe. Placing five consecrated hosts into her pyx, she turned the little key to lock the tabernacle.

Hearing a slight noise, she froze. When a hand slapped against her shoulder, Angie screamed.

"Why are you screaming, Ms. Pantera?" Mary sternly asked.

Placing her hand against her pounding heart, Angie shook her head. "Oh my God. You scared the crap out of me."

"My apologies," Mary replied. "Need to pay you for the week."

"Thanks." Still shaking, Angie studied the woman. *What kind of a game is she playing?* "I'll stop by after I lock up."

"Have you done any more of your wish-grantings?" Mary's voice seemed to slide from sarcastic to sweet and back again without notice. "Understand Luke is building a stage for you?"

"Tonight's the sisters' wish. The stage was their request."

"You already fulfilled two more wishes," Mary said, glaring at her. "Are those winners still alive?"

"Why wouldn't they be?" Angie frowned. Not wanting to be alone in the rectory with her, Angie almost grabbed the money from Mary before saying goodbye. She had a $190 tab to submit but thought it best to wait for Father Joe to return.

"I've been praying for Father Joe," Angie said, before darting out the door. "Any change in his health?"

"A little. We're optimistic."

"Adelaide and Trudy would love an audience. Any chance you're free tonight?"

Frowning, Mary shook her head. "I run the prayer service for Father Joe. Every evening at six. Perhaps *you* should join us, Ms. Pantera."

Staring at her boots and not the woman of her nightmares, Angie replied, "I'll try."

Driving Jakie's car into town, Angie stopped at the floral shop.

"May I help you?" a young girl asked.

"Is Ronnie in?"

"Off today."

Angie glanced into the flower-filled refrigerator behind the counter. "I'll take two dozen of the red roses. Wrapped separately, please. Tell Ronnie that the rec lady from the Home said the magical dandelions from South America grown by monks gave us a good show."

The young girl giggled. "Will do. By the way, today's your lucky day."

"How so?" Angie asked.

"Today's a BOGO. It's buy one dozen for fifteen and get the second free."

After a quick stop at Jared's Garage Depot to pay her weekly fifty and thank him again for the unbelievable Rolls, Angie experienced the same disappointment.

"Mr. Jared's out today." It was the same mechanic as the last time.

Angie made a fast stop at her cottage, changing into her black evening dress before heading back to the Home. Pleased with how very loose the dress felt, she grabbed her purse and keys from the table. As she threw her usual kiss at the framed photo of her twins, she reminded herself to give Maddie a call later.

Elder Luke never let her down. The slightly elevated mini-stage, accessed by a tilted plank, was built and ready. The man with the Christmas bulb face even placed three rows of chairs in front of it. Two spotlights, one on each corner, would no doubt highlight the sisters' act. The fireplace crackled with a dancing light that was dim enough for a theatrical effect. Classical music played in the background. A horizontal paper sign reading *SIMMONS DANCE ACADEMY* that Elder Luke attached to two clear rods decorated the back of the stage.

Walter prepared four kinds of tea sandwiches—crab salad with scallion, English cucumber and dill, curried chicken with golden raisins, and egg salad with caviar. The non-alcoholic punch, a frothy lemonade, looked more like meringue.

Wearing a blue cocktail dress, Jakie stood at the double doors waiting for the audience to arrive. Holding a dozen dance recital programs that Angie had printed, she read over one.

SISTERLY ACT

BEST OF FRIENDS, TAP

WHEN WILL OUR LIVES BEGIN, BALLET
FINAL CURTAIN & ANNOUNCEMENT

"Thanks for the help, Jakie."

"My pleasure." Jakie smiled.

"I have to say you're all looking sharp tonight," Angie said, serving sandwiches to Karun, Peter, and Eliza.

The doors opened and the sisters walked in, making their grand entrance. Wearing ankle-length, antique dresses, Adelaide swayed as she led Trudy by the hand. The room echoed with clapping. Angie showed the ladies to their seats. The small group talked, ate, and sipped the tea. When finished, Adelaide stood up.

"Ladies and gentlemen," she said, waving to the chairs stationed in front of the stage. "Please do take your seats."

As the lights dimmed, the classical music trumpeted through the room. Eliza took the middle seat in the front row. Karun and Peter sat to her right and left in the second row. Angie and Jakie sat in the back clapping the loudest. The sisters took center stage with Adelaide leading.

The small group watched in amazement as one ninety-something-year-old woman led the other across the stage. From one end to the other they danced interwoven with the melodies of the fugue.

Just as the performance was about to end, Jakie jumped up. Eliza had collapsed on the floor in front of the stage with sweat running down her pale face. Her eyes were shut. Angie grabbed hold of the shaking woman's arm, and together they pulled Eliza to her feet.

Jakie whispered, "We need to get her to her room."

Rose and Teddy walked into the dining room arm in arm, Rose in her blue gown and Teddy in his new tux. They sat in the back row. Several steps behind them, Spanks entered wearing his suit and a new bowtie. Sitting down next to Rose, he smiled. Together, the three read over the program.

Adelaide and Trudy bowed, acknowledging them. Twirling and swirling around, they were once again young and vibrant dancers ready for their final performance. Behind them, filling the stage, were their previous ballet and tap students—the same students who posed for the photos in their shadow box.

Holding hands, Trudy and Adelaide bowed to their audience, accepting the standing ovation with grace and humility. They were truly the superstars of the day. Spanks whistled and carried on in the old Spanks fashion with his hoopin' and hollerin'. Freely giving out their hugs and kisses, the students presented them with a dozen red roses each.

Trudy stepped forward. "Thank you, all. We would like you to know," Trudy gulped, "that I am the older one by a year."

The audience laughed.

"And . . ." Trudy gulped again. "We have an announcement. We've been living a lie all our lives. We're not really sisters. We're a couple."

They kissed tenderly as their tears flowed.

The audience clapped even louder. Spanks whistled from the last row. The students hugged each other, crying.

"Sixty-five years ago, Trudy and I met at a dance retreat. Our marriages were ending and we were both unhappy. We took the fact that our last names were the same as a sign. Together, we started our dream— the Simmons Dance Academy. Told everyone we were sisters."

"Everyone loved us. We had a huge waitlist of students," Trudy added.

"Together, we lived that way for a wonderful ten years," Adelaide said.

Although they were always careful to hide their secret, one day two of their students watched as they embraced and kissed. When the students told their parents, it was all over. A huge scandal broke. The sisters were shamed and forced to leave town to avoid prosecution. Fifteen years ago, at ages seventy-nine and eighty, the penniless couple found themselves in Birdsong. Their old car had died in the parking lot of the Chapel of the Little Flower. As he was for everyone, Father Joe was also there for them.

Eager to get back to her seat, Angie quietly opened one of the doors. She had left Jakie with Eliza, who seemed to be slightly feverish and dehydrated.

Angie arrived just in time to see the sisters holding their red roses.

Clapping, Angie took a step toward the sisters.

"Thank you for granting our wish, Angie," Adelaide said, bursting into tears.

"You're very welcome, Adelaide."

"Yes, thank you for granting our secret wish," Trudy said.

"You're *secret* wish?" Angie asked.

"Yes," Trudy replied. "Being able to tell everyone we're not really sisters."

"Not sisters?" Angie repeated.

"No," Adelaide said. "We're a couple."

Munching down on coconut cake with the others, Angie couldn't stop staring. After finishing off their chamomile tea, the *out-of-the-closet* couple walked arm in arm to their room, smiling the whole way. Angie kept scratching her head.

Angie called Maddie as soon as she returned home.

"The sisters are not really sisters." Angie laughed. "And no one ever knew."

"Mom, listen to you," Maddie said. "You're sounding like your old self again. Dad almost destroyed you. I hate him."

"Don't hate your father, Maddie. His mortality's just rearing its ugly head and he's reverted to being a child."

Maddie laughed. "You're impressing me with your spiritual mumbo-jumbo. Have you been seeing a therapist?"

"Just talking to a friend."

"I think this job is doing you wonders."

"You think?" Angie smiled.

The more they laughed, the more Angie felt as if she was truly home. Turning off the lights and climbing into bed, Angie felt content for the first time in a long time.

Jakie woke a little after midnight as her cellphone blasted one emergency alert after another. The alarm buttons for Karun, Peter, and the sisters echoed through her room.

"This cannot be happening!" Jakie yelled as she searched through the darkness for her robe.

Frantically, she raced down the stairs. The alarms had to be malfunctioning. What else could it be?

The cottage door vibrated with each loud bang that echoed through the small home.

"Ms. Pantera!" A man's voice blared through the thin night air.

Jumping up from a deep sleep, Angie's heart raced. After pulling on her black sweats, she stumbled through the darkness. Stubbing her toes on the leg of the couch, Angie hopped the last few feet.

"Coming. I'm coming."

"This is the police; open at once."

Pulling open the door, she found Officer Raines glaring at her. He looked as if he was about to panic. "I'm sorry to disturb you this late, but I need you to come with me."

"What's wrong?"

"Trouble at the Home," he replied, stepping inside.

"You could have called."

"Tried. No answer."

"Oh darn. I must have shut it off after talking to my daughter."

"Please hurry," he ordered.

Grabbing her coat and sneakers, Angie followed the officer into the bitter cold. She slid in the back door of his cruiser.

"Did someone die?" she asked.

"Not someone," he said.

"You mean there's more?"

The front of the Home lit up from the flashing colored lights. Three police cruisers and two medical examiner vehicles were parked at odd angles. Mary's old Buick was between them.

Angie followed Officer Raines through the open red door. Clutching her coat tightly around her, she prayed Jakie was okay. Lately the woman looked tired and lost most of the time. With her stomach tightening, Angie stood in the foyer watching the officers talk among themselves.

Officer Raines stepped up to a young police officer. "Where's the chief?"

The young man pointed to room number four.

Jakie emerged from the room. A much older man with a full head of grays followed behind her. He carried his large frame forcefully.

Angie ran up to Jakie. "Oh, thank God. I thought something happened to you. Is it Adelaide and Trudy?"

Jakie glanced at the floor. "Police Chief Bertrand," Jakie said, refusing to look directly at Angie, "this is Angie Pantera."

Angie nodded. "Hello. What happened here?"

"Ms. Pantera, I need to speak with you about last night's dinner."

"Of course," Angie replied.

Chief walked over to Officer Raines and the other officers.

"Are Adelaide and Trudy okay?" Angie whispered to Jakie.

Jakie's red eyes filled with tears. She shook her head. "All four of 'em. The sisters and Karun and Peter."

Angie looked away. "My God. All four? What happened?"

"All the alarms sounded at once. It was crazy." Jakie wiped her nose. "I ran from room to room like a crazy person. All dead."

"They all died at the same time?" Angie's mind whirled. How could four people die at the same time? "From what?"

"We don't know. Four residents dying at the same time just isn't normal." Jakie blew her nose again. "They're here investigating homicides now."

"Homicides?" Angie glanced over at the officers. "That's crazy."

"We're all suspects." Jakie again blew her nose.

The room spun around her, and Angie's knees buckled. As she fell backwards, Jakie grabbed her arm.

"Lean against me," Jakie whispered, reaching into her pocket. "Take this. It'll calm you down. It's gonna be a long night."

"Eliza? Please tell me Eliza's okay."

"Sleeping peacefully. Been out like a light all evening." Jakie helped Angie over to a chair. "Don't know how with all this ruckus. I've checked on her and her fever's gone."

"Good." Angie again glanced over at the officers. How in the world could four residents all die at the same time? What was going on around here?

Chief looked at Angie and Jakie. After touching one of the officer's arms, he turned and headed for them.

"Ms. Pantera," he said, "may I speak with you now? I understand there's coffee in the kitchen. Join me?"

The door to room number ten opened, and Eliza's head popped out.

"Eliza?" Jakie pushed her back into her room. "You shouldn't be out of bed."

"I'm feeling better. Tell me, did they die with a smile on their face?"

"How long have you been pretending to be asleep?" Jakie frowned. "Did you have your ear pressed against the door or something?"

"Come on. Don't give me that look. You'd have to be deaf not to hear what's going on out there. That police chief is the loudest of all of 'em." Eliza slapped her hands on her hips. "Well? Did they? I have to know. Did they die with a smile on their face?"

Jakie's jaw tightened.

"I'm the last one. I'm the survivor. Tell me. Were they smiling?"

"Yes, they were."

"Good. Then they're at peace. Now it's just me."

"Please, lie down." Jakie guided her back to her bed. "I'll be in later to check on you."

Eliza sat on her bed and smiled. "Soon." Eliza picked up the bottle of Obsession perfume from her nightstand. Spraying it into the air, she cocked her head and stuck out her tongue. "That's for you, Lucy." Placing her head on her pillow, she yawned.

Jakie didn't have the heart to tell Eliza that with four deaths, her wish-granting would be canceled. Standing next to Mary, the prayers of the dying over Adelaide and Trudy gave her reason to pause. Her residents were gone, actually gone, and they would not be coming back.

"Sit down, Ms. Pantera." Chief Bertrand pointed to a stool next to the counter.

Folding her hands in her lap, she glanced around the kitchen.

"How about some coffee?"

Angie nodded. "Thank you."

"Cups?" Chief Bertrand opened several cabinets and drawers, leaving them ajar.

Angie remained silent.

"Nice kitchen," he said, finding the cups. "Who's the cook?"

"Walter Heron, "Angie replied. "He owns Rose Petals restaurant."

"Haven't been there in a while," he said, filling up two cups with hot coffee. "I prefer eating at home. Cooking is a passion of mine."

Angie nodded.

"He's running some specials this week. I'll have to check 'em out."

"Walter volunteers here. He prepares our meals. Usually gone by the time I get here."

"Who set the stage up for you?"

"One of our elders," Angie replied.

"Elders?" Chief Bertrand would have known the elders if he attended Mass at the Little Flower. But the last time he set foot into church, let alone the Little Flower, was twenty years earlier on his wedding day. "There's more than one elder?"

"Five. Matthew, Mark, Luke and John."

"That's four."

"And Mary," Angie said glumly.

"Of course." He chuckled. "That would be Mary Mead. The woman praying over the deceased right now."

"The names are a little coincidental. But it's their real names."

Eyeing Angie, he added, "Who assists you the most around here?"

"Jakie."

"I mean, from the church."

"Oh, Luke."

"What do the other elders do for the church?"

"Luke told me that once. Don't really remember. You can ask Mary. She's Father Joe's assistant."

Taking a sip of coffee, the chief nodded. "Black? Cream and sugar?"

"Cream." Angie stared into her cup of black coffee.

"Like mine black." He pulled open the refrigerator. Grabbing the creamer, he handed it to Angie. "Tell me more about Mary Mead."

Walter Heron pushed open the kitchen door and waited for Jellybean to run in. Placing the fresh greens onto the counter, he reached down and petted his little friend. Orange fur floated around him.

"Been on your best behavior since sneaking in last week? You need to be a good kitty."

Picking up the leg of lamb, Walter glanced around his kitchen. Several drawers and cabinets doors were open. A pot of coffee, still on the warmer, wasn't a good sign. Especially with all the dirty cups scattered around the counters. This was not the way Angie left things after a wish-granting.

After he placed the lamb in the sink, a light knock rattled the kitchen door. Before Walter could dry his hands, Officer Raines entered from the dining room.

"Walter Heron?"

"Yes," Walter replied. He remembered the man from when Spanks died.

"Chief Bertrand would like a word with you down at the station."

Walter's heart pounded. "Regarding what?"

"The Home."

Sweat ran down the back of his flannel shirt.

Walter sat across from Chief Bertrand and wanted to cry. His heart raced and his head pounded. No longer able to hide his shaking hands, he shoved them under his legs.

"I confess," he blurted out. "I did it. Arrest me." He let out a heavy sigh.

Chief Bertrand and Officer Raines stared at each other. Leaning forward in his chair, Chief Bertrand grinned.

"Are we to understand you're confessing to the murders of Adelaide and Trudy Simmons, and Karun Nambeeson and Peter Peter?" He sat back, crossing his arms. "Raines, read him his rights."

"What? No!" Walter's eyes grew wider as his soul exploded. "Murder? No, not that."

"Mr. Heron?" Chief Bertrand whispered. "If not murder, then what exactly are you confessing to have done?"

Walter watched Chief Bertrand open a file on his desk. Standing behind him, Officer Raines remained silent.

"You buy and prepare the food for the residents?" Chief Bertrand asked.

Walter's skin crawled. "Okay. Okay." Walter rubbed his hands together. "I've been pilfering from the church. Okay, I said it. I'm a thief. Going to hell and my life's ruined."

The chief handed Walter a folded handkerchief.

"Restaurant's not doing so good," Walter said. "Economy's in the toilet, ya know. Been suffering for a while now." Wiping his forehead, he sighed. Walter twisted the handkerchief in his lap. "Don't tell Nancy. She doesn't know."

Chief Bertrand closed the file and tossed it into an open drawer. Sitting back, he eyed the frightened man. "Go home, Mr. Heron."

"You're not going to arrest me?"

"I get it. People don't go out much to eat these days. Have family in the restaurant business. Always complaining about cash flow." Chief Bertrand shook his head. "You need to make that confession to Father Joe. Not me."

"I can't," Walter whispered as he stood up. "He's in a coma."

"One more thing, Mr. Heron."

Walter titled his head.

"Don't leave town. Your meals were sent to the lab. You didn't add any unusual ingredients, did you?"

"My meals are just fine." Walter glared at the man. "That I can promise."

About nine in the morning, an officer tapped on the solid dark-blue door of a charming white cottage with a picket fence at the edge of Birdsong. The home of Elder Luke and his wife, Sylvia, was tucked away inside the local forest.

Opening the door, Sylvia tugged on her bathrobe. Holding a cup of hot tea, she smiled when she saw the badge. "How may I help you, Officer?"

"Morning, ma'am." The officer pulled off his hat and shoved it under his arm. "Is Luke Warner home? I need to speak with him."

"He's out back." She pointed to her left. "Chopping wood."

Walking around several burlap-covered bushes, the officer nodded at an older man. Dropping his ax, Elder Luke stepped up to him, wiping his forehead with a small cloth.

"Morning," the officer said.

"Morning."

"Are you aware of the deaths at the Home?"

Luke nodded. "Four of 'em, last night."

"Mr. Warner, did you notice anything unusual either yesterday or last night?"

"No. Nothing."

"Anything you can remember leading up to the dinner?"

Luke shook his head.

"Then I thank you for your time."

As the officer climbed into his patrol car, he glanced over at Luke, who was back to chopping wood. The snow-covered trees gave the officer a sense of calm. Concentrating on the sound of the axe hitting the wood, he chuckled. In a way, the noise was soothing.

Mary Mead was next on the list. Pulling up in front of Mary's house, he sighed. The front stairs were icy. He had to catch himself several times. No pretreating with salt, which usually meant the person lived alone. He knocked twice. As the door slowly cracked open, a stern-looking woman glared out at him.

"What can I do for you, Officer?"

"Chief needs to speak with you at the station."

"Talked to him last night." Mary pushed on the door, making the opening smaller. "Have nothing more to say."

"Chief has a few new questions. Be happy to drive you."

"Not going down there like a common criminal." Mary scowled.

The officer shook his head. "I can drive you or you can drive yourself. Either way, you need to talk with chief, today."

Mary huffed. "I knew that woman would be trouble. But Father Joe wouldn't listen to me. I'll take my own car."

Mary slammed the door.

Mary passed Walter on the steps of the police station. As their eyes met, he smiled, but she frowned. Pushing the door open, Mary sighed. She ignored the men at the front desk and steamed down the hallway. Not bothering to knock, Mary bolted through the door.

"You needed to see me?" she asked. "Again?"

"Ms. Mead," the chief said, pointing to a chair. "Please sit."

Mary sat down so hard that the legs screeched, leaving deep marks on the polished wooden floor. Officer Raines held back a chuckle.

"Ms. Mead, with Father Joe still in a coma, you're in charge of the parish."

"Told you such last night." Mary crossed her arms. "Father Joe asked me to handle things while he was away. We hold a prayer every evening for his recovery. Maybe you should come. Say a few words."

Chief ignored her invitation and opened a file folder. "Who do you report to?"

"The diocese. In Caribou."

"Name?"

"Of the diocese?"

"No. Who's your point of contact?"

"Bishop Lansing. Mostly, I speak with his secretary, Magdalene Oquoque. We call her Mrs. O. The bishop's a busy man."

"What do Elders Matthew, Mark, Luke and John do for the church? And what are their full names?"

"They're volunteers. Matthew Rays oversees the church maintenance. Mark Shafer is our groundskeeper. Luke Warner oversees various small duties, and John Leland helps out wherever needed." She stared at chief. "John's been in Boston from the start watching over Father Joe."

Chief glanced down at his notes and frowned. "The Caribou Diocese has agreed to sell the Home. To the university?"

"Yes. After the last resident has moved on to heaven."

"The church is to receive about ten million for the property?"

Mary's eyes narrowed. Taking in a deep breath, she let it out slowly. "Was not privy to that info."

"Only one resident left alive?"

Mary's mind pulled in Eliza's funny smile. Would she be next on Ms. Pantera's list? "Yes, there's one left."

"Eliza Finney?"

"Yes, Eliza Finney."

He scribbled something in the folder.

"Chief Bertrand," Mary said, glaring at him, "you're not implying that the church had anything to do with the deaths?"

"From what I read, the church has the most to gain. That is, once the last resident has, how did you put it, moved on to heaven."

Mary looked away.

"Thank you for your time, Ms. Mead." Chief closed his folder.

Mary stared at the two men.

"You're free to go." Chief motioned for her to leave.

"Something I need to say."

"And what is that?" Chief asked.

"You need to take a closer look at Angie Pantera."

"Why is that?"

"That divorcee showed up here with barely a penny to her name. Father Joe took her in without a question. Gave her the job as recreational director." Mary snapped her fingers. "Then our residents start dying off, one at a time. And, on top of that"—Mary's voice rose until she was almost screaming—"commissioned her as a Eucharist minister! That's unheard of."

"You're not a fan of Angie Pantera, are you?" He glanced at Officer Raines and grinned. "Thank you, Ms. Mead. We'll be in touch."

"Will I see you in prayer this evening?" she asked, her voice sweet and alluring again.

"Probably not. But I wish the father well."

Mary stood.

"Ms. Mead, if you see or hear anything unusual, we'd appreciate knowing about it."

"Of course, Chief Bertrand. Of course."

Chapter 14

After lunch, Chief stopped by the Home for a second time. Sitting in his cruiser, he stared at the bright red door. The place was definitely huge. Not to mention impressive. Ten million dollars was a lot of money. Especially for a church. Stepping into the lobby, he surveyed the grand staircase leading to the second floor. He could almost taste the wealth that once oozed from this place.

"Something I can help you with, Chief?"

"Ms. Pantera," he said, pulled from his thoughts. "Just the person I wanted to see."

"Have you had lunch yet? I was about to make myself a sandwich. Would you like one?"

"Don't mind if I do." He followed her into the kitchen.

"I just fed our last resident her lunch." Angie pulled a covered bowl from the fridge. "I hope you don't mind chicken salad."

"Love it." Chief sat on a stool.

"Walter's chicken salad is the best."

"Who runs this place?"

"On a daily basis?"

He nodded.

"Nurse Jakie. I believe you talked to her last night."

He nodded again.

"She cares for the residents, mostly." Angie placed a plate in front of him. "Then there's Ms. Fettore."

"Ms. Fettore?"

"Our part-time administrator. She's only temporary."

"Part-time?"

"Tuesdays and Thursdays." Angie placed a sandwich on his empty plate. "Didn't come in this past Thursday, though. I think the weather scared her off."

"How can I get in touch with Ms. Fettore?"

Angie shrugged. "She comes and goes on her own schedule. Assigned by the Caribou Diocese." Angie placed her plate next to Chief's and sat. "Why?"

He shook his head and took a bite. "What brought you to Birdsong?"

"Divorce. Wanted a start fresh."

"Ah, yes, divorce. Been there, done that." He took another bite. "Why Birdsong?"

She smiled. "Serendipity."

"Serendipity?"

"I made a wish. A feather selected Birdsong." She laughed. "A place I never heard of."

Finishing off his sandwich, he pushed his plate to the center of the counter. "That was very good, thank you."

"You're welcome." Angie stood and placed both plates into the sink.

"What do you do here besides grant wishes?"

Angie giggled. "Father Joe hired me to be the recreational director. 'Make it your own,' he said. So, I did. He also asked me to distribute Holy Communion three times a week. He can't do it if he's not here."

"No, I guess not. How are you able to distribute Holy Communion if you're a divorcee? Isn't divorce frowned upon by the Church?"

"Father said the Church was more forgiving these days. I made confession and he commissioned me. Are you Catholic?"

"Born and raised."

"Have you attended any of Father Joe's prayer services?" Angie scooted her stool a little closer.

"Don't do church anymore."

"Sorry?"

"Left the military hating God."

"Oh, why?"

"Desert Storm. Made me question if there even was a God. And if there was, why such annihilation?"

"You carry a lot of anger with you."

"Unfortunately." Chief finished off his water. Handing Angie the empty glass, he smiled. "Tell me about these wishes."

"Just a fun game. Once a week I pull a name or wish from the treasure box. Then I grant it. Started with the dandelions. What a show that was."

"Show?"

Angie sighed. "This is going to sound a little weird." She smiled. "But as each resident made their wish and blew on the huge dandelions . . . I've never seen anything like it. These things were huge. Bought them from the floral shop in town. Once I got them here, the puffs took on a life of their own. When the residents blew on them, the little seeds flew all around us." Angie waved her arms in the air. "Those flowers teased us and their seeds grew in numbers."

"Grew in numbers?"

"It started with a few hundred seeds. But after they got into the air, they became thousands. Then they swarmed around and around the room. Reminded me of a flock of birds."

Chief chuckled.

"Ronnie, the store owner, said that the flowers were grown by monks from the Andes Mountains. She said they had special spiritual and magical powers."

"Magical powers?"

"I believe her."

He shook his head.

"It was strange. I would never have believed it if I didn't see it with my own eyes. The residents got a big kick out of it. Ms. Fettore didn't. That was also her first day here."

"Anyone else see these seeds flock around the room?"

"Eliza, and I think Jakie did. They fell when Ms. Fettore came into the room."

"Fell?"

"Yes. When Ms. Fettore yelled at us about the mess, the seeds just fell. Covered the floor just as if it was snowing."

"Well, that *is* quite a story. Thank you for your time. And thank you for lunch." Walking toward the back door, he added, "No more wish-granting. Understood? At least until I can get a handle on all of this."

Angie frowned. "What about Eliza? It'll break her heart."

"Too many deaths. Don't feel comfortable about it. You're not leaving town anytime soon, are you?"

"Wasn't planning on it."

After work, Officer Raines stopped into the Every Day Is an Occasion floral shop. Maybe he'd buy his wife some flowers. A young woman with pink hair was writing something on a display board.

"Are you Ronnie?" he asked.

"Who wants to know?"

"You sold some dandelions to Angie up at the Home?"

"Yes. She bought a few. They were sent here by accident. I was afraid they'd go bad."

"Do you have any left? I hear that they're magical. Wanted some for my wife."

"Sorry, sold out." She giggled. "I have to do a lot of self-promoting to make a living in this town. Who's going to buy dandelions unless you embellish a little? Arrest me. I'm guilty of false advertising."

"Fine, I'll take a dozen roses instead."

"I'll throw in a professional discount just for you."

As he opened his cruiser's door, Ronnie dragged the display board outside.

SATURDAY & SUNDAY SPECIALS
MAGICAL FLOWERS
DISCOUNTS GALORE
PROMISED TO MAKE SOMEONE'S DAY SPECIAL

Officer Raines had said that all the questions were just routine. With four people dying on the same night, everyone was a suspect. As Jakie and Michael took their seats, Chief opened his file. Shifting in her chair, Jakie stared at him.

"Ms. Sterling, twenty years ago you worked for Boston General, correct?"

Jakie nodded.

"As a floor nurse?"

Jakie nodded, again.

"You and four others were questioned about the unexpected deaths of five elderly patients."

"I thought those records were sealed," she said.

Michael stared at his mother.

"You can't seal a murder investigation," Chief replied.

Jakie tightened her grip on Michael's hand. "The media and protestors chased my son home from school. He was only ten then. Scared the *bejesus* out of him." Jakie's stomach tightened as her fear grew. "The state found no evidence against me or the other nurses. Ruling came back as natural causes."

Chief glanced down at the open folder again. "I'm aware that the case was dropped. However, with these recent deaths, we may want to take a closer look."

Jakie jumped from her seat. Slapping her hand on his desk, she winced. Taking in a deep breath, she belted, "My residents died of natural causes. They were in their nineties. People die of old age all the time. We don't live forever."

"You might want to consult a lawyer before saying anything else."

"Why does my mother need an attorney?" Michael stood and grabbed his mother by the arm. "She didn't do anything wrong."

"Let me handle this, Michael." Jakie's voice quivered. "Please."

Standing, Chief closed the folder. "You're free to leave . . . for now. But do not leave town until our investigation is over."

"I'm not leaving town," Jakie replied. "I have no reason to."

Stepping into sunlight, Jakie cried inside her son's arms.

"He's an ass," Michael said, wrapping his arms around his mother. "He can't do this to you. He has nothing on you."

Jakie glanced up at her son. "I need to tell you something."

"You didn't kill those people, did you?"

"Of course not. You know me better than that."

"Get into the car," Michael said. "It's cold."

Jakie pulled a tissue from her purse. As her son started the engine, she smiled. "I wanted to shelter you and Olivia for as long as I could."

"Shelter us? From what?"

"I have cancer. The doctor said there's nothing more they can do."

Michael glared at her. "What are you talking about? You're fine."

"No, I'm not. Doctor Bolton said I have very little time left. I've been thinking about quitting. Been thinking about coming home to you and the family."

"Of course," Michael replied. "Yes, of course."

Michael leaned over and hugged his mother. As he cried on her shoulder, Jakie rubbed the back of his head just as she did when he was a little boy.

"I'm at peace with this. Your father loved me with all his heart, and you're the best son a mother could want."

Michael pulled away. "I knew something was wrong. You've lost so much weight. And you're always so tired."

"We don't live forever," Jakie replied. "Let's call and tell my beautiful grandbabies I'm coming home."

"You gonna finish that?" Eliza pointed to Angie's uneaten sandwich. Angie pushed it over to her. "It's yours."

"Thanks." Eliza giggled.

Angie watched as Eliza took one bite after another. What was going on with her? The woman was smiling and happy as a clam. She walked with a bounce. No grieving, not even a tear. Maybe she was in shock.

"Don't be so sad," Eliza said, finishing off the sandwich.

"They're gone." Angie sighed. "I can't help but be sad. The police are investigating their deaths because they all died at the same time. That isn't normal."

"Piff." Eliza waved her hand in the air. "What's so strange about four old people dying?" She leaned over and motioned for Angie to come a little closer. Eliza whispered, "They died with a smile on their face. That means their wish was granted."

"Eliza." Angie sat back in her chair. "A wish is only a wish. These people are dead."

"But they died in peace." Eliza laughed. "And Adelaide and Trudy's secret. Who'd have known they were a couple? They kept it a secret for so long. Too long, as far as I'm concerned."

Angie rubbed her nose. "I keep meaning to ask about the perfume you wear. What's the name?"

"Obsession. I had just a little left. I dropped the bottle last night. It broke. Was saving it for Lucy. For when you grant my wish. It was her favorite, ya know."

"About your wish . . ."

"Bishop Lansing's office. Mrs. O speaking."

"This is Officer Raines from the Birdsong Police Department. Is Ms. Fettore available? She didn't show up at the Home this past Thursday." The sound of shuffling paper filled his ear. "Hello?"

"Come by my office tomorrow. Ms. Fettore broke her leg. I'll have to find her phone number for you."

"I'll call you tomorrow morning."

"No," Mrs. O replied. "I prefer you to just come by."

The phone fell silent.

The following morning, Officer Raines entered Bishop Lansing's office. Instead of a woman greeting him, a priest sat at the front desk holding a phone to his ear. Shuffling papers across the desk, he tapped his keyboard.

"I'll get back to you," he said, hanging up. "Sorry, have a hell of a problem here. How can I help you?"

"Mrs. O? I spoke with her yesterday regarding the administrator for the Home of the Little Flower. A Ms. Fettore. I'm here for her contact information."

"I'm sorry. She's no longer with us."

"Who? The administrator, Ms. Fettore?"

"No," the priest chuckled. "Mrs. O."

"She quit?"

"Not exactly. Mrs. O's experiencing some memory problems and confusion. I'm Monsignor Gabinez, the bishop's assistant."

Officer Raines nodded. "Sorry to hear that."

Monsignor Gabinez looked down at the cluttered desk. "Mrs. O worked yesterday. Left late and didn't return home. Her friend called the police, and when they found her she kept talking about a journal she misplaced. She's at the Caribou Medical Center. Probably dementia or something."

"I must speak to Ms. Fettore. Can you provide me with a phone number?"

"Don't know anybody by that name." The office phone rang. "Give me a second. Let me take this call."

Officer Raines listened to the one-sided conversation. After hanging up, the priest scribbled on a notepad. Handing it to Officer Raines, he nodded.

Officer Raines read over the scribbled note. It included a phone number and address but no name.

"Thank you," Officer Raines whispered.

Answering the ringing phone, Monsignor Gabinez gave him a thumbs-up.

Officer Raines called the number and received a "no longer in service" recording. Driving to the address, he knocked on the door. A woman with crutches and a cast covering her right thigh opened the door.

"Ms. Fettore?" Officer Raines asked.

"Who?"

Mary missed Father Joe. Sitting in the front pew, she waited for the rosary service to start. Father Joe was the lifeblood of the chapel. Mary frowned as she focused on the statue of St. Therese. With a full heart and heavy soul, she begged for help.

"Please. Please help us. We need Father Joe to return."

Mary glanced around the chapel. A good turnout tonight. The place was full. Angie sat quietly in the back. Mary frowned. That woman was a curse. Seven residents dead, and the police investigating everyone, including her.

"Welcome and thank you for coming to pray for our beloved Father Joe. Let's begin."

ELIZA FINNEY
MY WISH IS TO TAKE A BUBBLE BATH WITH LUCY!

Angie sat in the Home's dining room rereading the wish. Cupping her hand to her face, she sighed. Chief said no more wish-grantings. *Who is he to order me around, anyway?* Not granting the last wish wasn't fair to Eliza. Maybe she could keep it a secret. Eliza swore she'd not say a word to anyone. She even crossed her heart and hoped to die.

Since she was spending the evening with her family, Jakie would be back late. Ms. Fettore was a no-show, again.

"Hi, Angie, what ya doing?"

Angie smiled at Eliza. "Nothing much."

"My wish. You have my card. Oh, thank you for granting my wish. Just like you promised." Eliza smiled.

"Eliza, I can't—"

"Thirteen years ago I met her," Eliza said. "A very special cat. Injured and abused. Was part of a struggling circus." Eliza sat in the chair across from Angie. "She needed me. Lucy was a superstar. People came from all over just to watch her jump into a tub with bubbles." Eliza laughed. "How she loved Obsession perfume. I'd spray it on her tongue and she'd lap it up." Eliza stuck out her tongue and pretended to spray perfume on it.

"Lucy is who, exactly?" Angie asked.

"My tiger. Who else? The most beautiful cat in the world."

Angie frowned. "You do realize that I cannot grant a bubble bath with a real tiger. We might be able to pretend."

"Of course. I understand." Eliza giggled. "Oh, Lucy. We'll be together again, soon."

Needing toiletries for her trip to Boston, Mary drove toward the pharmacy, passing Officer Raines sitting in his police car. *The man is a menace.* She pulled into an empty spot and stepped into the freezing rain. As she ran into the store, Angie Pantera stepped out holding a large paper bag.

At the counter, Mary looked around as if searching for something. "That woman who was just here. Do you have any more of what she bought?"

The girl pointed to a colorful display. "It's on sale 'til the end of the week."

Mary nodded.

After paying for her items, Mary stepped outside. Officer Raines was still in his car. Stepping up to the window, Mary knocked three times.

"You wanted to know if I noticed anything unusual." Mary smirked.

Angie used the excuse of paying Tom in order to borrow Jakie's car. At the pharmacy, Angie picked up a medium-sized stuffed tiger that was on sale for five dollars. The only Obsession perfume available set her back fifty dollars. Then she had to buy a three-pound sirloin steak. Eliza demanded it for her tiger. That cost fifteen and thankfully was on bulk sale. Angie didn't understand why a raw steak. She dared not ask Walter for it. That would have raised suspicion.

The wish-grantings amounted to $275, and she held no hope of a full reimbursement. Practically a week's pay.

After three trips to the kitchen carrying a large cooking pot, the bubbles were at the rim of the galvanized tub she found in the closet. Taking the stuffed tiger, she sat it next to the plate with the raw steak. Angie laughed. *Now, where to put the bottle of perfume?* She briefly wondered what would happen if someone walked in on them. Would she be arrested? Of course not. It wasn't illegal to grant a wish—even if that police chief ordered her not to go through with it.

As she stepped out of the dining room, her stomach tightened. She still had time to back out. But could she tell Eliza that she couldn't go through with it? No, she couldn't. Angie's heart pounded as she thought of Rose, Teddy, Spanks, Karun, Peter, Adelaide, and Trudy. Their rooms remained locked by order of the police chief.

Angie knocked on room number ten. Eliza opened the door dressed in a cream-colored, silk nightgown. Giddy with excitement, she bounced on her toes.

"This was Sherry's." Eliza twirled around, showing off the garment. "Been saving it. This was hers, too." Eliza turned her head to show off the silver comb holding back her whitish blonde hair.

"I guess I do owe you this wish," Angie whispered. "You look beautiful. Can you please put on a sweater or something? Don't need you to catch a cold."

"Silly," Eliza said, darting from her room. "I'm not cold."

Angie chased Eliza down the hallway and into the dining room. At the sight of the bubbles, Eliza screamed.

"Perfect. Just perfect!"

Sitting down to dinner, Angie served Walter's meatloaf dinner. Every few seconds, Angie stopped eating to stare at Eliza. *Will she last through dinner?*

"I catered to seventy-five cats once. The reserve survived entirely on donations." Eliza spoke with her mouth full. "We had lions, tigers, jaguars, panthers, leopards, cougars. Big cats from circuses, TV shows, and movies. Sometimes they came from people who bought them believing they'd make perfect pets. Can you believe that? A lion for a pet?"

"You weren't afraid of 'em?" Angie sipped on her tea.

Eliza shook her head. "Afraid of such beautiful creatures? No way. I'd never turn my back on 'em, though. Especially at feeding time. Nah, I wouldn't change my time with them for anything." Eliza pulled up her sleeve, showing off a long scar. "Comes with the territory."

"That from Lucy?"

Eliza shook her head. "Lucy loved me like I was her momma. I'd fill her tub with water and bubbles. Tourists loved to watch Lucy jumping in and trying to eat 'em. One day I discovered she loved this perfume. A woman gave it to me as a gift. If I sprayed the perfume into the air, Lucy would lunge up like it was a rain shower." Eliza laughed. "She would lick me on my face as if she was thanking me. Real smart cat that Lucy was. Always looked forward to her bubble baths and the perfume."

"Since we're done with dinner, would you like to dunk the stuffed tiger into the bubbles in memory of Lucy?"

"Oh yes. Let me spray some perfume on her first."

As Eliza sprayed the stuffed tiger, a noise from the lobby echoed through the dining room.

"Did you hear that?" Angie's stomach churned.

"Hear what?" Eliza asked, concentrating on the stuffed animal.

Staring out the window, Angie saw nothing. The strange noise again echoed through the room.

"Stay put. I'll be right back." Angie pushed open the double doors and peered out. "I keep hearing a strange noise."

Eliza held the stuffed tiger over the bubbles and grinned.

Walking toward the closed red door, Angie screamed at the same time as Eliza.

Officer Raines sat in his cruiser just outside the Home. Only Angie Pantera and Eliza Finney would be here tonight. He still had questions after talking to the woman with the broken leg. Obvious someone had their information crossed. If it wasn't the woman with the broken leg, then who was working as the part-time administrator? The woman said that she was hired by Mrs. O, but that she never started work. She broke her leg.

Calling Mrs. O's friend didn't help to solve the mystery, either. It seemed that Mrs. O didn't even know who Mrs. O was, let alone who Ms. Fettore was supposed to be. After sharing with the chief what Mary told him about the stuffed animal and perfume from the pharmacy, he was assigned to keep tabs on Ms. Pantera's whereabouts.

So far, the Home was nothing but quiet. No reason to go inside. How would he start the conversation? Ms. Pantera, what're you doing with that stuffed tiger? Nah, better to just sit it out and wait. Maybe tomorrow he'd ask Jakie Sterling about Ms. Fettore. Maybe tomorrow he could connect more of the dots. As for now, he would just sit and wait.

"Ms. Fettore?" Angie glared at her. "What are you doing here so late?"

Ms. Fettore wore her usual dark suit with her hair pulled back, looking stern as ever.

"Good evening, Ms. Pantera."

"Good evening to you. You're working tonight instead of in the morning?"

"Yes. After tonight, I'll be leaving the Home for good."

"You mean because of the deaths?"

"No need to worry, Ms. Pantera. They are home with Our Father."

"Okay?" Angie's mind whirled. It wasn't right for this woman to be here so late. Taking several steps backwards, Angie whispered, "I should get back to Eliza. We're having dinner now."

"Yes. Eliza's wish is being granted, isn't it? Yes, it is time. I lost track."

Angie's heart pounded as she stared at the woman. *What game is she playing now?*

"Ms. Pantera? His love is greater than all. Is it not magic when we are within His love? Miracles, Ms. Pantera. Miracles are real and an extension of His love for us. Have faith. Do not waver. All will be divine. All will be shown."

Angie took a few more steps back. "What are you talking about?" Obviously, this woman was losing her mind.

"Isn't that what you wished for, Ms. Pantera?"

"What I wished for?" Angie repeated. "I didn't wish for anything."

Ms. Fettore grinned. "'Take my little rhyme. Promise not to change my mind. But do change my life, to make it again divine.'" Staring at Angie as if she was looking right through her, she added, "'Please.'"

Angie was flabbergasted. "How could you possibly know about that? I never told anyone about that."

"Will you give Father Joe a message for me?"

Angie nodded.

"Please let him know that they will come. That *they* will build it."

Ms. Fettore turned and walked to the red door and stepped outside.

"I don't understand," Angie said, stepping forward.

Turning around, Ms. Fettore replied, "You will." She closed the door behind her.

"Ms. Fettore!" Angie pulled open the door and ran outside. "Ms. Fettore, wait!"

As a stormy wind whipped across the yard, Walter's orange cat jumped out from behind the burlap wraps, hissing several times before darting through the red door.

"Ah, man," Angie yelled out. "Ms. Fettore, wait!"

Ms. Fettore was nowhere in sight. The yard was empty.

"Ms. Fettore?" Angie yelled. "Ms. Fettore, where are you?"

Darting around the mansion, Angie bounced against something soft before landing hard on the frozen driveway, staring up at Officer Raines.

"Lucy!" Eliza screamed. "I knew you'd come back to me."

Eliza stood on the ladder where she always stood when spraying Obsession on Lucy's tongue. But this time, no wire cages. Just the growing bubbles overflowing the galvanized tub. A 600-pound Siberian tiger sat in front of Eliza. The tiger closed her yellowish eyes and greeted Eliza with a chuffing sound. Her long, sandpapery tongue scrapped against Eliza's cheek.

Rubbing the large cat under her neck, Eliza's heart warmed. "You're my girl. Aren't you, Lucy? I know your stripes by heart." Eliza held out the steak. "I have a snack for you."

Lucy devoured the meat in only a few bites.

Eliza stood at the top of the tank. "Make room for me, Lucy. I'm coming in."

The bubbles splashed over the sides as Eliza jumped in to play with Lucy.

"Ms. Pantera," Officer Raines asked, hovering over her. "What's going on?"

Angie reached out her hand. "I'm, I'm—"

Officer Raines pulled her up. "You're what?"

"I'm looking for Ms. Fettore. She was just here a second ago."

"I've been here all evening. No one left the Home except for you."

"She was just here. I swear."

"It's cold. Let's go inside. Where's Eliza Finney?"

"In the dining room. I heard a noise in the lobby. Ms. Fettore was just standing there. She was acting very weird."

Sitting on Lucy's back, Eliza plowed through the bubbles.

"What a good girl you are."

Lucy let out a gentle *roar*. Eliza jumped off Lucy and brushed off the bubbles. Lucy jumped up, placing her paws on Eliza's shoulders. Towering over her, she roared again.

"Shhh," Eliza cooed. "We don't want Angie to spoil our fun."

Jumping out of the tub, Lucy shook, and the bubbles rained around Eliza. Eliza laughed.

"It's time to rest, Lucy."

Eliza punched the button and the dining room doors sprang open. Together, Eliza and Lucy walked into the lobby. Eliza placed her hand on Lucy's neck, leading her to her room. Room number ten. Left behind on the marble floor were two sets of soapy footprints—one human and one animal.

Chapter 15

Angie ran into the dining room with Officer Raines close behind. Everything was as she had left it—the table set for two with the soapy galvanized tub and the perfume bottle. But Eliza and the stuffed tiger were nowhere in sight.

"Eliza probably went to her room," Angie said, holding her stomach.

"Take me there," Officer Raines ordered.

Silence filled the hallway. Angie stopped and knocked.

No answer.

Opening the door, Angie saw Eliza curled up with her stuffed tiger on her bed, smiling. Her nightgown was soaking wet.

"She's sleeping," Angie whispered. "Must of gotten tired and came to bed."

"She's wet. And what's that she's holding?"

"A stuffed tiger."

"No. In her hand."

Angie took the note. Smiling she handed it to the officer.

Thank you Angie! For granting my wish with Lucy!! You are the best Rec person The Home of the Little Flower ever had!!! Eliza

Officer Raines picked up Eliza's hand. Staring at Angie, his eyes narrowed and he frowned.

"What's wrong?"

"No pulse," he said. "I believe that Eliza Finney has died."

"What? No!"

"I'm sorry, Angie, but you give me no choice." Officer Raines pulled out his handcuffs. "You're under arrest."

"Arrest for what?"

"The murder of Eliza Finney."

Angie's tears fell. "I didn't murder Eliza. I—"

"You have the right to remain silent . . ."

Something moved within the shadows as Officer Raines explained her rights. It looked like a large cat's paw.

"What's that?" Angie screamed. "Look over there. I saw something."

Officer Raines ignored her. Pushing her down the hallway, he radioed the station asking for backup.

"There, please. Look," Angie begged.

Officer Raines stopped walking and turned around. No shadow, nothing.

Sitting in the back of the cruiser and staring up at the red door, Angie cried. Something in the shadows grabbed her attention. Straining to see through the darkness, Angie could have sworn that the burlap covers over the bushes were moving.

She arrived at the police station without a word exchanged and was immediately placed in a jail cell. Angie pulled the cell's blanket closer around her shoulders. Staring at the iron bars, she cried. Yesterday, Eliza was in good health and looking forward to her wish. And now, just twenty-four hours later, she was dead. Grateful that she'd given Eliza Holy Communion before breakfast yesterday, Angie leaned against the pillow. *Who can I call? Who would take the time to help me now?* Maybe she'd call Jakie again. Maybe this time she'd answer.

Chief sat at the far end of the Rose Petals bar and sipped on a cold beer. Off duty but still in uniform, he dug into his dinner of short ribs. His cellphone buzzed. *Officer Raines.*

"You arrested her? Damn, I told her not to grant wishes . . . That's it, then. She was the last." After taking another bite, he wiped his hands. "On my way." Chief pointed at the bartender, then down at his plate. "Need this to go."

Seated a few stools from the chief, Tom Jared put two and two together. Angie was the only person granting wishes these days. He'd heard the rumors. Four people on the same night. A bit strange. Then again, they were all in their nineties. Would someone connect him to the deaths since he helped out with the Rolls Royce? Ever since Angie arrived in town, strange things were happening.

"Nancy?" he said. "Gotta go."

Tom pushed away from the bar, not looking forward to another late night at the garage. Shaking his head, he chuckled.

After hanging up with the chief, Officer Raines dialed Jakie and a man answered. "May I help you?"

"This is Officer Raines. I need to speak with Jakie Sterling."

"She's resting. I'll let her know you called."

The medical examiner's van pulled away with Eliza's body tucked inside. Staring up at the full moon, Chief knew there was a serious problem. Something was going on around here, but without good evidence, he had no case. No one to charge. Although Eliza Finney's circumstances looked to not be normal, the medical examiner determined, once again, death by natural causes. Until all the bodies were autopsied, there was no proof of foul play.

If these were indeed murders, he had five suspects—Mary Mead, Nurse Jakie, Angie Pantera, Walter Heron, and the missing administrator, Ms. Fettore. Mary was on her way to Boston to see Father Joe, and Nurse

Jakie was with her family. Angie was in a holding cell for the night, and Walter was at his restaurant. But where was the mysterious Ms. Fettore?

Pulling away from the Home, Chief listened as the town's clock struck the first midnight bell.

With the light of dawn, Walter boxed up the day's meals for Eliza, Jakie, and Angie. His hands were full when his cellphone buzzed from his pants. Sitting the boxes back on the counter, he stared at the number. It was the police station.

"Hello? . . . I understand."

Placing the food back into the refrigerator, he sighed. It was time to talk to Nancy. He grabbed a bottle of water and took a swig as he walked into the main part of the restaurant. Instead of the water effortlessly sliding down his throat, he gagged and spit it out, shocked at the sight before him.

Outside his French doors, the roses on the snowy patio were in full bloom. Below their flowered branches, their burlap coats lay open as if on display. Walter stepped outside.

"It's February. How in the world?"

Walter snapped several pictures with his cell, messaged them to his wife and then called her.

"Mornin', my love." He laughed. "You're not going to believe what I'm looking at. Our roses are in full bloom."

"What are you talking about?" Nancy asked.

"I'm going to rent a dozen heaters 'cuz I know people will want to sit out here for this one. It's unbelievable. February. February and we have roses!"

Minutes later, Elder Luke would have the same reaction. Sylvia, his wife, picked up her cup of English tea. Sitting down at her breakfast nook, she glanced out at her snowy backyard. Her tea fell into her lap as she stared at the thicket of red roses in full bloom. Each of the burlap coats had been blown off and were now lying off to one side.

"Luke? Luke? Get down here!" she yelled. "You won't believe this."

Elder Luke stood next to his wife and stared out at the colorful sight. "Do you think they're in bloom at the Home, too?"

Astonishment quickly rippled over the tiny town in north-central Maine as the townsfolk awoke.

Jakie opened her eyes. Her young granddaughters stood at the foot of her bed. They were jumping up and down and screaming.

"Grandma!" the oldest one yelled out. "Grandma, wake up. Wake up. The Rose Fairy came last night."

Pulling on her bathrobe, Jakie stood behind the excited girls and looked out the bedroom window. The ground, covered in a blanket of fresh snow, glistened in the morning sunlight.

"Oh my." Jakie laughed. "The Rose Fairy did come to Birdsong last night."

"Can we make a wish now?" the oldest one asked. "Can we please?"

"Yes, we can make a wish now," Jakie replied, hugging them. "But don't tell anyone. Or our wishes won't come true."

Elder John shivered as his dogs darted into the freezing sunlight to do their morning business. Instead of a blanket of pure white snow, his backyard was filled with colorful flowers.

"Oh my God." Looking up at the clear blue sky, he made the sign of the cross. "What a signal, my Lord. Father Joe *will* definitely come home to us now."

Mary Mead, replacing Elder John, had left right after prayer service to drive to Boston to be with Father Joe in the morning. The trip's only excitement occurred on her way out of Birdsong. She had pulled over to let Officer Raines by in his police car with blue lights flashing. *No doubt he caught another lowlife*, she thought.

Arriving at St. Aloysius Rectory before midnight, she heard a voice from the shadows of the living room.

"Mary Mead!"

Gasping, Mary took a step backwards. "You frightened me, Father."

Father Francis stepped out of the darkness. Reaching over, he flipped on the overhead lights. "Put your bags down. We need to talk."

Mary had prepared for this moment, but, raising her hand, she shook her head. "No. It's only been a few weeks. I will not hear this."

"We must be prepared," Father Francis said, stepping a little closer. "We are Father Joe's only family."

"We've been praying for him. He just needs a little more time."

"I won't allow this to go on much longer," he said. "Father Joe wouldn't want it this way. Kept alive by a machine is not living, Mary."

Tossing and turning all night, Mary decided to arrive at the hospital at dawn.

Mary peered around the hospital room's door. Her heart pounded as she stepped into Father Joe's room. Wires and tubes ran from his body to various machines and back again. Feeling dizzy, she stepped softly up to his bed.

"You're looking good, Father." Mary wiped away a tear. "Better than I expected." Allowing her eyes to trail along the valleys and ridges of the blanket, her heart broke for the critically ill man she held so dear to her heart. "You're down a few pounds. Nothing you can't regain if you put your mind to it."

Grabbing the closest chair, Mary pushed it to the bed. Sitting down, she sighed.

"I need to tell you everything that's happened." Mary rubbed her hands together. "You know about Spanks and Rose." She rubbed her eyes with the backs of her hands. "I guess I'll just tell you everything."

The clock ticking away beside his bed, Mary shared her stories with Father Joe. Just as she mentioned Eliza's name, the machines beeped. She glanced up and watched as the monitors sprang to life.

"Father?" Mary whispered.

A nurse came to Father Joe. As she checked his connections, Mary's heart pounded.

"What's happening?"

"Sometimes there's a glitch," the nurse said, walking away.

"Okay, back to Eliza," Mary said as her cellphone rang. "Yes, John."

"Have you heard the mornin' news?"

"What news?"

"Turn on the TV, Mary," John yelled. "We've gone national."

"What do you mean, we've gone national? What are you talking about?"

"It's winter here."

"Tell me something I don't know."

"You don't understand. The roses. The roses are in bloom. And only here. Only here in Birdsong. People are postin' pictures everywhere. A TV crew from Boston just arrived. The summer roses have bloomed, Mary." John paused, breathing heavily. "Turn on the TV. See for yourself. I think it's a sign."

Mary searched the nightstand for the remote. Finding it in a drawer, she clicked the *on* button.

"And there's something else I need to tell ya. Eliza Finney passed away last night. They've detained Angie. Not sure why."

"Angie was arrested? I knew it. I knew it. I saw Officer Raines whiz by me with lights flashing. Must've had the culprit. Finally caught her in the act. Poor Eliza." Mary yelled so loudly that the lines on Father Joe's machines jumped. "And she killed the others. I knew we shouldn't have hired her."

Mary listened as the newscaster stood in the parking lot of the Home, pointing to the blooming roses. Mary stepped closer to the TV with her back turned to the bed. She didn't know what to concentrate on: the flowers or Angie sitting in a jail cell. Mary smiled. With the plan complete, she could finally rest.

The news jumped to another reporter standing in the garden of the Rose Petals restaurant. Walter was giving the reporter a tour.

". . . this is LM Neuhouse reporting live from Birdsong, Maine . . ."

"Jesus, Mary, and Joseph!" Father Joe's voice blared through the room. "What's all this crap that's on me?"

Twirling around, Mary lost her balance. The controller flew across the room, bouncing twice before hitting the wall. The batteries rolled under Father Joe's bed as the controller glided to a stop under the nightstand.

"Father Joe?" Mary whispered.

Father Joe flailed as if trying to sit up.

"Nurse!" Mary yelled from the door. "Nurse, come quick!" Mary ran back to the bed. Leaning over, she glared at Father Joe. "You've decided to come back to us?"

"What are you talking about? And what are you doing here? Where's John?" Father Joe stared up at her. "I had some good tiles. And I want my points. Where's my Scrabble board?"

"You remember that?" Mary asked.

"Why wouldn't I remember it?"

"You've been out for a couple weeks." Grabbing a tissue, Mary blew her nose.

"I have a terrible headache." Father Joe touched the bandages that covered his head. "What's that sound?"

"Well, look who finally decided to wake up," the arriving nurse said, inspecting the machines. "How are you feeling?"

"He said his head hurts," Mary replied.

"Normal," the nurse said. "I'll call the doctor."

"Did you say something about Angie being arrested?" Father Joe asked. "That she killed someone?"

"Yes, the local police arrested her for Eliza's murder. She probably killed the others, too."

"Others?"

"Yes. All the residents have gone on to heaven."

"I need to get back to Birdsong." Father Joe tried to push himself up.

"Father, you mustn't move," Mary said, pushing Father Joe back onto the pillow. "Wait for the doctor."

"Angie Pantera couldn't hurt a fly. I would sooner think *you* had something to do with their dying."

Mary frowned. "What?"

"For the good of the church, your heart's in survival mode."

A doctor and nurse stepped in. Reading over Father Joe's chart, the doctor smiled. "Feeling better, Father Joe?"

Drawn back to the local news, Mary watched as the reporters talked to different people she knew.

"Call Tom Jared," Father Joe barked. "Tell him what I told you."

Mary watched as a female reporter talked with the pharmacist. Grabbing her cellphone, Mary's eyes remained glued to the broadcast, where colorful roses of all shades stood out against the blanket of white snow.

"Oh my," Mary said. "It *is* a sign, Father. A real sign."

Tom wiped his hands. Grabbing his cell, he glanced at the name—Mary Mead.

"Tom? Good news!" Mary stated. "Father Joe woke up, and he has asked for a favor."

"Thank goodness he's all right. Whatever he needs." Tom glanced around his full garage. His work was stacking up. "Always been there for me. So, I'm there for him."

Listening to Mary's directions, Tom picked up the keys to Angie's silver Honda. He finished it just last night. Clicking off his phone, he glanced out the dingy shop's window. The view reminded him of a town fair; the streets were packed with strangers.

Tossing the keys into the air several times, Tom walked to the police station. People were running up and down the street, yelling out different things. One man screamed that it was a sign of the end times. Another was trying to convince everyone that they were being invaded by aliens. At one point, Tom thought he saw a news truck, but what would the national news be doing in Birdsong? As he approached the front desk, the man in uniform there barked out orders.

"Chief wants everybody on duty. Everybody!" The officer pointed to several men leaning against a wall. "That means you. With the media streaming in, it's gonna get crowded. Chief doesn't want trouble."

Several officers darted from the lobby. Another officer spoke into a radio. A couple more stepped into the men's room, laughing.

"I need to speak with Chief," Tom said, knocking on the counter.

"He's busy."

"Please. Tell him Father Joe sent me."

"Father Joe's in a coma," the man replied. "Everyone knows that."

"Not any longer," Tom replied. "He directed me to speak to Chief. It's about Angie Pantera."

"Wait a sec," the man said, picking up the phone.

Tom stepped away from the counter and glanced out the window. Two reporters were directing one cameraman to different locations. Tom laughed. Across the street, a woman was yelling at a truck that was blocking her car. Chief was right; it wasn't even noon and the place was going nuts.

"Hey, Tom," the chief said, holding out his hand. "Something wrong with one of our cars?"

"No." Tom shook Chief's hand. "Guess no one told you. Father Joe asked me to come on behalf of Angie Pantera."

"No longer in a coma? Amazing!"

"Woke up about an hour or so ago. Seems to be fine."

Chief smiled. "Glad to hear that."

"Father said Angie wouldn't hurt a fly. He wants to know if you're charging her with anything."

"No. Just detaining her for her own good. Told her no more wish-granting. Wouldn't listen. And now the last resident is dead."

"Respectfully, Chief, don't you think she served her punishment by spending the night here?"

"She's being released now," Chief said, shaking his head. "Mostly, I just wanted to scare her a little. Are you going to wait for her?"

Tom nodded. "I think I should."

"I'll tell her to find you out front."

"Thanks, Chief."

Tom stepped outside. Bumper-to-bumper cars lined the street. This town was definitely getting interesting.

"Tom?" Angie wrapped her arms around his neck. "It's so good to see you. I thought I'd be here forever."

"Can't keep you but overnight without a charge. And granting a wish isn't against the law. At least, not in any book I know of."

"Murder is," she said.

"Did you murder someone?"

Angie shook her head.

"Then they can't keep ya but overnight. Got a present for ya," he said, tossing her keys in the air.

"It's fixed?"

"Yep, come on. I'll show ya."

Angie followed Tom through the crowd of reporters and nosy townsfolk. "I still owe you a lot of money."

"Not worried," Tom replied. "I trust you. Father Joe is worried about you."

"How can he be worried about me? He's in a coma."

"Woke up this morning. First thing he wanted was me to come rescue you."

"Father Joe woke up? That's great."

"Mary called saying Father wanted me to get you out of the clink." He laughed. "But Chief said they were releasing you anyway. Didn't have anything to keep you on."

"I'm so tired and hungry. I just want to go home." Angie jumped behind Tom as a man wearing a suit ran past. "What's going on around here? All this excitement over Eliza?"

"No," Tom replied. "The roses."

"Roses?"

"Yeah," he said, pointing over at the Rose Petals restaurant. "Some scientists in town are yelling about climate change."

"Climate change? Roses?"

"Let's get some breakfast," he said, pulling her into the crowded restaurant. "I see an empty table."

Angie sat. "I could eat a horse."

"Two coffees," Tom said to Nancy. "And two of your morning specials."

"Scrambled good?" Nancy asked.

Tom and Angie nodded.

"You married, Angie?" Tom asked.

Angie shook her head. "Divorced. You?"

"My wife died three years ago. Breast cancer."

Walter had said to seat everyone. After a few hours, Nancy lost count. There were so many coming in just wanting to look at the colorful roses. The heaters would arrive any minute. But their customers refused to wait, demanding to be outside next to the magical flowers. Clearing the snow off the patio was easy, but dragging the tables and chairs out of storage was not. As Walter worked, Nancy watched a reporter and cameraman film a segment.

"Another big story here in Birdsong," the reporter said to her cameraman. "Eight mysterious deaths up at the nursing home. Four on the same night. And . . . they died after being granted a wish."

Angie devoured her breakfast of scrambled eggs. As they talked, she watched the frantic people vying for peeks of the rose bushes.

"A couple of times, I hid from you when you came in." Tom laughed. "Not proud, mind ya. Just so damn behind. Everyone chewing me out these days. After hiring two helpers, finally got caught up."

Angie giggled. "I wondered why you were never there."

"Wish I could have been there for Father Joe more," Tom said. "When my wife was diagnosed with cancer, Father Joe was there for us."

Angie patted his hand.

"After she died, I worked. Sometimes took on more than I should have. It helped to stop my feelings and all."

Angie nodded.

"Don't have kids. Lots of married nieces and nephews. Otherwise, I stay to myself."

Angie studied him. Tom didn't look polished. His messy blonde hair needed a good cut. His hands were calloused and fingernails dirty. Stained coveralls and dirty face, Tom looked like a working man. So unlike her ex-husband, Jay.

"Listen to me, talking about my problems like an idiot." Tom smiled. "Tell me about you."

"Not much to tell. I have twins, Maddie and Kevin. Grown now. I was married for twenty-five years. Thought our love was made in heaven. Turned out to be a big fat lie. Ended up here. Serendipity brought me."

Glancing at his watch, Tom sighed. "Can't believe we've been talking for more than an hour. My guys are probably wondering what happened to me." Tom grabbed the bill and stood up. "Need to get back. You okay?"

Angie nodded.

"Your car's parked near the front. You've got the keys."

"Thanks again, Tom. For everything. I'll drop off the next payment on Friday."

"I'll be there." Tom grinned.

Angie sipped her coffee, watching as Tom paid the bill and walked out the door. With Walter and Nancy so busy, she decided it was time to give up the booth. She joined the people on the patio and stood under a heater.

From the corner of her eye, she spotted a familiar face. Sitting with her son, Michael, Jakie sipped on a steamy cup of something hot. She looked frailer than ever. Angie waved.

"Well, well. Who gave you a get-out-of-jail-free card?" Jakie quipped. "Chief doesn't play games. Still wants to grill me about Ms. Fettore. I

called the station earlier, but you already left. Sorry, about last night."
Jakie glared over at Michael. "*Someone* turned off my cellphone."

Michael stood and nodded to Angie. "I'm going to the restroom."

"You know about Eliza?" Angie asked, sitting down in Michael's chair.

"I heard."

"About Father Joe?" Angie grinned.

"The best news so far. I think I'm up on everything."

"Tom told me Father was worried about me."

"I heard that, too. Did you get your car back?"

"Finally." Angie giggled. "I guess we're both gonna need new jobs."

Jakie frowned. "Just you. I'm retiring." She took a deep breath. "These roses are beautiful, aren't they?"

Angie nodded.

"This is my favorite place to come in the summer. Flowers are early this year."

"Overheard someone say it's climate change," Angie said.

Jakie laughed. "Strange days since you arrived. Those jumbo dandelions and your wish-granting. Then the residents leaving this world with a smile on their face. Eliza's wish was no different. And these blooming roses. Every rose in Birdsong bloomed at the exact same time. All in the middle of winter. Climate change has nothing to do with it. More like a miracle, if you ask me."

Thinking about Ms. Fettore showing up in the lobby last night, Angie frowned.

"Hey," Jakie leaned over and touched Angie's hand. "I don't mean it in a bad way. I think you're the best thing that's happened to this place in a long time."

Angie sighed. "Actually . . . I'm feeling Mary's daggers in me right now."

They both glanced at a reporter and her cameraman walking past.

"They've been filming here all morning. Interviewing anyone who'll give them the time," Jakie huffed. She turned back to Angie. "Somehow, you reignited the faith in me. I thank you for that, my friend."

"I didn't do anything." Angie shrugged. "I just needed a friend and you stepped in."

"There's something about my health I need to tell you," Jakie whispered. As Jakie explained, Angie grabbed hold of her friend and cried.

"Can't wait to tell my wife," Luke said, holding the burlap to his chest at the Home. "Just think, I'm gonna be on TV."

The reporter shook her head. "Who's the recreational director for the old folk's home? I'd like to speak with her. Heard they let her out of jail earlier this morning."

"Her name's Angie Pantera," Luke said, bending to pick up another burlap bag. "Not here right now. Why?"

The reporter stepped closer to the bushes. "Know when she'll be back?"

"Nope." Luke shook his head,

"Heard you had a few deaths recently."

"A few. Heard that too," Luke replied.

"Wanna tell me about them?"

Jakie sat cold and exhausted, her head dipping as if nodding off.

"Come on, Mom. Time to get you home," Michael said. "Haven't you had enough of these roses?"

Michael turned up the heat in his mom's room and tucked her in.

"I'll check on you in a bit. I'm gonna make some soup for later. Get some rest."

When he returned, Jakie didn't move.

"Hey, lazy bones. You gonna sleep all day?"

Straightening her covers, he studied his mother's face. Her large smile made her look peaceful, almost happy.

Chapter 16

Father Joe awoke in the middle of the night in the midst of a shadowy nightmare. With shaking hands, he wiped the beads of sweat from his forehead. It was important that he return to Birdsong—immediately. He had to get to the tabernacle. The nightmare was a warning. Not to mention, there were funerals to attend. It was also important that he speak to Chief personally. If he didn't return this afternoon, something terrible would happen.

His recovery had been inexplicable, as if nothing ever happened to him. No sign of an aneurysm. No sign of a bad knee or the surgery. After telling the nurses where they could put their pain meds, he agreed to attend rehab once back in Birdsong. He had sent Mary to fetch his release papers from the nurse's station. Instead of papers, Mary followed Dr. Yates into Father Joe's room.

"I'll consider releasing you after we conduct one more test," Dr. Yates said, reviewing the chart.

"Oh no. I'm outta here today," Father Joe huffed, his voice raspy but firm. "It's a four-hour drive to Birdsong." Turning to Mary, he grinned. "Will your Buick make it home?"

"Of course." Mary crossed her arms and scowled.

"Then you have me until ten this morning. I know my rights, Doctor."

"Based on your test results, I have no medical reason to hold you.

Except for my own peace of mind. Please, I wish for one additional MRI."

"As long as we do it immediately."

"I heard you, Father. You will be leaving before ten."

Mary pulled her ringing cellphone from her purse and stepped from the room.

Dr. Yates checked over Father Joe's vitals. "I heard that the roses are blooming in Birdsong. Seems that your small town is in the news."

"Most unusual." Father Joe leaned over as Dr. Yates listened to his breathing. "Then again, a lot of unusual things are happening in Birdsong lately."

"We're up to nine funerals, Father." Mary raised her head and stared at the ceiling. "Jakie Sterling passed away yesterday afternoon. Her son, Michael, is a wreck. I didn't know she had cancer. Did you?"

Father Joe shook his head. "She was a good woman. I'll miss her. Had no idea she was ill."

"Neither did anyone else." Mary frowned.

Sitting up straight, Father Joe pointed at Mary. "What's going on? I left *you* in charge and the place is falling apart."

Mary's cheeks flushed. Stomping over to the door, she grabbed the handle. "I told you NOT to hire that woman!"

"Angie had nothing to do with any of this."

"Nothing to do with any of this?" Mary stomped back to his bed. "She had everything to do with ALL of this. She killed those people!"

"And I suppose she made the roses bloom, too?"

An orderly with a wheelchair peeked into the room. "Ready, Father?"

"I most certainly am." Father Joe stood, pulled his gown tighter around his waist and sat in the chair. "Think about it, Mary. You're being ridiculous."

As she waited, Mary read over the discharge papers. Blood thinners daily. Rehab three days a week. Follow-up visit in seven days. Later, as she pushed Father Joe down the hall, the nurses shouted out their goodbyes. With the cold wind slapping against their backs, Mary wondered if one of them would be Angie's next victim.

Stepping into the rectory, Father Joe prayed silently to himself. It was good to be home. As it was in his dream, it was as now in real life. He nearly sprinted to the tabernacle and stared at the chalice-shaped ciborium. Reaching forward, he took a deep breath.

Mary answered the rectory's doorbell. Nodding, she motioned for the woman to follow her into Father Joe's office. "This officer's here to see you, Father," Mary said, stepping aside.

"Me?" Father Joe stood up. "And how may I be of help?"

"I have a warrant for the confiscation of all Holy Communion remaining in the Chapel of the Little Flower." The officer held out the warrant. "Here."

Mary gasped.

Staring at the officer, Father Joe smiled. "The officials must believe that the Holy Communion Angie distributed to the residents was tampered with."

"It was poisoned?" Mary asked. "So, that's how she did it."

"I believe the police would like to think so." Father Joe laughed.

"You're not going to oblige them," Mary said, placing her hands on her hips. "That's sacrilegious."

Taking the warrant from the officer, he read over the papers. "This way."

"Father!" Mary yelled.

"Mary, that is enough." Walking past her stomping foot, Father Joe shook his head.

Mary followed the two into the chapel. After Father Joe wiggled the key in the lock, the tabernacle easily opened.

"Step aside, Father." The officer pulled out a labeled plastic baggie.

"Are you Catholic, my dear?" Father Joe asked. "You are about to hold the body of Christ."

The officer stepped back. "No. I'm not Catholic. Will this kill me?"

"Not necessarily," he replied.

Father Joe removed the silver chalice-shaped ciborium. Looking into the heavens, he said a silent prayer. After a pause, he lifted the cover and held it out to the waiting policewoman. Father Joe grinned.

Mary screamed. "Father! It's empty."

"Really?" Father Joe grinned, again. "How odd."

Mary slapped her hand over her mouth. "Oh my God. There were seventy-five consecrated Communion hosts in there when I left."

"Yes," Father Joe said. "Seventy-five exactly. I consumed them a little while ago." He looked over at the young officer. "Protecting the living body of our Lord and Savior, Jesus Christ. We wouldn't want him to be unholy disrespected, would we?"

It was just as it was in his dream.

"The idiot ate the hosts just before I got there," the young officer said to the police chief.

"He ate what?" Chief slapped his desk.

"I said, he ate—"

"I heard you," he yelled. "Didn't expect Father Joe to return this early."

"Anything else you want me to do, Chief?" she asked.

Having grown up as an altar boy, the chief could only laugh. "If Father Joe drops dead, then I'll have a case." He laughed a little louder. "Be at the church by six this evening. There's a special Mass to celebrate Father Joe's recovery. Need you to direct traffic. We're expecting a big crowd."

"Hi, Maddie," Angie said into her cellphone. "How're you?"

"Birdsong's on TV!" Maddie yelled. "You have roses blooming in the snow?"

"Crazy, I know. Kevin emailed me about it, too." Angie wiped her nose.

"Are you okay?"

"Jakie died," she said, holding back a sob. "From cancer. Her son, Michael, called. She told me yesterday at the restaurant. Didn't look well."

"I'm sorry, Mom. I know you were friends."

"I need to tell you something." Angie's stomach tightened. "We lost some more residents. In fact, they're all gone. That means they'll be closing the Home. I'll be looking for a bookkeeping position. Heard the Holiday Inn may be hiring. They just reopened after the fire."

"That's good, isn't it?"

"Maybe. With all this craziness about the roses, the manager said they're sold out."

"Hope it works out for you. You deserve a break."

Angie's phone beeped. Seeing Mary's name gave her the chills.

"Gotta run, sweetie. Another call."

"Okay, love you, Mom."

"Hello, Mary." Angie took in a deep breath.

"Good news, Ms. Pantera. Father Joe has returned."

"Wonderful."

"He would like to speak with you in the rectory."

"Chief Bertrand requested I come to the station. Has some questions about Ms. Fettore."

"So does Father Joe. So, stop here first. It will only take a minute. Do hurry."

"Yes, of course. "

Angie grabbed the stack of receipts. The $275 would come in handy right now. It was almost a week's worth of salary.

Father Joe was waiting at the front door and gave Angie a hug.

"Good to see you." She stepped back. "For a man just out of a coma, you're looking exceptionally well. And you're not using the crutches anymore?"

"I feel great," Father Joe laughed. "Had a good long nap."

Angie laughed, too.

"You've lost weight," he said.

"A little. All that walking up and down Ridge Road. Took a while to get my car back."

"Tom Jared did you good?"

Angie nodded. "He did. And he was there for me when I got out of jail."

"Quite a bit has gone on since I left. I'm so sorry about what you've been through." Father Joe sighed. "We must talk."

Mary walked into Father Joe's office carrying a large picture frame.

"You have to take care of this now, Mary?" Father Joe asked.

"Matthew picked it up this morning. I felt it only proper to place our St. Therese back as quickly as possible."

Father Joe shook his head. "Very well. Hang the painting."

Angie smiled, remembering the glass shards she swept up for him many weeks ago.

Mary tried to balance the portrait on a nail. "Need the step stool." Mary sat the portrait down and left the room.

"The woman doesn't want to miss a thing." He motioned for Angie to sit. Father sat at his desk. "How did you like your job? Mary tells me you granted the residents wishes."

"Yes. You said to have fun and make it my own. Each week I picked a name and granted a wish." Angie sighed. "I guess I started off on the wrong foot with Ms. Fettore."

"How so?"

"I bought these gigantic dandelions for the residents. When they made a wish and blew on the flowers, they made a huge mess." Angie explained the whole story.

Father Joe laughed. "Then their wishes were not a normal request."

"Let's just say that Ms. Fettore wasn't happy. I planned to make the best of their requests. At dinner I used special props. I tried really hard."

"I knew you would. I always thought you'd be perfect for the position. Do we owe you money for the props?" Angie held out the receipts. "I'll have Mary pay you right away."

"Thank you, Father. I wasn't worried."

"Sounds like you made them happy. They each died with a smile." He stared at Angie. "Now the important question." He leaned a little closer. "Who is this Ms. Fettore?"

"You mean the part-time administrator from the diocese?"

Mary returned carrying the step stool. As she picked up the painting, she kept glancing over her shoulder.

"The diocese did not send out anyone named Ms. Fettore," Father Joe stated.

"Jakie informed me of her," Mary said, leveling the frame against the wall. "Never heard her first name. In fact, Luke never saw the woman at the Home."

"Thank you, Mary." Father Joe sat back and crossed his arms. "What can you tell me, Angie?"

"About Ms. Fettore? Not much. She only came in on Tuesdays and Thursdays. Stayed in her office mostly."

"They're all gone now, Ms. Pantera. Except for you," Mary said, still turned away from them.

Angie frowned. "She's right. I'm the only one who can identify Ms. Fettore. Maybe that's why Chief Bertrand wants to talk to me."

"The diocese is selling the Home to the university. Was to take place once the last resident passed," Father Joe said.

"Yes, I remember. You told me that when I took the job, Father. I already assumed I am out of a job."

"No, Angie, that's not why I'm mentioning this. I just learned about a very special clause."

"Clause?" Angie asked.

"Yes. The church was given only three years from the time we signed the contract to transfer ownership. If the university didn't take ownership within that time period, the contract would be voided. That would mean that the church lost ten million dollars."

"So what?" Angie didn't understand. "They could write another contract."

"No," Father Joe chuckled. "According to the contract, if the Home wasn't sold by the end of three years, the church would lose the ten million dollars."

"That's a lot of money," Angie replied.

"We were in the last few months of the contract," Father Joe said.

"And our residents started dying as soon as Ms. Fettore started," Angie piped.

"Exactly," Father Joe replied. "If the last resident hadn't died by this spring, the deal was off."

A loud bang echoed through the room. "Sorry," Mary said, not turning around. "Dropped the hammer."

"Do you need it?" Father Joe asked.

"No," Mary laughed. "I'm good."

"Does Chief Bertrand believe Ms. Fettore had something to do with their deaths?" Mary asked.

"Don't know," Father Joe said. "The bishop's secretary, Mrs. O, would be the only one to know, and she's having memory problems right now. And this Ms. Fettore has disappeared into thin air. Can you tell me what she looked like?"

Stepping away from the portrait, Mary slapped her hands on her hips. "There! Safe and sound and back where you belong."

"That's Ms. Fettore!" Angie stood, gazing at the picture. "Ms. Lilleth W. Fettore."

"Where?" Mary asked, glancing around the room.

Angie pointed to the portrait of Saint Therese. "Right there. That is her."

Father Joe printed Ms. Fettore's full name on a sheet of paper. Studying the letters, he laughed. "It's an anagram."

"What is what?" Mary asked.

"*Lilleth W. Fettore* is *The Little Flower*," he said, laughing. "It's an anagram."

Boom! Again, the wire snapped and the portrait of St. Therese fell to the floor, the glass shattering.

"Jesus, Mary and Joseph!" Father Joe yelled, glaring at Mary. "So, I didn't break it the first time. It's your inability to hang a portrait properly."

Mary made the sign of the cross.

Rubbing her hands against her pants, Angie stared at them. "Father . . ."

"Yes."

"I was afraid to say something earlier 'cuz it's so crazy."

"You must tell us everything," he replied.

"The night Eliza died, Ms. Fettore was at the Home. Before she ran out of the house, she said something that didn't make any sense. She said something about 'His love was greater than everything.' And then she said something about 'magic.' Oh, and that miracles were real. Yes, I remember that part. And that they were an extension of *His love* for us."

"Sounds a little like a prayer," Mary replied. "Maybe she was praying over Eliza."

"No," Father Joe said. "It means something. Do you remember anything else?"

Angie stared at the shattered glass. Feeling her heart pounding, her mind whirled. "Yes, she said to have faith and not to waver."

Father Joe nodded.

"And after Rose died, Ms. Fettore told me that I was stronger than I knew, and that God worked in mysterious ways."

"Anything else? . . . It's okay, Angie. I believe you."

Looking up, a tear fell. Angie took in a deep breath and whispered, "Tell Father Joe that they will come. That they will build it."

Mary gasped.

"When Ms. Fettore left, I ran after her. But she vanished. Officer Raines was sitting in his car outside the door and he didn't see her either."

"Officer Raines?" Father Joe asked.

Mary gasped again. "I told him about the stuffed tiger."

"You told an officer what?" Father Joe frowned.

Mary nodded. Grinning at Angie, she whispered. "Did Ms. Fettore have a message for me?"

"No," Angie said, glaring at her.

Angie kept glancing between the sullen faces of Chief Bertrand, Father Joe, and Mary. She hated being there and wanted no part of it. Her head ached and her heart pounded.

"I'm not sure what's going on in this town," Chief Bertrand said, shaking his head. "But I don't like it." He glanced at the notepad sitting next to Angie's treasure box. "Roy Spankler, deceased. Rose Maquire, deceased. Theodore Chumley . . . deceased. Peter Peter—is that his *real* name?"

Mary nodded.

Shrugging, Chief Bertrand continued. "Adelaide and Trudy Simmons, deceased. Karun Nambeeson, deceased. And last but not least, Eliza Finney. All died after having their wish granted by Ms. Pantera."

Shifting in her chair, Angie grinned.

"Granting wishes is not illegal," Father Joe said.

"No, it is not. But when people die, Father, and at the same time," Chief Bertrand replied, "then things seem a little mysterious."

"I understand that the circumstances do not look right," Father added.

"Jakie Sterling died," Chief Bertrand said, frowning. "The last time the coroner's office was this busy was during the Asian flu back in the nineties."

"Jakie died from cancer," Father Joe said. "Not from a wish-granting."

Chief Bertrand nodded. "Ms. Pantera, are you positive that no one else other than you, Jakie or the residents knew of or talked to Ms. Fettore?"

Angie nodded. "I don't believe so."

"Mary," Chief Bertrand said. "Ms. Fettore's assignment supposedly came from the Caribou Diocese. And in the report, it says that no one from the church ever saw or met with her. Is that correct?"

"Correct." Mary crossed her arms. "However, Mrs. O from the diocese—"

Chief Bertrand raised his hand. "Mrs. O cannot be questioned at this time." He sighed. "Currently, we have a description from Ms. Pantera that Ms. Fettore not only resembles Saint Therese, but that she is Saint Therese. We all know that there's no way that Ms. Fettore can be a saint. Especially a dead one."

"We have proof," Father Joe said, sitting up straighter in his chair.

"Proof?" Chief Bertrand glared at him.

"The roses are in bloom and it's winter. And"—Father Joe pointed to the heavens—"only in Birdsong. This is a sign. A miracle. Saint Therese has spoken!"

"Father," Chief Bertrand replied. "Honestly, do you—"

"Saint Therese is known as the Little Flower because of the roses. In every painting, she's holding a bouquet of roses and a cross. And don't forget about the anagram." When Chief Bertrand scowled at him, Father Joe lowered his voice and eyes. "I showed you earlier."

"Coincidence. I can make many names from these letters."

Mary uncrossed her arms and leaned forward. "We prayed, Chief. The Elders and I. We prayed for nine days. A novena for Saint Therese's help. We prayed the ninth day just before Father left for his surgery." Mary sat back and smiled.

Scratching his head, Chief Bertrand smirked. "Is that what you want me to explain to the environmentalists and media? That the blooming roses are a miracle from Saint Therese? And that she showed up, personally? Maybe I should tell everyone to just go home now, that the mystery was solved by you three." He held out his hands.

Father Joe stood. Placing his hand on Angie's shoulder, he smiled at Chief Bertrand. "That's *exactly* what I plan on saying."

"You could probably get away with such as statement, Father. I cannot. My job is to find and question Ms. Fettore. The church stands to collect ten million dollars." Chief Bertrand glared at Father Joe. "And let's not forget about the contract that had an expiration date. A date that's only a few weeks from now. Seems pretty cut and dried to me."

Father Joe slapped the chief's desk and glared at him. "From what

I've been told, everyone died from natural causes. No *poison* was found in their blood. No trauma found on their bodies. Therefore, a funeral for each resident will take place as planned next Tuesday. They lived together as a family, so they'll have a funeral Mass as a family. Unless you have proof of foul play, I will need my residents to be returned to me no later than Monday morning. I do not believe I can be any clearer than that."

Chief Bertrand shook his head and frowned.

"I also demand to have that treasure box returned to the church. Ms. Pantera bought it. I've reimbursed her for it. Therefore, it is church property. And don't touch the eight cards that are inside it. Those are mine, too. I believe they are part of the miracle. Our residents asked for a final wish. God granted that wish. Why else would they die with smiles on their faces?"

Picking up the portrait of Saint Therese, Chief Bertrand walked around his desk. Opening the office door, he motioned to Officer Raines. "Find this woman!"

"Looks like a nun," Officer Raines said.

"Put an APB on Lilleth W. Fettore. Add Canada in the search. The woman looks exactly like this saint. Brown eyes, brown hair. No makeup."

"We're looking for a nun?"

"Well," Chief laughed, "exclude the headgear."

Officer Raines took the portrait with both hands and frowned. "Largest photo we've received to date."

Chief Bertrand took a deep breath.

"Okay, Chief," Officer Raines said, walking away. "I'll have Mrs. O look at it, too. Maybe she'll see something we're not."

Chief Bertrand frowned. "Why do I doubt that?"

Chapter 17

Wearing a long white robe, Mary Mead poked her head out of the sacristy and watched as Elders John and Luke ushered people to a seat. Seeing Angie talking to the Boston reporter, she leaned back and sighed. "This is not good," she whispered.

"Are we ready, Mary?" Father Joe, dressed in his vestments, looked as healthy as ever.

"They're standing wall to wall, Father. They're overflowing into the parking lot."

Father placed the green stole around his neck. "Wonderful news. It's important everyone hears me tonight. Too bad there isn't enough sitting room. Gonna be a cold one tonight."

"They're here to see you, Father."

"No, Mary," Father Joe replied. "They're here to see God. The Little Flower has brought the faithful back to us."

"I'll make sure the volume is at its highest. The outdoor speakers Matthew installed should help."

"Did you see Angie out there?"

"She's in the back row talking to that nosy reporter from Boston. Tom Jared's sitting on her other side. They're packed in like sardines."

"Good man, that Tom Jared," Father Joe said. "I'm ready, Mary."

Father Joe entered the chapel with Mary walking behind him. The people stood. Their excitement vibrated through the small chapel.

"Thank you," Father Joe said from the altar. He motioned with his hands and the crowd silenced. "It's wonderful to be back. We're surrounded by miracles." Looking over the expectant faces, his heart pounded. "It all started with a nine-day novena. Our church elders prayed to Saint Therese. They only requested a little help while I was away. What we received was tenfold. My aneurysm disappeared. Our roses bloomed in the snow. The Little Flower has spoken to us."

The word "roses" echoed through the room.

"His love," Father Joe said a little louder, "is greater than all, and it is not magic within His word. Miracles are real and an extension of His love for us. Have faith. Do not waver."

He glanced at his flock. "We're stronger than we think, and our God works in mysterious ways."

LM Neuhouse stood her ground outside the chapel doors, searching the faces. Angie was nowhere in sight. There wasn't much room in the street, and the dispersing crowd was now causing a traffic jam in the parking lot.

"I need you to move to the street with the other reporters," a female officer said.

"It's too windy down there," LM replied.

The officer yelled at a couple of kids running through the packed people. Turning back to LM, she scowled. "I thought I told you to get down to the street?"

LM moved back a few feet.

The officer glared. "Get your ass to the street, now! I'm not going to say it again."

LM frowned as she and her cameraman walked down to join the other reporters.

"Keep an eye out for a middle-aged woman with blonde hair. I was actually sitting next to her inside," LM said to the cameraman.

"Are they done in there?" he asked.

LM shook her head. "I snuck out. We'll grab her coming out. Get ready. It'll be over soon."

The climate change scenario had granted her enormous overnight ratings with her Boston station, the only station that would hire her after she lost everything. It had been seven long years, and she had to rise above, maybe one day to go national again. Maybe, this time, to stay there.

"Here they come." LM grabbed her cameraman's arm.

The cameraman stuck up his thumb. "Recording in . . . three . . . two . . . one."

"Roses still in need of hibernation," LM said, forcing a smile from time to time, "are found blooming throughout this sleepy central northern town of Birdsong, Maine. We're just fifty miles from the Canadian border. It's a miracle. Father Joe from the Chapel of the Little Flower claims that the roses are a sign from Saint Therese. However, the environmentalists are whooping it up. They feel vindicated saying that the blooming roses validate their claims of climate change. In some fashion, perhaps this event is their miracle, too. Proof that climate change is real. At least here, in Birdsong, Maine."

Glancing back at the chapel as the congregation let out, she sighed. Still no sign of Angie Pantera. Staring into the camera, LM grinned. As the cameraman panned the crowd, LM adjusted her jacket. When the camera panned back to her, a large, evil grin spread across her face.

"Aside from the miracle with the blooming roses, this little frozen town also has a murder mystery on their hands. The recreational director was granting a last wish to each resident of the local nursing home. And after their wish was done, so was the resident. Now this little diocese has eight murders to investigate. And at the center of the investigation is the recreational director . . . a Mrs. Angie Pantera, a recent divorcee."

Glancing over her shoulder, the snow-covered lawn was now empty. *Where did that woman go?* To break this story, it was now or never.

"We also have a missing person. Lilleth W. Fettore from the local diocese is also at the center of these murders. What does Angie Pantera know about Lilleth Fettore? After all, she was the last person to have seen her at the Home the night the last resident was found dead. And according to Ms. Pantera, Lilleth Fettore is an exact double of the legendary Saint Therese. A woman who's been dead for over a hundred years!" LM lowered her microphone.

"Cut. Did you get a good picture of that portrait?" The cameraman nodded. "Good. I guess we'll have to interview Angie Pantera tomorrow."

"Good take," the cameraman said, laughing. "You'll get some heads turning with this one."

"I'm hungry. I want to try that Rose Petals restaurant," LM said, walking past a short woman who was glaring at them. "Do you want my autograph?"

"No, thank you," the steely gray-haired woman said.

Walter couldn't believe his stupid good luck. Instant fame for Rose Petals, and a lot of money. All within forty-eight hours. Just two days ago, he was trying to decide which person to lay off first. Now he could use another chef and bartender. Not to mention more waiters, busboys, and dishwashers. Receiving deliveries by the hour, Rose Petals was now the center of the blooming rose phenomenon. Everyone in town stopped by his restaurant to see the beautiful flowers. Even though it was approaching nine, people were still waiting to be seated. Walter devoured every minute and every dollar.

He and Nancy barely spoke. When she entered the kitchen, he dropped the large spoon. Pulling her into his arms, he kissed her. His brother, the temporary chef from the next town over, yelled at his teenage son, who had just dropped a large tray of dirty dishes in the corner.

"Don't have time for this," Nancy said, pushing Walter away. "Mass just let out and everybody's coming straight here."

"Father's back?" he asked.

"Yep. Customers said he's talking about miracles. And he's including himself as one."

"Have to see him." Walter released his grip. "I'll be able to repay every last cent with the way things are going." Walter frowned. "If he forgives me."

"Of course he'll forgive you. You gave your time for free. Every day you prepared the meals for his home. How much did he ever pay you? Nothing, that's what."

"No. I took the church's money secretly."

"So we fell on hard times. He'll understand."

"Father signed every bill I gave him." Walter shook his head. "Never questioned even one."

"Everything will be okay." Nancy turned to leave. "Gotta seat the customers."

The back door opened. Walter smiled when Tom walked in with Angie behind him.

"Hi, Walter," Angie said, giving Walter a hug. "I've missed your cooking."

"Hope you don't mind," Tom said. "My truck's in the back. It's crazy. Couldn't find any parking."

"No problem," Walter said. "You fix my car, I let you park. We're real busy today."

"We'll sit at the bar," Tom replied. Taking Angie by the hand, he smiled. As they walked past the boy lugging a crate of dirty dishes, he chuckled.

Winding through the crowd, Tom aimed for an empty space near the back.

"Can I get you a drink?"

"Red wine," she replied.

Glancing around the room, Angie shook her head. Not an empty seat anywhere. People walked in, added their names to a list, and walked back out. Nancy looked ragged. A couple of waitresses didn't look familiar. She wondered where Walter picked them up from.

"Here we go," Tom said. "Nancy said she'd get us a table as soon as one clears."

"Good," Angie replied, taking a sip. "Oh no."

"What?"

"It's Mary. And she's seen me. Now what does she want?"

"Glad I found you," Mary said, panting.

"What'd you do? Run?" Tom asked.

Ignoring him, she stared at Angie. "Luke said you were here. Good thing that you left through the sacristy."

"Luke told us to," Angie replied.

"I told him to tell you that," Mary said, grinning. Taking in a deep breath, she let it out slowly. "Saw that reporter spying on you. Her name's LM Neuhouse from Boston. I watched her and she's doing a segment on the residents. Said your name several times."

"Why would she say my name?"

"As the potential killer. She also mentioned Ms. Fettore. That reporter asked about you yesterday."

"I know. Luke told me." Angie took another sip.

"You need to leave," Mary said. "She's outside with the cameraman. I think she's looking for you."

"I don't care. So what if she finds me? I didn't do anything wrong."

"Reporters go for the jugular. If I were you, I'd leave before she spots you. Don't go to the cottage. I have a spare bedroom you can use until this blows over."

Angie's mind swirled. Such kindness wasn't normal for this woman.

"We are church family. Just trying to help you out. Protect you."

"Thanks for your concern. I'll be fine."

"Maybe you should listen to her," Tom said. "Things could get ugly with that reporter nosing around. Maybe you should hire a lawyer."

"A lawyer?" Angie glared at Tom. "I didn't do anything to those residents except grant their wishes."

"I believe you. But reporters twist their stories. You know, to get ratings. You can use my guesthouse. You're welcome to use it until this passes. I'm never home anyway. With my work schedule so heavy," he said, "you'd have all the privacy you need."

Mary tugged on Angie's sleeve. "Two o'clock," Mary mumbled. "The woman in white." Mary's eyes darted away and then back again. "LM is here."

Tom took Angie's wine out of her hand and placed it on the counter. Leading her through the kitchen, he nodded to Walter.

"I'm tired," Angie said. "A lot to take in. But I'm staying put."

"My guesthouse is there if you need it."

"I'll keep it in mind."

Streams of sunlight inched their way onto her bedcovers. Angie tugged until she covered the top of her head.

After tossing and turning throughout the night, the good and bad lay heavily on her mind. That bookkeeping interview couldn't come fast enough. Father Joe told her not to worry about paying him rent. At least, not yet.

Right now, the bad seemed to be outweighing the good. Rolling onto her side, Angie cringed. Her stomach hurt.

I didn't kill anybody. I didn't . . . Her thoughts refused to go away. *Why didn't I just talk to that reporter last night? Why did I allow Tom and Mary to pull me away?* That reporter seemed friendly enough when they met in the chapel. It should have been safe. It was Father Joe who said he'd protect her. That the church would stand behind her. Why would she doubt his word?

Bang!

Angie stared at the cottage's front door.

Bang! Bang!

"Who in the world!" Angie grabbed for her robe. "Not another policeman."

When she opened the small door, a woman stepped inside. Holding a microphone close to her face, she stated loudly, "LM Neuhouse reporting live with Angie Pantera!"

Angie took a step back, wrapping her robe tighter around her waist. The cameraman aimed right at her.

"Were you hired by the Catholic Church to—"

"I . . . I . . ." Angie grasped for the right words.

"This is private property!" Mary stated, rushing up the cottage steps. "The police chief has issued a gag order. None of us are allowed to talk to the press. I'm asking you politely to leave, or I will call the police." Mary pushed Angie into the bedroom. LM started to say something, but Mary pushed her onto the front porch. Slamming the cottage door, she sighed. "Damn reporters."

"Why are you here?" Angie asked.

"I saw the news van out front," Mary replied. "I'm here to protect you."

Angie sat on her bed and stared at the floor. "Why do I need your protection when I didn't do anything wrong? Why can't I tell that to the reporter?"

Peeking out between the living room curtains, Mary shook her head. "She's outside. They're trying to film you."

"I think I can take care of myself," Angie said.

Mary clenched her fists. "That woman reported on national TV that the residents' deaths were orchestrated by the diocese. And that Ms. Fettore and *you* are accomplices. That reporter has named you as a murderer. What do I have to do to get you to understand? That woman has announced on live TV that you killed all eight of our residents. Do you want to live out your life in a prison cell?"

"She called me a murderer?" Angie's eyes widened. "Are you kidding?" Angie walked over to the window and peeked out. "I'm innocent, and I'm going to tell her that!"

"You talking to her will only make things worse. Don't say a word to her or her cameraman. People like that are vultures. They'll make you look however they want in order to get a story."

Through the window, LM's voice echoed through the room. "Ms. Pantera . . . when you took the position of recreation director did you already know Lilleth W. Fettore?"

Angie glanced at Mary and frowned.

"Ms. Pantera," LM yelled. "Were the deaths of the eight residents concocted under the pretense of a wish-granting hoax?"

Shaking her head, Mary glared at Angie.

"Ms. Pantera, did the church ask you to take care of them—literally— in order to guarantee the sale of the property for ten million dollars?"

Mary pointed at Angie. "What did I just tell you?"

Sitting, Angie wiped away a tear. "What should I do?"

"Tom Jared offered you the use of his guesthouse. You should be safe there." Mary looked through the curtains again. "Good, they're leaving."

Angie glanced over at her cellphone. Maybe Tom's offer wasn't such a bad idea after all.

Friday afternoon, Elder Mark was working just outside the cottage. It was his job to keep an eye out for that reporter. With the coast clear, Angie climbed into the back of Mark's van. Carrying only a small suitcase, her whole body shook.

"I feel like a thief," Angie said, sitting as low as she could. "This whole thing is nuts."

"Small town, Angie," Mark said, pulling away from the rectory. "People talk. That reporter pushed her way into the chief's office. Demanded to see his files on the residents."

"Really?"

Mark chuckled. "Chief threw her out. Barred every reporter from the coroner's, the funeral home, and the examiner's office."

"Unreal." Angie tried to see out the window.

"More reporters are picking up the story. Calling in from all over. Chief has one pain-in-the-ass situation."

"Can't wait for this to be over."

The van bounced through the snow-packed roads. As Mark drove deeper into the woods, Angie struggled with her seat.

"Where're we going?" Angie glanced out the window at the trees.

"Tom's house is tucked away good in these woods. That reporter won't find you out here."

The van stopped at a Victorian-style house with a wraparound porch. Sunlight couldn't penetrate the thick evergreens. The front porch lights reflected spiral shapes across the white yard.

"Guesthouse to the left," Mark said, turning off the van.

"Tom said he'd leave it open for me." Stepping into the frigid air, Angie scanned the area. Tall, snow-covered evergreens framed the large yard, shading the house from the afternoon sun. The roses in full bloom added the only color.

"Thank you," Angie said, grabbing her small suitcase.

"Busy time right now," Mark replied. "Probably won't see you for a while. You take care, Angie."

"I'll be fine."

Angie waved at Mark. Entering the small guesthouse, the pit of her stomach clenched. Not from hunger, but from uncertainty. Uncertainty of where she was and where she was going. Flipping on the light, her heart warmed. The place was beautiful and comfy.

Getting to know Tom felt good. With each word they exchanged, Angie gained respect for the man she only knew through aggravation over her car. Took Tom awhile, but now her car hummed just like new. Just like he promised her many weeks ago. After putting her clothes away, Angie lay down on the brass bed. No TV, but there was Wi-Fi.

She liked Tom. She liked him a lot. However, there was a problem. The man was still in love with his past—his deceased wife.

Chief Bertrand found Officer Raines walking back and forth in front of the Chapel of the Little Flower. He looked irritated. Several people carrying signs that said *Atheists Against the Church* didn't seem to be paying him any attention. Waving at Officer Raines, Chief Bertrand pulled over.

Two protesters holding up photos of Lilleth W. Fettore chanted as they walked. "Eight hadda die. Eight hadda die. Fettore and Pantera gotta lie!"

That crazy reporter is opening the way for all the nutcases to come out. As if Chief didn't have enough on his plate already. First, the environmentalists accusing Birdsong of being the center of climate change. How ridiculous. Then there were the activists and the faithful. And now, townspeople claimed that their roses were being stolen right off their bushes. His entire staff were stretched to the limit, working round the clock. Something was about to explode, and he hoped it wouldn't be him.

"Yes, Chief?" Officer Raines asked as he stepped up to the patrol car window.

"You good?"

Officer Raines nodded. "Just some crazies. I'll threaten them with a night in jail and they'll leave."

Chief Bertrand laughed as he pulled away from the curb.

Sunday morning, Chief Bertrand held a news conference outside headquarters. It was time to state the obvious.

"All eight are still being autopsied," Chief Bertrand said. "We should have the results shortly. Lilleth W. Fettore is considered a person of interest. If anyone knows of her whereabouts, they should call my office."

"What about Angie Pantera, the recreational director?" LM yelled out from the crowd. "She's her accomplice."

"Angie Pantera is cooperating with our investigation," he said, scanning the crowd.

"Angie Pantera is a person of interest now, too," LM yelled.

"We are waiting on the test results," Chief Bertrand said. "We will know more shortly."

"How shortly, Chief?" LM yelled.

"Shortly," he repeated. "This ends our news conference. Thank you." The chief walked away as a slew of questions bombarded him from all sides.

With the atheists still protesting in front of the chapel, Father Joe kept busy with the overflowing Masses. After the last one, he entered his office, exhausted.

"It's our little joke, Father." Mary laughed, staring out the window. "Those crazies are carrying the face of our Saint Therese, and they don't even know it."

He lowered his eyes. Chief would never accept what happened as a miracle. Ms. Lilleth W. Fettore was, in fact, the Little Flower. How could he ever get Chief to believe?

"Mary, please make the calls for me. The funeral Mass and burial will proceed as planned on Tuesday for all eight of our residents. Jakie Sterling's is still scheduled for tomorrow."

"That's if the chief gives the okay," Mary replied.

"I'm confident that he will. How's Angie?"

"According to Mark, she's safely tucked away in the woods."

The doorbell rang, and Mary left to answer it.

The church would be covering Jakie's funeral expenses. She was to be placed next to her husband. Jakie's son, Michael, left a message informing him that Rose Petals offered to hold the reception for family and friends, free of charge. *Good man, that Walter.*

Mary returned carrying a big box. "Delivery, Father. It's from Walter. And there's a note."

"More food then I know what to do with," Father Joe said, taking the note from Mary.

"I'll make room in the fridge," she said.

Father Joe read.

Regards Father Joe,

I have, thankfully, been so busy that I haven't had the time to chat. I'm glad you're back with us. After the luncheon for Jakie's family may we speak?

Sincerely, Walter

Elder Luke walked into the office with two barrel-sized rattan baskets, one under each arm.

"What in the world do you have there, Luke?" Father Joe asked.

Luke tipped over the baskets and hundreds of envelopes spilled to the floor. "You're not going to believe this. I went up to the Home to secure the roses and found these baskets filled with mail. Opened up a couple of 'em. They're all the same." He pulled an envelope from his pocket.

"Protesters?" Father Joe asked.

"No. They're wishes. Wishes with a donation to the church. Here, listen. *Dear Father Joe, I wish to have a better relationship with my daughter—Betsy Thomas.*" Holding up a five-dollar bill, Luke smiled. "And this one: *Dear Father, I wish my son, Greg, God's protection while on Tour in Afghanistan—Matthew Cole.*" Holding up a ten-dollar bill, he chuckled. "They're all the same."

"Betsy Thomas?" Father Joe grinned. "Hadn't been to Mass in years. But she was there this morning."

Elder Luke chuckled. "I'll take these baskets back to the Home. I think we'll be seeing more of the same."

"Would you mind taking a little detour?"

"Sure thing, Father," he replied. "Where to?"

"Tom Jared's place. Need to get a box of food to Angie. And tell no one where she is staying."

Chapter 18

"Mom, exactly what kind of trouble are you in?"

"Didn't want to worry you. Trust me, Maddie. By tomorrow this will blow over. I'm innocent. The autopsies will prove it. It just that there's this reporter in town—"

"I'm coming out. I can fly into Caribou and rent a car."

"No, Maddie. Please don't. I'm okay."

"Are you really?"

"Yes. I am. My friends are taking care of me. Don't say anything to Kevin. I don't need him worrying needlessly." Angie sat on the edge of the bed holding back her tears.

"I'll call tomorrow," Maddie replied. "If anything changes, I'm flying out. Love you."

"Love you, too. We'll talk more then."

Feeling more like a prisoner than a guest, Angie stood in the kitchen and stared at the box of food Luke had brought over from Father Joe's. There was enough here to share with Tom. Angie had only spoken with him once since she arrived, and that was by cellphone. He had apologized for not being there more but did promise that they would go to Jakie's funeral together.

Angie placed the containers into a shopping bag she'd found under the sink. She slipped on her boots and coat and walked to Tom's house, following the wraparound porch to the back door. The kitchen light was on. Maybe Tom was home.

The door was unlocked. Peeking in, she called "Tom. Are you home?"

No answer.

Taking steps toward the fridge, she yelled out again. "Your door was open. I have lots of food from Rose Petals. Can't eat it all by myself. Thought you'd like some dinner."

Still no answer.

"I'll leave it in your fridge."

Angie emptied the shopping bag and tossed it in the trash under the sink. Wanting to leave a note, she searched for some paper and a pen. Peeking into the living room, she saw several framed photos of Tom and Emma, his deceased wife. Their wedding photos were of a much younger and happy couple. Several photos of them later in life lined the walls. There were so many. She glanced from frame to frame. If only her marriage could have been so full of love and devotion. Emma was such a beautiful woman. And Tom was so handsome. Feeling deprived and jilted because of her uncaring husband, something stirred inside her. Could she ever see herself dating Tom?

"Ms. Pantera!" Tom's loud voice echoed through the room.

Angie jumped. Jerking around, she stared at the angry and surprised man.

"What are you doing?" Tom sounded angry. He called her Ms. Pantera again.

"Tom, you startled me. I had extra food that Luke dropped off. I thought you might like something to eat. Put the food in your fridge. Wanted to leave a note. But couldn't find any paper."

Tom glared.

"You just decided to let yourself in without me here?"

"I'm sorry," Angie said, aiming for the back door. "I'll leave. So sorry to intrude." The door slammed and, guided by a half moon, Angie stumbled down the stairs. Hitting the snow-covered lawn at a full run, she almost fell several times. She locked the door behind her and climbed into bed with her coat and boots still on. Pulling the covers over her head, she curled into a little ball, holding her head between her hands.

What a mess she'd made of her life. How worthless of a person she had become. She couldn't make it as a wife and now she couldn't make it as a friend. Why did she ever come to Birdsong in the first place? Granting wishes of joy to ninety-year-old residents, what a stupid idea. Because of her big heart, she was now labeled as a murderer. Hiding away from the world because of some rude reporter. She felt worthless. Strangers looked at her as if she wore two heads on her shoulders. She was trapped in a world that was decided by serendipity. Why serendipity? It wasn't even a real thing. Something she'd made up to replace someone she loved. How stupid was she to ever believe she could be truly loved or happy?

"Stupid, pathetic me. I wish I was dead!"

Angie cried herself to sleep.

At dawn's first light, Father Joe walked into his kitchen. His stomach growled.

"What's for breakfast?" In the fridge, Walter's leftovers seemed to be jumping around to get his attention. Pulling out a sleeve of eggs and a half-eaten steak, Father Joe's mouth watered.

Ding-dong.

"Hope it's not another delivery from Walter. Fridge can't hold any more."

Opening the door, Father Joe stared at the man dressed in a dark suit. He looked tired.

"You clean up pretty good. But you're a little early for Jakie's funeral." Father Joe chuckled.

"Morning, Father," Tom said, wiping his eyes with the backs of his hands. "Was wondering if I could have a few minutes of your time?"

"Of course. Cooking steak and eggs. Hungry?"

"Another time," Tom said. "I need your help. Stayed at the garage last night. Couldn't sleep."

"You look as if the world's resting on your shoulders right now." Father Joe placed a frying pan on the stove. While cutting up the steak, he watched Tom from the corner of his vision.

"It's about Emma."

"Sit down at the table." Father Joe grabbed a cup and filled it with coffee. Placing it in front of Tom, he frowned. "Emma died years ago. She's haunting you in your dreams or something?"

"Something like that."

"Cream?"

Tom nodded.

"Walter sent over so much food I can't find a darn thing in this fridge. Sent a box over to Angie last night, too." Finding the creamer, Father Joe sat it down next to Tom.

"Angie filled my fridge with some last night." Tom stared into his cup.

"Thank you for sheltering Angie from that reporter."

Tom looked up and frowned. "That's why I'm here." He twirled his wedding band on his finger.

Father Joe placed the steak pieces into the pan.

"Truth be known, after Emma died, I hated stepping into that house. Too many memories. Spent most of my time at the garage. Slept there, too, on a cot."

"That's not living, my son." Father Joe stirred the sizzling steak. "You're hiding from the world. And that's not what Emma would have wanted for you."

Tears dribbled down Tom's cheeks. "I miss her so much. We were happy. Why did God take her from me?" He glanced away, wiping his eyes again with his hands.

Father Joe cracked an egg. As it sizzled into the butter, he replied, "I wish I had that answer. But I don't. God has his plans. Plans we're not privy to. In the meantime, it's time for you to let go. To say goodbye to Emma. You need to accept her passing."

Tom stared up at Father Joe. "How do I do that? How do I let go of someone I loved so much, and still do?"

"I spent several chemo sessions with Emma," Father Joe replied. "Remember?"

"When I was too busy," Tom said, nodding.

"She told me that you'd show up here someday. She knew you'd come for my help. And here you are, three years later."

Tom looked away.

Father Joe cleared his throat. "Emma knew I'd have to prod you along. She gave me a message for you. When you finally came to me, she asked me to tell you something. Her last wish was for you to live and love again. She wanted you to remember her. But she also wanted you to fall in love."

Tom sniffled and blew his nose on a napkin.

"She knew that, someday, someone wonderful would come into your life. And when that happened, she wanted you to love again. Wholeheartedly and without guilt. Without remorse."

Tom knocked on the guesthouse door. There was no answer. He knocked again. He turned to leave. After a few steps, the door opened.

"Tom?"

Angie stood in the doorway, clutching the collar on her robe. Water dripped from her hair.

"I'll be ready in about—"

"Forgive me, Angie," Tom said. "I'm such an idiot to take it out on you. I acted like an ogre yesterday. I invited you here. You're the first woman who's been in my house, other than—"

"No, Tom, you were right. I was wrong. I should have honored your privacy. I'm the one that should be apologizing. It won't happen again. I've packed. After the funeral, I'll go back to the cottage. I can handle that reporter."

He looked deeply into her eyes. Red and puffy. She'd been crying just like he had. Maybe even all night. He felt like he had been kicked in the gut. For the first time in years, his heart demanded more. He was attracted to Angie and he wanted more of her. He had proved that to himself by sliding off his wedding band and tucking it into his pocket after leaving Father Joe's.

"Angie," Tom whispered. "Don't leave because of my stupid behavior yesterday. Please, stay."

"It's for the best."

Reaching out, Tom grabbed Angie by the arm and pulled her into a strong embrace. Staring into her Caribbean-blue eyes, he kissed her tenderly, and she kissed him back.

The hearse arrived at the Chapel of the Little Flower with Jakie tucked away inside. Protestors chanting "Eight hadda die, eight hadda die, Fettore and Pantera gotta lie" seemed to be setting the stage for everyone's emotions. Michael Sterling pulled his SUV into the parking lot. Glaring at the protestors that were being pushed back by the police, Michael gripped the steering wheel a little tighter. His heart pounded as he remembered the devasting lies spewed against his mother when he was only ten. For years he hid in his bedroom closet and cried.

"We're honoring the memory of my mother, your grandma," he said. "Don't allow them to interfere with that."

The five-year-old stared out the window and stuck out her tongue.

"There'll be none of that, young lady." Olivia pulled her daughter away from the window. "She has so much of your mother in her, Michael."

"And that's a good thing." Michael took his wife's hand and kissed it. "Let's do this for grandma. Together."

The little girl took her little sister's hand and grinned. "Grandma's in heaven now. She's watching us."

The little sister nodded.

LM and her cameraman filmed from across the street. The protestors and their chants would cause even more havoc in the small town if their antics ever made it to the evening news.

Glancing down at Angie, who was trying to hide from the camera, Tom laughed. "Feeling like a spy yet?"

"No. Just silly. Guess I'll be doing this all day," Angie sighed. "Mary said to park behind the rectory and enter through the sacristy. Hopefully the police won't let the reporters into the funeral."

Father Joe smiled as they entered. With Mary's help, he was working with his vestments.

"Glad you heeded my instructions," Mary said. "*She's* out front with those ridiculous protestors." Mary frowned. "Walter closed the restaurant to the public this afternoon. The family luncheon should be private."

"I hate skulking around like this," Angie said.

"I know," Father Joe replied. "It'll be over soon. The police chief said he should hear from the medical examiner's office soon."

"Come," Elder Luke said from the doorway.

Angie followed Luke into the chapel. As they walked past the closed casket, Angie reached out and lightly touched it.

I'm really going to miss you, Jakie. You were a good friend. May you rest in peace.

The chapel, filled with family and friends, looked to be standing room only. Luke found them a couple of seats in the middle row on the side of the Little Flower. Angie's eyes darted between a photo of Jakie and the statue. As a tear ran down her cheek, Angie held back a sob.

"You okay?" Tom asked, cupping his hand around hers.

"Sure," Angie replied, accepting the lie.

Angie's stomach hurt. Would anything in the autopsies come back to bite her? With her name plastered across the news, would the bookkeeping interview be canceled?

As the services played out, Tom handed Angie one tissue after another. When Jakie was laid to rest next to her husband, Angie said her final goodbyes.

Walter watched as Nancy worked on clearing the tables. He had prepared Jakie's favorite pies and cakes for her family's luncheon. Taking in a deep breath, he needed to relieve the tightness engulfing his chest. It was time.

"Father?" Walter leaned over and whispered. "May I have that word with you now?"

Father Joe looked up at him. "Certainly." He wiped his mouth before setting his napkin on the table.

Walter ushered Father Joe through the kitchen toward his office. They walked past Jellybean, who was curled up in a basket.

"Got yourself a cat?" Father Joe chuckled.

"Brought him over from the Home." Walter wiped the sweat from his brow. "Father, I have a confession to make."

"Usually we make confessions in the chapel."

Walter took in another deep breath. "I've been stealing from the Home for over a year. My restaurant was suffering. I'll pay back every last cent with interest. I promise. If you decide to press charges, I'll understand."

Father Joe stared at the broken man. "Tell me something I don't already know."

Walter's eyes widened. "You knew and you still signed the bills?"

"You're a good man. I knew you'd come around eventually. How many years have you volunteered to cook the meals for free? Ten years? You never asked for a dime. You are forgiven. No need to pay us back. Glad you won't need to be stealing from us anymore." Father Joe laughed. "Nice to hear that the business has picked up."

"Ever since the roses bloomed." Walter reached out and shook Father Joe's hand. "Thank you. My conscience will be cleared when you receive my donation to the church."

Father's cellphone rang. He glanced at his watch. "About time. We should have our answer soon."

"I'll give you privacy." Walter stepped out of the office and closed the door.

LM Neuhouse stood as close to the police chief as she could. He stepped up to the microphone and frowned. Chief Bertrand opened the folder.

"He's looking like a man who got his answer," LM whispered to her cameraman. "That could only mean one thing: guilty as sin." LM smiled. *I was the first to report on this little scandal. More doors should open for me now.*

"Good afternoon," Chief Bertrand said, glancing out at the large crowd. "We've received the official report from the medical examiner's office in Caribou."

LM raised her microphone.

"According to the medical examiner, Roy Spankler, Rose Maguire, Teddy Chumley, Karun Nambeeson, Peter Peter, Adelaide Simmons, Trudy Simmons and Eliza Finney—" Chief paused and smirked at LM. "They all died from natural causes."

"What?" LM screamed out as the other reporters yelled their questions.

"You want us to believe that four of the eight people died at the exact same time from natural causes?" LM squawked.

Chief shook his head. Glancing down at the report, he smiled. "Yes, 1:30 a.m., to be precise."

"What about Angie Pantera and Lilleth Fettore?" LM asked.

"Angie Pantera is no longer a person of interest. We still need and would like to speak with Lilleth Fettore," he said. "We are still looking for leads as to her true identity. What we do know is that the Caribou Diocese never hired a Lilleth Fettore. Nor have they ever heard of her before, which leads to other pending charges."

LM Neuhouse yelled, "Do you have any positive leads, Chief?"

"We did, Ms. Neuhouse. So far they've been false or dead ends."

"Then what you are saying, Chief, is that you're concluding your investigation of Lilleth Fettore?"

"No. That is not what I'm saying. Don't put words in my mouth. What I am saying is that Ms. Fettore may have disappeared and that our investigation remains open." Chief Bertrand cleared his throat. "This concludes our news briefing. Thank you." Stepping away from the podium, he ignored the shouts and questions. Especially those from LM Neuhouse.

"This is all BS," LM said, walking away and waving her microphone in all directions.

Nancy placed a piece of chocolate cake in front of Angie. "This was Jakie's favorite."

"Looks good," Angie replied, taking a bite.

"Not much of an appetite?" Tom asked. "Been moving your food more than eating it."

"First time for everything." Angie tried to laugh. "Lots on my mind."

"Angie?" Father Joe's voice stirred her emotions. "Natural causes. Never any doubt in my mind."

Angie beamed.

He tapped her shoulder. "Enjoy your cake. Hear it was Jakie's favorite."

Tears flowed.

"What's wrong?" Tom asked.

She grabbed his hand and squeezed it. "It's over. It's finally over." Taking another bite, she smiled. *May you rest in cake-heaven, my friend.*

Driving herself to the job interview a couple hours later, Angie felt confident she could handle anything and everything. Even if she ran into that reporter, LM Neuhouse, who was still nosing around.

"Been so busy around here, haven't had time to keep up with the world," the Holiday Inn manager said. He glanced over her resume. "You're qualified, Ms. Pantera. No question about that. And I do need a bookkeeper. The job's yours if you're interested."

"Oh, yes," Angie replied.

Light snow continued to fall all afternoon. Protestors now carried posters of dollar signs instead of replicas of the Saint Therese painting. The era of Kerr Bird Song was officially over. The Home of the Little Flower would be sold.

Stepping out of the cottage, Angie stood on the porch. It was great to be home. As she walked up to the chapel, a familiar voice echoed through the trees.

"You're looking happy today," Tom said, pecking her lightly on the lips.

"Got myself a new job. Bookkeeper at the Holiday Inn. Start tomorrow."

"Congratulations. How about a dinner celebration?" Tom asked.

"Would love it. Want to get back to a normal life."

"By the way, no Ms. Neuhouse across the street." He pointed at the protestors.

"Amen to that."

Holding hands, they walked into the chapel. Being the first to arrive they sat in the front row. Eight urns sat side by side on a table in front of the altar. The photos placed in front of each one warmed Angie's heart.

As the chapel filled with mourners, Angie couldn't stop staring at the photos. She would dearly miss each of them.

Father Joe stood tall. Glancing down, he said, "Something of a miracle happened here in Birdsong while I was sleeping."

There was some nervous laughter.

"I see new faces and old faces that I haven't seen in a while. I think I know why you're here. Your faith has brought you back. You want to hear more. Understand more. Most of you didn't know these wonderful eight people. Yet, you're here." He smiled "You see, they all had a last wish. A wish that I believe God granted."

Father Joe looked down at Angie.

"Roy Spankler." Father Joe walked over to the first photo and picked it up. He chuckled. Turning the photo toward the crowd, he said, "We called him Spanks."

With each photo, Father Joe gave a little story about the resident and their final wish that God granted. For the first time in a long time, Birdsong's populace held themselves not only as fellow citizens but as family and friends.

It was all Angie could do to hold back her tears.

Father Joe and Mary stood in the mausoleum after the service. Elder Mark grinned when his stomach growled.

"Sorry, my friend," Father Joe said. "No luncheon planned for our eight residents."

Mary nodded.

"Okay," Father Joe said. "Let's get a move on so we can get some lunch. I want Spanks near his second wife, Michelle. Unfortunately, we have no idea where Rose's husband is interred. Therefore, we'll place her next to Teddy."

Mary laughed. "Just the way Teddy would have wanted it."

"Trudy and Adelaide will be here," Father Joe said. "I want Karun and Peter somewhere near the others. And with Eliza. She needs to be near her sister." He looked over at Mark.

"Got it, Father," Mark replied.

"I have the princess's photo for Karun, *The Vitruvian Man* for Peter, and the stuffed tiger for Eliza," Mary said.

Father Joe lowered his head. "Let us pray."

Upon leaving the cemetery, Father Joe chuckled. "Mary, may I use your cellphone? I have one more thing I must do. Hope I'm not too late."

Chapter 19

L
M signed her name on the invoice. As she pulled her luggage toward the door, the Holiday Inn manager stepped in front of her. "Ms. Neuhouse?"

"Yes."

He handed her a note. "This is for you."

"Thanks."

> *Ms. Neuhouse. Will you please meet with me @ 4pm this afternoon. It will be worth your time.*

It was a little before four. The message was from Father Joe Methuen. The meeting place was the rectory.

LM walked up to the rectory's door. *Why does this priest want to speak with me?*

Shrugging, she shook her head. Maybe the supreme being had something better for her waiting just beyond this door. Pressing on the doorbell, her mind wandered to where she didn't want to go.

Once top dog in her field with a highly rated morning news show, *The Neuhouse Factor*, she had fallen from grace after being caught paying guests to sensationalize their stories to improve her ratings. She had written several books about politics and cultural issues, which remained popular.

But that wasn't enough to save her career or reputation in broadcast journalism. She was fired, and after a couple of years of trying to play the part of the stay-at-home mother, her marriage had fallen apart. An old college friend working as a news director at a small Boston network affiliate gave LM a chance to start over as a local news reporter. It was a rookie beat-reporting job, but at least it was something.

Mary answered the bell. "Welcome, Ms. Neuhouse. I'm Mary Mead, Father Joe's assistant."

"We've met. Father Joe summoned me." LM forced a grin.

"He's waiting for you in the office."

LM followed Mary down the slender hallway. Stepping into the office, Mary stepped to one side.

Father Joe extended his hand. "Thank you for coming, Ms. Neuhouse."

"It will be worth my while?" she said. "I have to admit you've piqued my interest."

"Please take a seat." Father Joe stepped aside, revealing the person sitting near his desk. "I'd like to formally introduce you to Angie Pantera."

"Been looking all over for you," LM said, glaring. "And here you sit, waiting for me to come to you."

Angie nodded.

LM sat down. "You'll give me your undivided attention now?"

"The church is offering you a job."

"Offering *me* a job?" LM laughed. "You've got to be kidding."

"It involves Lilleth W. Fettore."

LM's jaw dropped. "You've also been hiding Fettore from the police?"

Mary giggled.

"Not at all. Chief knows exactly where we have her hidden." Father Joe smiled and pointed to a portrait on the wall.

LM glanced around the room. "Where is Fettore? Is she here?"

Mary giggled again.

Father Joe again pointed to the portrait. "Ms. Neuhouse, meet Lilleth W. Fettore. Also known as our Saint Therese, the Little Flower."

LM stood up and walked over to the glassless frame. "Is this some kind of a joke? Because I don't find it very funny."

"No joke," Father Joe replied. "Please, Ms. Neuhouse, sit back down. Hear me out before you make a decision."

LM sat down and frowned.

"The church would like for you to write a book about Birdsong. About the recent happenings."

"You want me to write about your roses blooming now?"

"No, Ms. Neuhouse. The miracles." As he explained, his smile grew. "We want you to write about the miracles we've experienced. The church will eventually publish our findings. But the public is hungry now. Are you Catholic, by any chance?"

"I used to be. The church left me a long time ago. I'm assuming you already know about my past."

"I do. And I trust you. The church welcomes you back. You write the book . . . our story, and the royalties are yours. You'll also have control over the dramatic. We'll cover your expenses, to a point, and we both benefit. And you're free to use our real names. Our identity." Father Joe glanced over at Angie. "However, there is one exception."

"Exception?"

"Angie."

"Mary Mead is spelled M-A-R-Y . . . M-E-A-D," Mary said from the back of the room.

Father Joe laughed and held up his hand. "You will create a fictitious character instead of using Angie's name."

LM stared at Angie. "And why is that?"

"Because I don't want to be turned into a freak show. And Father Joe has promised that I wouldn't be. I believe him. I just want to live my life and not be on the nightly news."

Father Joe opened his desk drawer. He pulled out a curved box. Tucked away inside were several folded index cards. He handed them to LM.

"For inspiration," Father Joe said.

LM picked up the cards.

"Take a photo of the cards," Father Joe said. "The church will not release them. The nonagenarians still have dreams of unfulfilled fruition." He winked at Angie. "Angie granted them an opportunity of experiencing life in its simplest form: a special dinner, a date, a dance. Instead, our residents asked for a chance at fulfillment that only God can grant."

Standing, LM pulled out her cellphone and snapped a few pictures. "I'll think about it."

Wishes? She didn't have to believe what Father Joe said, she just had to write about it. Besides, what did she have to lose?

Chapter 20

Wearing winter coats, Father Joe and Mary stood near a newly constructed grotto for their Little Flower, Saint Therese. Two pillars framed a stone altar and statue. Above the wide mail slot was a sign labeled *WISHES*. Elder Luke emptied it daily. Envelopes and written requests were coming in regularly now. As the snow fell, Father Joe watched the faithful arrive. It was Sunday afternoon, a day to say prayer and make a verbal wish in the grotto.

"Busier than usual," Father Joe said.

Mary, working with a checklist, glanced up. "Did you say something?"

"Just commenting on those arriving."

"Oh." She looked out at the group of faithfuls. "Seems to be crowded this afternoon. I saw Chief Bertrand in Mass this morning with his ex-wife. Asked if he had any leads on Lilleth Fettore."

"And what did he say this time?"

"Same thing. Still working the case, but there were more pressing priorities." Mary looked back at her checklist.

Enjoying a moment of peacefulness, Father Joe gazed upon God's handiwork. High on the ridge, the new foundation for a church and expanded nursing home was just starting to form. He was excited about the medical facility that would be built next year. Construction trucks and workers were busy on most days. But not Sunday.

Thank you, Little Flower. Father Joe's eyes pierced to the heavens. *You did all of this. We couldn't have done it without you.*

He thought back to when the bishop told him of the pending sale. *When the last resident has gone on to heaven . . .* Seemed more like a lifetime ago.

Little did they know then that the sale would never go through. Bishop Lansing, at the behest of church members, was forced to forgo the sale. Seemed these grounds were holy after all. A flood of calls from around the world came from people wanting to reside at the Home of the Little Flower—and they were willing to pay.

His heart warmed, contemplating the miracles showering over them, a downpour that all started with a novena.

A new hotel was under construction just across the street. Several restaurants and franchises fighting for space helped to boost the economy. People started moving here because of new jobs. Because of all the interest, Father Joe opened the chapel for round-the-clock prayers. He chuckled as Mary wrote in her notes.

Birdsong's roses were labeled Official Miracle Roses. Every day it seemed that a new product from Birdsong was available online. People couldn't seem to get enough of this town.

Father Joe glanced at the rose bushes covered in burlap. The climate change group had hoped they'd bloom again this winter, but they did not.

"Well, that's done," Mary said, turning the page. "Can't wait for Walter's new barbeque restaurant to open."

"What did he name it again?" Father Joe asked. "Something about a cat?"

"Yes, he named it Jellybean's BBQ."

"That's right."

"How will he cook for the new home if he has two restaurants?"

"He won't be cooking anymore. Just managing." Father Joe clasped his hands. "Any word from the diocese about the new help?"

"They're working hard on the executives for the Home and medical facility. No names yet."

"It's in their hands. We have enough to worry about."

"I dropped a wish in the mail slot," Mary said, grinning. "Wanna know what I wished for?"

"Retirement?"

Squinting, Mary stared up at him. "No, I wished that you'll stay with us and that I remain your assistant for many years to come."

"Jesus, Mary and Joseph. Will I ever get a break?" Lifting his arms, he looked at the gray clouds gathering overhead.

"If I didn't know you were joking, I'd get mad." Mary frowned.

"Do you know what I wish for daily?"

"Besides a new church and your parishioners to come back?"

"You do know me well, Mary."

Little Flower's words came to his mind. *They will build it. They will come.*

"I do have a wish for you, though."

"Oh?" Mary's eyes brightened.

A car came to a stop near the grotto. A man dressed in coveralls stepped out and approached them.

"Straight from the Garage Depot, Father." The man handed Father Joe a set of keys.

Father Joe turned to Mary. "I wished for you to get rid of that clunker. If you'd be so kind, please give this man your old keys. Here is your new car."

Mary wiped away a tear. Hugging Father Joe, she struggled to hold back her emotions.

"I'm never leaving."

"No break, then."

They laughed.

Angie glanced at her reflection in the tall store windows as she jogged past. Stopping at the next store, she winked at her image.

Over the last year, Angie maintained a healthy diet and exercised regularly. Losing thirty pounds was easy while training for a marathon. Angie never felt better, and she definitely looked the part. Her longer hair made her look younger. Now, when she was around her daughter, people asked if they were sisters.

Angie was pleased with LM's bestseller. She stopped to look at a poster of the book cover displayed in the bookstore window. Angie laughed as she remembered the months she spent working side by side with Father Joe and Mary Mead, explaining to LM Neuhouse about the Little Flower.

"It began with a nine day novena . . ." Father Joe had started.

LM glanced over at Angie before writing down anything.

"And don't forget Father's miraculous healing," Mary added. "After all, he was in a coma for weeks."

"And," Angie said, "the anagram. Lilleth W. Fettore spells out *The Little Flower*. And the Little Flower is Saint Therese."

"What name will you use for Angie?" Father Joe asked.

Angie perked up. "May I?"

LM nodded.

"Marilynn Lionne."

"Marilynn Lion?" Father Joe repeated.

"Correct, spelled with two *n*'s and an *e*."

"How did you come up with that name?"

"Since Eliza referred to me as a big cat, why not?"

"I like it." Father Joe chuckled. "Marilynn Lionne will have dark hair and not blonde?"

"Correct," LM had promised.

Needing a break from running, Angie stopped at the statue of Saint Therese. She read the plaque.

Our Lord does not look so much

at the greatness of our actions,

or even at their difficulty, as at the love

with which we do them.

The Little Flower

"Sorry that I let you down," Angie whispered.

Many times over the last year, Angie had wondered about Ms. Fettore. She worked directly with the woman for weeks, and now her memory brought back only little flashes. One thing that wasn't very clear was how Ms. Fettore had known about her wish—a wish that Ms. Fettore recited word for word. Angie glanced around and shrugged. Not wanting anyone to see her talking to a statue, she backed away. If Ms. Fettore was the real Saint Therese, then it was better if no one knew about their past relationship. Angie would be labeled as a nutcase. No, better to allow LM's book to stand on its own.

Turning down her block in the Garden District of New Orleans, Angie smiled. Almost home. She jogged past the historic homes and stopped at an iron gate. From the front, one could look all the way through her house and into the backyard. Walking down her cobblestone path, Angie breathed in the aroma of the blooming flowers.

"Hey, beautiful," Tom said, flipping over the grilling chicken. "You home already?"

"It's after two, and I still have to shower."

"I better hurry, too. Cy and his family will be here any minute."

Walking over to her husband, Angie kissed Tom on the lips.

"Love you, babe." Tom wrapped his arms around her.

"I'm so lucky."

In the shower, Angie thought back to Tom's proposal the previous year.

Angie's eyes had lit up when she handed him that final envelope. "Woohoo. I'm all done with you, Mr. Jared. My last payment." She amused herself remembering their earlier confrontations over her car.

"I certainly hope not," Tom said with a wink. "I'm only taking this because you keep insisting." Tucking the envelope into his jacket pocket, Tom exchanged it for a diamond ring he pulled out. He took her right hand into his, sliding the ring on her finger.

"We've been so happy together these last three months, me especially."
He smiled. "Marry me, Angie. I love you and promise to always."

Glancing down at the ring, her heart raced. Angie fell back into the
warmth of his blue eyes and smile. The love she felt for him in that
moment was overwhelming. Tears ran down her cheeks. "Yes. I'll marry
you. I love you, Tom," she had cried. This time, Angie finally cried out of
joy and happiness. "Let's call Maddie and Kevin," she said.

The bottle of champagne arrived along with Nancy and Walter's
congratulations.

The bishop had awarded Angie an annulment. With Maddie and
Kevin by her side, Angie walked down the aisle to a beaming Tom waiting
for her at the altar. Father Joe celebrated the Mass with Mary assisting.
Family and friends attended.

"The only way this day could be better," Angie said, "is if my residents
and Jakie could be here."

"Don't doubt they're here in spirit," Tom replied, taking her hand.

After the reception at Rose Petals, Maddie informed Angie of Dad's
latest news.

"His girlfriend left him," Maddie said with a smirk.

"Well then, your father's going to need you and Kevin more than ever
now." Angie smiled, thinking what a difference a year made.

Shortly thereafter, Tom put his home and business up for sale.

"Always wanted to live in New Orleans and broker antique and exotic
cars," Tom said. "What do you think, Angie? You up for that? We'll buy
our home there. Make a new life together. Join a church."

Shaking her head Angie had said, "Do you believe in coincidence,
Tom?"

"I do believe things happen for a reason. If that's what you mean."

The shower over, Angie thought of her wish. *Take my little rhyme.
Promise not to change my mind. But do change my life, to make it again
divine.*

*I wished to live in New Orleans, and here I am—by way of Birdsong,
Maine.*

Another True Story

One hundred miles north of Quebec City, seven elders of the Church of Sacre Croix knelt in novena prayer. A little boy playing with a toy car in the last pew listened. His grandmother's voice echoed through the pews.

"We pray for Your help, dear God. We raise our voices in glory to *You*, and ask for Your guidance. Our church is in need of repair. Our youth are leaving. Our seniors are suffering. We ask for Your help, dear God."

She took her grandson by the hand and led him from the church. The little boy held his toy car close to his chest.

"This is the last day of our novena," the grandmother said. "The ninth."

"So, what happens now?"

"Now?" she replied. "Why, we wait."

"Wait for what?"

"Wait for the miracles to happen." The grandmother pushed the button and waited for the lights to change.

"Is it magic?"

"No, no, my *petite chouc*." She smiled. "Magic is not real. Miracles are real."

The following week, the little boy sat in the back pew and waited for his grandmother's prayer group to end. As they finished, the little boy watched the elders sit back down. He rolled his car along the rail and heard a car driving across the pebble parking lot.

"Grandma," the little boy yelled out. "Someone's here."

As the church doors opened, the little boy watched the lady walk in. She winked at him. The little boy glanced over at the elders. The small group didn't notice the stranger.

"I'll tell them you're here," the little boy said, jumping to his feet. "What's your name?"

Leaning forward, the woman whispered into his ear.

The little boy ran between the pews. "Grandma! Grandma! There's a lady here."

The elders looked up.

"Where?" his grandmother asked.

The little boy looked back at the empty aisle. "She was right there."

"What did she say to you?" his grandmother asked.

"She said to tell you everything will be okay. She said to tell you that Lilleth W. Fettore had arrived."

St Therese of Lisieux, France, was a Carmelite nun canonized on May 17, 1925. She believed that her mission of doing good on earth would continue after her death and proclaimed that from heaven she would let fall a shower of roses. She became known as the Little Flower.

Acknowledgments

A special thank you to John Koehler, Joe Coccaro, Hannah Woodlan, and Kellie Emery.

A heartfelt thanks to Lynn Moon, editor extraordinaire.

And a thank you to all the octogenarians and nonagenarians in nursing homes who have allowed me the privilege of walking amongst their angels.